CLASSIC IN THE DOCK

CLASSIC IN THE DOCK

A case for Jack Colby, car detective

Amy Myers

This first world edition published 2015
in Great Britain and the USA by
SEVERN HOUSE PUBLISHERS LTD of
19 Cedar Road, Sutton, Surrey, England, SM2 5DA.
Trade paperback edition first published
in Great Britain and the USA 2015 by
SEVERN HOUSE PUBLISHERS LTD.

British Library Cataloguing in Publication Data

Myers, Amy, 1938- author.
  Classic in the dock. – (A Jack Colby mystery)
  1. Colby, Jack (Fictitious character)–Fiction. 2. Antique
  and classic cars–Fiction. 3. Alfa Romeo automobile–
  Fiction. 4. Murder–Investigation–Fiction. 5. Detective
  and mystery stories.
  I. Title II. Series
  823.9'14-dc23

ISBN-13: 978-0-7278-8513-5 (cased)
ISBN-13: 978-1-84751-615-2 (trade paper)
ISBN-13: 978-1-78010-666-3 (e-book)

All Severn House titles are printed on acid-free paper.

Severn House Publishers support the Forest Stewardship Council™ [FSC™],
the leading international forest certification organisation. All our titles that
are printed on FSC certified paper carry the FSC logo.

Typeset by Palimpsest Book Production Ltd.,
Falkirk, Stirlingshire, Scotland.
Printed and bound in Great Britain by
TJ International, Padstow, Cornwall.

To Sally
with much love

Author's Note

Classic in the Dock is Jack Colby's seventh recorded case. He still lives at Frogs Hill Farm in Kent, where his classic car restoration business is based and from which he carries out his car detection work for the Kent Car Crime Unit. This is a fictitious name, as are several of the place names in this novel, including Plumshaw; the North Downs, however, a designated Area of Outstanding Natural Beauty, is familiar territory to Jack, as are the Greensand Ridge where Frogs Hill is situated and the landscape around it, and they are far from fictitious. As regards the Alfa Romeo featured in this story, it is a fictitious contender in the 1938 Mille Miglia. Those that took first, second and third place in it are factual, as are the hardships endured by the Italian civil population and Partisans in the north of the country during the Second World War and the Allied involvement there.

My thanks for his enthusiasm and help in writing this book go to my husband James, without whose car-buff knowledge it would not have been possible to tell the story of Jack Colby's seventh case. He also runs Jack Colby's website for him at www.jackcolby.co.uk. During my career as an editor of military books, I had the privilege of meeting Michael Lees, whose memoir *Special Operations Executed* was helpful about his time in the Apennine Mountains in the last desperate months of the Second World War, as were Philip Warner's *Special Air Service*, SOE agent Charles Macintosh's *From Cloak to Dagger* and Eric Newby's inimitable *Love and War in the Apennines*.

My thanks are also due to my agent, Sara Keane of Keane Kataria Literary Agency, and to the unrivalled team at Severn House, in particular to my editor Rachel Simpson Hutchens and to Piers Tilbury who must have been hiding out at Frogs Hill to produce such splendid cover designs for Jack's classics.

Amy Myers

Jack Colby's list of those involved in his latest case:

Jack Colby: myself, the proud owner of Frogs Hill farmhouse and classic car business

Louise: my partner in love

Len Vickers: irreplaceable crusty car mechanic in charge of the Pits, the barn we use for car restoration

Zoe Grant: Len's equally irreplaceable number two

Pen Roxton: investigative journalist who treads a fine line between friend and bête noire

Harry Prince: local garage magnate, ever hopeful of buying me out

Dave Jennings: head of the Kent Car Crime Unit for whom I work (on and off)

DCI Brandon: of the Kent Police

Giovanni Donati: famous classic car artist and friend of the Colby family

Maria Donati: his long-suffering wife

Umberto Monti: owner of La Casa restaurant and Giovanni's ally

Martin Fisher: garage owner in the village of Plumshaw

Andrew and Lucy Lee: managers of the Hop and Harry pub in Plumshaw

Peter Compton: head of the long-established Compton family at Plumshaw Manor

Hazel Compton: his second wife

Bronte Compton: their granddaughter

Stephanie Ranger: Peter Compton's daughter by his first wife

Paul Ranger: Stephanie's husband

Jamie Makepeace: grandson of George Makepeace and engaged to Bronte

George Makepeace: the bogeyman behind Plumshaw's push for development

Nantucket Brown: Plumshaw's peacemaker

Giulio Santoro: former racing driver

ONE

Not in the Pits? Not working at their favourite occupation?
Even if the unmistakable roar of a very special car
heading for Frogs Hill Farm was the attraction, it takes a
lot for Len and Zoe to down tools and rush out to see what was
going on. Or, rather, what was coming *in*. A hand waved in greeting
from my unexpected guest.

'*Ciao*, Jack!'

Giovanni had hit town, as the phrase goes, although as Frogs Hill
is set in the midst of the Kent countryside overlooking the green
and fertile Weald of Kent, the word 'town' hardly applies. 'Hit'
does. Giovanni, lithe and graceful as always, slid out of his priceless
bright red Ferrari 1972 Daytona Spyder. I'd heard its unmistakable
sound coming along the lane and had rushed out to see what glorious
fate was bringing our way.

Giovanni came over to hug me. For good measure he hugged
Zoe and Len too, a tribute to which Zoe responded with alacrity.
Len wasn't so keen, being roughly forty years older than her and
of the generation that views casual hugs with suspicion. They work
in the Pits, our name for the Frogs Hill classic car restoration barn,
which thankfully for their employer – me, Jack Colby – is a harmo-
nious arrangement.

'What are you here for? A tune-up?' I joked to Giovanni.

Delighted though I was to see him, he must have driven his
precious Daytona all the way here from Bologna, and Kentish lanes
are hardly ideal for such an immaculate car, especially one famed
for road speeds of 170 mph. Nor would Giovanni seek out Frogs
Hill on a mere whim and without prior notice. Frogs Hill is not a
place for casual calling.

'The Glory Boot, my friend,' was his answer.

All was explained. A world-famous artist, Giovanni is older
than I am – in his late fifties – and was a chum of my father's
before I joined his fan club too. Some of his early works hang in
the Glory Boot, which was Dad's name for his prized collection

of automobilia, kept in a specially built annex of the farmhouse. Giovanni does have a surname too – Donati – but he's so famous he's known everywhere simply as Giovanni.

'Need a bed for the night?' I enquired. My partner, Louise, was away for a few days and it would be good to have company, especially Giovanni's.

'*Grazie*, Jack. Tonight we drink. Tomorrow I go to Plumshaw.'

Instant alert! '*Plumshaw?* What on earth for?'

Every time I go there Plumshaw strikes me as an unhappy village. No such thing? Just as human beings can exude signals that all is not well, so can houses, cars and villages. I'd heard hints of a village feud which might account for it in Plumshaw's case.

Giovanni hooted with laughter, but it was Zoe who broke in impatiently: 'Get up to speed, Jack. The Alfa Romeo.'

I had indeed been asleep at the wheel. There had been a rumour in the car world so unbelievable that I had not given it much attention. Plumshaw Manor, it claimed, was the home of a classic Alfa Romeo that had been resting there on its laurels since the 1940s.

'One of *the* Alfa Romeos?' I asked Giovanni, not sure I had the story right. 'The 1937 Alfa Romeo Spyder 8C 2900B, only thirty-two or thirty-three ever built?' The doubt about the number is because it depends on whether one assembled in 1941 from spare parts is counted, and now on whether the car found in Plumshaw was the real McCoy.

'*Si*, Jack. I paint *la bellissima* Alfa Romeo Spyder.'

Even Len's face registered extreme emotion.

Some hours and a bottle of Chianti later, I was in the picture – perhaps literally, knowing Giovanni's artistic pranks. He paints classic motor cars lovingly true to every tiny detail but in an idiosyncratic surreal setting that always manages in some brilliant way to heighten each car's 'persona'. My father's beloved Gordon-Keeble (now mine) appears at a sixties' coffee bar in the sky with Sophia Loren, Popeye and John Lennon.

'Do you know the Comptons, Giovanni?' I asked carefully. The family that owned Plumshaw Manor had the reputation of being stuck in a time warp where feudal attitudes lingered, albeit without oppression. Peter Compton, who was over ninety, was considered patriarchal and eccentric; his word was law, although for all practical purposes his son Hugh ruled the manor estate. He was generally liked, I gathered, but even so the idea of the carefree Giovanni painting in the midst of this family enclave gave me instant misgivings. I couldn't see the mix.

'No. No matter, Jack. I paint the car and Mr Hugh will like it.'

If the story I had read was true, this Alfa Romeo had been kept in a barn at Plumshaw Manor and was badly in need of rescue. Its true place was in motor racing history. Although a roadster, the 2900B had been aimed at the racing scene and had triumphed in the Mille Miglia road race. It had dazzled the 1938 race, the last before the Second World War broke out; one of them had won the race, another had come second and a slightly different model third. And one of these rare beauties was apparently living in retirement only half an hour's drive from Frogs Hill.

Giovanni and I spent so much time that evening chewing over the delightful details of the Alfa Romeo and curing our consequent thirst with Chianti that the Glory Boot visit had been delayed. Its moment finally arrived, however.

'And now, Jack, we go to the Glory Boot,' Giovanni demanded. 'Your health, my friend.' He raised his glass.

'To the Glory Boot,' I echoed, by now somewhat unfocused.

Giovanni was no stranger to the collection, and once inside the Glory Boot annex he forged his way straight to his objective. To my surprise, this was not to study his own early paintings – well, not immediately – but the trunkfuls of old photographs and newspaper clippings that my father had hoarded in the belief that, unsorted and uncatalogued as they were, someone somewhere sometime would find them invaluable. As apparently Giovanni did now.

Usually these trunks merely provide a place on which to perch, as apart from the old car seat or two there are no chairs in the Glory Boot. One stands in respectful contemplation, but there is only a narrow path between the piles for such solitary musing. Half an hour later, the path had disappeared under discarded pictures and newspapers as Giovanni fought his way through to whatever he sought.

'What exactly are we here for?' I asked plaintively.

No answer. I continued to wait, wondering whether the trunk on which I was perched would be next in Giovanni's mad pursuit of some cherished item.

'This,' he cried in triumph twenty minutes later, waving it under my nose. 'This' proved to be a faded photograph and, since he was alternately jerking it around and planting kisses on it, I had to work hard to see the subject of the picture. When I finally focused on the image, it was unmistakable. It was a 1930s race and an Alfa Romeo was centre-stage.

'The Mille Miglia,' I said. 'Nineteen thirty-eight.' I was beginning to focus again.

'Yes, my friend. In all its glory.' Another kiss. 'And this is the car.' He pointed at the centre-stage Alfa Romeo.

'The one at Plumshaw Manor?'

'Yes. I am sure of it. This car was the one that had to drop out just before the end. The mechanic was taken ill and its driver, Giulio Santoro, abandoned the race to drive him to a hospital.'

'How can you be so certain?'

'Because all the other 2900Bs can be accounted for. This one could not be found. It had disappeared.'

'*Disappeared?* How could it?'

Giovanni was staring hard at the photo as though it could reveal the answer to my question. 'I do not know,' he said finally. 'Santoro himself owned the car after that race, but Mussolini then ruled Italy with the king a mere puppet and Santoro was no fascist. When Mussolini joined Hitler in 1940 and war came, Santoro would have had to serve in the army. Who knows what happened to the car then.'

'For it to have made its way to England and to a Kentish barn is quite a step,' I pointed out. 'Hugh Compton is only in his mid-forties so he can't have been involved, although his father might have been.'

Giovanni grew querulous. 'I am here to paint it. That is all. It will be the best painting I have ever done. It will be my masterpiece and I shall be even greater than I am now. My Maria will be proud of me. She will walk on diamonds.'

'Uncomfortable,' I joked.

He ignored me, but in any case Maria, his long-suffering wife, is used to putting up with Giovanni's whims. She appeared in one of his paintings as Boadicea standing in a 1936 Mercedes-Benz as her chariot and facing a terrified Roman warrior army rigid with fear in Model T Fords.

'So now I have found my photo, let us drink more good Italian wine,' he declared.

My photo, I noted, wondering whether I would ever see my bed again. It was already midnight. Then our twosome unexpectedly became three.

'Make mine cocoa please.'

To my befuddled amazement, Louise was standing at the doorway, as calm and beautiful as ever, with her dark hair fastened back with a blue scarf. She was clearly tired, however, and naturally surprised to see a visitor. I hadn't even heard the door open. She must have had a long day on the set and this week she was filming near Tunbridge Wells, a fair drive from Frogs Hill.

She came reluctantly to join us and I hastened to introduce her to Giovanni.

'I've heard a lot about you, but we haven't met before,' she said to him, her voice somewhat stilted.

Louise is a celebrity, being a famous actor on stage and screen, but she studiously keeps her private life to herself. She's therefore on guard against any potential intruder into this situation, although Giovanni wouldn't come into that category.

'That is a pity,' he replied gallantly, and Louise received a kiss on the hand that she had extended in welcome.

'Giovanni's staying overnight, Louise,' I said brightly to fill the conversational gap that followed.

Another hesitation. 'Sir Galahad awaits you,' she replied. She still hadn't relaxed.

Giovanni not unnaturally looked puzzled until I explained. 'Our guest room always has a bed made up so we call it the Galahad Room, as King Arthur's Round Table always kept an empty chair waiting for the noble knight's arrival.'

His face cleared. 'He has arrived. I am he.' Typical Giovanni.

Considering that Louise and I have only been living together for six months – and that for much of that time she had been filming away from Frogs Hill – I was childishly proud of the fact that we had already established a joint tradition, even if she didn't seem to view Giovanni in the role of a holy knight. She was tired of course, and an unknown guest was probably the last thing she wanted.

That was all there was to it, wasn't it?

* * *

By the next morning, my Chianti-fogged head had cleared sufficiently and Giovanni had a happy smile on his face when he descended for breakfast. Louise had already left, so we would have time to ourselves until he had to leave for Plumshaw after – he informed me firmly – lunch at the Half Moon, my local pub in Piper's Green. That's our nearest village, although it's small and lacks a church, technically rendering it a hamlet. Pluckley is our nearest sizeable village, about three miles away.

Before lunch, we had a happy chat about Alfa Romeos and a tour of the Pits with Len and Zoe. This is a great honour, especially as I'm (to them) merely the figurehead owner who is occasionally allowed to assist with a job if so permitted by my devoted staff. Devoted, that is, to their work. Their attitude to me is changeable, but in times of need they are staunch allies, good friends and an essential part of my life, as I am of theirs.

This morning, Len and Zoe were more interested in the Ferrari Daytona than in work on my humble behalf.

'Four cam?' Len was overcome.

Giovanni nodded. 'The GTB/4. You drive it,' he added generously.

Did he mean me? No way. Only one of us was allowed to take the wheel, and that was Len.

Giovanni is as unpredictable in life as he is in his art, and to single Len out was a good move. I thought Len would refuse, but he didn't. Giovanni even let me accompany him, while he remained in the Pits with Zoe. It was a memorable trip. Even the tractor we met in the single-track lane obeyed the message about giving precedence to the Daytona. It was the tractor that drove off into the muddy field to allow us to pass in style, with its driver gawping at the red beauty gliding by. He would have doffed his cap if he'd been wearing one. We did a circular tour while Len clutched the wheel, muttering under his breath and clearly in complete communion with this wonderful car with its blood-red colour and matching upholstery as fiery as it was unforgettable.

When we returned from lunch, Giovanni announced his departure, promptly throwing his luggage into the Daytona with a careless abandon that would have most classic car owners shivering in their shoes. Louise was already home for the day and Giovanni kissed her hand in farewell, which caused her to blush. She has to cope with a lot of adulation in her career, so the blush was quite a tribute to Giovanni, I thought somewhat uneasily.

'Come and stay with us on your way home,' I told him. 'We all want to hear about the Alfa Romeo.'

'I will, my friend, I will.' A wave of the hand and he was off.

I put an arm round Louise as we returned to the farmhouse. 'What did you make of Giovanni?' I asked, perhaps stupidly.

'Great fun,' she said quickly.

I had to ask. 'Had you met him before?'

She seemed surprised. 'No. I did think he looked familiar, but only because I'd seen his photo in the press.' She looked uncertainly at me. 'Why? Have I dropped a line or two from the script?'

'Not from mine.' So that was all. I laughed at my overactive imagination. 'My stage directions command that we exit left and enjoy the rest of the day together.'

'Good. No work to do?'

'No.'

Len and Zoe had given no indication that they couldn't do without me, and I hadn't anything else clamouring for attention. Most of my own work is for private clients hunting down the cars of their dreams, past or present, or freelance work for the Kent Car Crime Unit. Car crime has been decreasing in Kent, although I can't claim any personal hand in this achievement, and as a result I hadn't been called upon for some weeks. This was to the detriment of my ability to pay the mortgage on Frogs Hill, but it did mean that I was able to enjoy the most wonderful May. The fields and the woods were greener than I could ever remember, wild flowers were covering the verges and meadows, sheep were happily grazing, I was king of the world and Louise was my queen. The rest of the day lay before us.

'Then let the trumpets sound,' Louise announced gleefully. Giovanni was forgotten.

Or so I thought. The very next day, however, my instinct that Plumshaw was not a happy village was reinforced when its local garage owner and restorer, Martin Fisher, popped into the Pits. He loves classic cars, but isn't a specialist and so he consults Frogs Hill Classic Car Restorations when he gets a knotty problem. Such consultations are usually a trio, with Len and Zoe holding forth with their professional expertise, although sometimes I add my own gut instincts.

Today he and I had the chance of a one-to-one after he had finished his high-tech discussions on a Bristol, so I interrogated him over the Compton family. I tried to sound casual since I could be treading on marshy ground.

Martin's younger than I am – in his mid-thirties – and passionate about his job. He has to be, as he's an independent operator with only a couple of lads to help run Four Star Services. Mostly they deal with customers' daily drivers, but that makes him all the more enthusiastic about the classics when he has the opportunity. That seemed to be now.

'That Alfa Romeo, Jack. Quite something. The Comptons asked me to take a look at it – maybe they'll let me restore it.'

He shot a look at me, perhaps guessing (correctly) that I would consider this a job way out of his league. By the time he had extolled its glories, dust, rust and all, and I had been suitably impressed, I was able to ask him about the manor. I still couldn't see laid-back Giovanni fitting, however temporarily, into a Kentish family grown from strong feudal roots and still firmly entwined with them. Martin was only too eager to talk though.

'There's an atmosphere about that place. Hits you as soon as you turn in the gates,' he said. 'That's if the resident killer dogs let you. Weird they are.' He grinned. 'The Comptons, not the dogs. You won't believe this, but Peter Compton still takes a daily feudal drive round the village. Expects his workers to doff any hats they might be wearing.'

'And do they?'

'If they're wise.'

'The son sounds more reasonable.'

'They're all weird if you're a Makepeace. Makepeaces versus the Comptons is what Plumshaw is all about.'

'That's the traditional village feud I've heard about?'

'Yes. Plumshaw is two villages,' he replied. 'There's old Plumshaw, with the church and the Comptons and all that, and there's new Plumshaw, with the housing estate, my garage, the hotel and a convenience store.'

I understood what Martin meant. With so much building going on in the south-east this divide in villages is to some extent to be expected, but in some cases the growth sits like a massive carbuncle on one side of an ancient village so that neither is comfortable inside its skin.

I made this point to Martin and he nodded. 'New Plumshaw is run by the Makepeaces and old Plumshaw by the Comptons. Never the twain shall meet except in the church, or my garage, or the pub. Feelings are usually kept underneath the surface, but at the moment they're surfacing in a big way. What with the Hop and Harry and all that.'

'The *what*?'

'The pub,' he reminded me. 'Legend has it that Henry VIII, good king Harry, courted Anne Boleyn there, but more likely Harry is just a shortened Harrow. Anyway, it's stuck in the middle of a nightmare at present and there's going to be trouble. You know there's only the one road that really goes through Plumshaw, and it's only a minor road at that. The pub stands at the point where the old Plumshaw meets the new.'

I usually approach Plumshaw from the Ashford to Canterbury road, as the other direction involves such twisty and narrow lanes that driving along them means facing opposition from oncoming vehicles every few seconds. There's a limit to the amount of fun to be had from manoeuvring on to verges, avoiding hidden ditches, or backing long distances for a passing place.

As I recalled, from my direction the manor and the church are on the right, and on the left are some clusters of cottages and a narrow lane, the sort that boasts a signpost bearing names so enticing that Louise calls them 'tomorrow lanes', because you always think that next time you drive past you'll stop and explore them. As one turns the bend to the south on the main Plumshaw road, the hotel, garage, secondary school and housing estates lie beyond it. The pub sits just on that bend.

'So what's the problem with the Hop and Harry?' I asked.

'There's a plan afoot for more land to be developed behind it and to the west, a massive new housing estate and a big industrial one.'

'Nothing unusual about that,' I said sadly. Times move on, although in my opinion they don't need to sprint.

'This one depends on a new road to be carved out, which will take traffic in a jiffy to the Ashford rail terminal, the major A20 road and the motorway to Folkestone and on to Dover.'

I saw where this might be leading. 'And where would this road be?'

'The Hop and Harry pub sits bang in the middle of the only possible route.'

I hardly needed to ask. 'Who owns the pub?'

'The Comptons.'

'I take it they don't want to sell?'

'No, especially to the Makepeaces or their developers. The Makepeaces own the farms that would be sold for the development. You'd think the Comptons would be only too keen to sell; their farm's obviously struggling.'

'Can't they put ancient history aside?'

'History is never ancient,' Martin said gloomily. 'It's just beyond our fingertips and if we stretch we can touch it. Plumshaw's stretching.'

Plumshaw was indeed an unhappy village and Giovanni had driven blithely into it. Luckily, he was there for the Alfa Romeo only. Old village vendettas wouldn't affect him.

I was wrong.

Giovanni had planned to be at Plumshaw Manor for about ten days, working on his masterpiece, and so I had not expected to hear from him until at least a week had passed. When, therefore, he rang that very evening, only a day after he had left, I was surprised to say the least.

'A bed for the night?' I merrily quipped, only belatedly aware of the tremor in his voice.

'I have a bed, Jack. I am arrested.'

I thought I'd misheard. '*Arrested?*'

I hadn't misheard.

'I am in a police station.'

His voice struck a chilling note and I was appalled. 'For what?' My mind flashed through the options. Careless driving? Licence out of date?

'Murder, Jack.'

TWO

Eight-thirty on a May Friday morning. Events move in the fast lane when life switches into top gear, and that's how it was now. Giovanni was being held at Charing HQ in connection with the murder of Hugh Compton. I still couldn't take it in. I'd seen nothing on the news or in the press about any murder anywhere in Kent since Giovanni had left, and no mention of Plumshaw. I was so stunned that all I had been able to do on the phone last evening was to assure Giovanni I would sort out a solicitor for him right away. The first step was not hard. I had immediately contacted his agent in London (who had been about to depart on a weekend break when I rang and rapidly changed his mind). He said he'd summon the best solicitor for criminal cases in London, who would, I was informed, set off to rescue Giovanni immediately.

Now Zoe appeared in my kitchen, demanding to know what I was doing about this nonsensical story. How on earth had she heard the news? From a neighbour who knew a policeman, apparently. Before I could make any kind of reply to her, I heard a car arrive outside – and I recognized it from its loud gurgling noise. I rushed to the door to see my favourite bête noire, Pen Roxton, journalist for the *Kentish Graphic*, drawing up in a cloud of smoke in her old Vauxhall, her nose quivering for an inside story.

'What have you got for me, Jack?' she yelled out of the car window, simultaneously opening the door and tumbling out in her eagerness to grab me (not in affection). 'You're not fobbing me off this time. This guy – he's your mate, yes?'

'Which guy, Pen?' I asked sweetly.

'That cocky artist friend of yours, Giovanni, full of himself and pumped up with hot air.'

'Kind of you,' I said drily.

She grinned. 'Tell me about it, Jack.'

'You tell *me* – I only just heard about it and no details at all. Where was Hugh Compton's body found?'

She looked at me thoughtfully, which meant she was sizing up her best attack mode, not that she was giving any consideration to my feelings about the mess Giovanni was in. 'It hasn't been found – yet. Your chum was *found* though, *found* yesterday morning covered in Compton's blood and out of his tiny mind. He *found* himself, he said, in King's Wood. Challock way, isn't it? Drove to Plumshaw Manor for help – he *said*. They called the rozzers.'

Knowing Pen of old, I wondered how long she had been prowling around the manor before she found a victim to spill a few beans with which she could build up a delectable dish for her readers.

'Why call the police?' I asked. 'I realize Hugh Compton couldn't have been there when Giovanni returned, but why assume he'd been the victim of a crime? Suppose Giovanni merely took him to a station to get a train or to see a lady friend?'

She regarded me pityingly. 'Blood, Jack. Blood.'

'Why is it presumed to be Hugh's, dear Pen? Why not Giovanni's own blood, or that of a passing stranger or a dead chicken?'

'Waiting for you to tell me, Jack. Know Hugh Compton, do you? He wouldn't dare have a girlfriend, not with that father. His wife fled long ago. Divorced. Anyway, any sensible chap would keep his mobile phone on.'

Pen's not daft. She had a point. 'Did he have his with him?'

'Immaterial,' she said grandly. 'The family believes their Hughie boy is missing and probably dead.'

This wasn't looking too good, even though the basic premise that Giovanni could have left here on Wednesday to stay with total strangers and decided to murder one of them within hours was crazy. As far as I knew, there was only one subject in which Giovanni and Hugh Compton had a common interest, though for different reasons. 'Is the Alfa Romeo missing?'

'Wouldn't know. Giovanni was driving some Italian job.'

'The Italian job is probably his own car – a rare and valuable 1972 Ferrari Daytona,' I pointed out.

'Whatever. He drove it to Challock woods, murdered Hugh Compton in it, dumped the body and drove the car back. Not too bright, your chum. Come on, Jack. You must know something.'

'Giovanni told me nothing about what happened and there's a limit to how much even I can find out in the thirty-five minutes I've been operational today,' I shot back savagely. 'All I really know is what you've just told me. So now tell me more.'

'What's it worth?' She didn't mean cash.

'No pre-bargaining, Pen.'

'Exclusive when he's convicted?'

'What I love about you, Pen, is your consideration for other people's feelings. Giovanni won't even be charged without a body.' She snorted. 'Don't bank on it. Still . . .' She considered her position for a moment, as I knew she would. 'OK, do your best for me. Usual terms apply though, so play fair, Jack.'

'Always, Pen,' I replied through gritted teeth.

'That old wreck in the barn is what they quarrelled over, so everyone thinks. Blood everywhere in the barn too.'

Subtract a lot for Pen's love of overstatement, but it still didn't sound good. 'In the Alfa Romeo?' I asked with horror.

'Dunno.'

'But the car is still there?'

'No idea, but if it is it's probably full of blood too, like that red job of Giovanni's. That's why they've charged him.'

'They've already *charged* him?' There's a big difference between arrested and charged.

'Well, arrested anyway,' she amended to my relief.

'OK. Who says, Pen? Who's your source for all this blood? The milkman? Someone's auntie in Scotland?'

'Nope. Anyway, a witness saw your mate trying to scrub the blood off at King's Wood. He's glued to the frame all right, Jack.'

For once I agreed with her. If the DNA matched, the story would go that Giovanni had killed Hugh, taken the body off in his car, concealed it in some secluded place and then tried to clear up the mess as he panicked. Conceal it where? The coast, a river, a quarry, the woodland? Why go back to the manor, however, unless he was a braver man than I'd given him credit for? He could be cocky, as Pen had said, but he was clever. Did that make him a cunning villain? Hardly.

I made one last assault. 'Any particular reason your informant thinks Giovanni would want to kill Hugh Compton?'

She shrugged. 'Simple, Jack. They came to blows over Compton's Alfa Romeo, your mate killed him by mistake and then panicked. Hot-headed, these Italians.'

'Is that your informant's view too? And he or she is . . .?'

She waggled a finger at me. 'Sources, Jack. Can't reveal them.'

'To me you can. You made me a colleague, remember?'
She hesitated. 'Landlord of the Hop and Harry pub.'

'He'll be staying here?' Louise looked appalled.

I couldn't blame her. She had come back at eight in the evening
on Saturday to find not the relaxation she needed but Giovanni
alternately shrieking and sobbing on my shoulder, almost literally.
Usually she takes most situations in her stride but this one was a
different matter. Being an actor, she managed to hide her reactions
in Giovanni's presence but when we were alone in the kitchen she
let fly.

I would not normally have been enthusiastic about a longish stay,
as Giovanni's idea of a quiet evening is that it goes on twice as
long with twice as much alcohol, twice as much smoke and twice
as much loud music. But this time it was different.

'He can't put up at a hotel in the state he's in,' I explained.

Giovanni had been released without charge that afternoon. The
normal twenty-four-hour period within which he should be charged
or released had been extended by a further twelve, and then by
courtesy of a magistrate's court hearing yesterday evening for
another twelve. He'd been warned not to leave the country and to
leave an address at which he could be contacted, and had come
straight to Frogs Hill. Sending him away had not been an option.

This Giovanni, however, was a far cry from the one who had
flashed in so boldly in his bright-red Daytona three days ago. This
time he had arrived not in his Daytona, but in a hired BMW arranged
by his agent, and he looked careworn, defeated and even physically
smaller.

'I am not a murderer, Jack,' he had pleaded as he came into the
farmhouse. He didn't have to tell me that. The very idea of it was
nonsense. Planning a crime would be beyond his powers and even
in his cups he wasn't one to lose his cool. Spur of the moment
passionate outbursts weren't his way of doing things. I remember
Dad telling me about a time when Maria had taken exception to
one of his lady friends (a failing of his). Frying pans were flying,
but Giovanni merely ducked, took her seriously (or appeared to)
and kissed her.

Louise didn't look as though a kiss would pacify her. 'How long
will he be here for?' she asked.

'I don't know,' I admitted.

'Great.'

I revved myself up for a showdown. 'What's wrong, Louise? The extra work? My being distracted? Dislike of Giovanni?'

'None of those.' The words emerged as a mutter.

'Then what?'

'I can't tell you, Jack. Mainly perhaps not being able to cope with more than one life at a time. Anyway,' she concluded firmly, 'it will only be for a day or so. I've got a short run at the Albion in London. Rerun of that solo show I did on the Bloomsbury Group. Evenings and matinees, so I'll have to stay in London.' She keeps a small flat there for just such a purpose.

'You hadn't mentioned that before,' I said. 'Is it on the calendar?' We both carefully mark our joint calendar with every expected movement as soon as it's on the horizon.

'Only just came up.'

That was highly unlikely and we both knew it.

'Anyway,' she continued, 'I'll cook myself something and leave you two to talk things over. Poor Giovanni,' she added somewhat belatedly.

'I don't think Giovanni's up to very much talking tonight, and nor am I. Not if I'm going to be without you for weeks.'

She didn't reply to that and I wasn't surprised. I'd stepped over the boundary. When a star wanders there's no point in shouting 'Come back' at it. Just wait for it to touch base again.

Dejected, I left her microwaving a ready meal. This wasn't how it was meant to be. Something had gone wrong and I couldn't see how to mend it.

Then I had a brainwave. I'd take Giovanni to the pub for a meal and give Louise space. Giovanni was somewhat reluctant, convinced that the world would be gossiping about him. That seemed unlikely as so far his arrest was not widely known, but I assured him that as he wasn't in his Daytona and we would drive there in my Polo (my beloved Alfa – not a Romeo alas – had been retired). That way we would be reasonably anonymous, even if some people recognized him from previous visits as the Great Artist Giovanni. That cheered him up and off we went.

Once he had eaten a large lasagne at the Half Moon followed by an apple crumble and custard, he began to relax. He took a careful slug of red wine, clutching his glass as if it were about to be wrested from him by the great DCI Brandon himself, the gimlet police chief at Charing HQ.

'Now I tell you about it, Jack. This Hugh Compton, he is not interested in painting so why should I kill him?'

'Tell me why the police think you did.'

'Because of the blood and they do not believe my story.'

'Which is? Tell me, Giovanni, right from the beginning – what happened.'

'I do not know, Jack. I know we quarrelled, but the next thing I know I am in this wood and there is blood.'

'How much? A smear? Or more?'

'More. Much more. On me, on the seat, on the door – I cannot get rid of it, so I drive back to find out where Mr Compton is and what happened. But they say Mr Compton is missing and send for the police. The police do not believe me, so they take me in and take sample of blood and spit for testing.'

So far the story was as clear as mud. 'Start again from the beginning,' I told him. 'Tell me everything that happened that evening. Can you do that?'

'I have been talking about it for two days, Jack. Why not again?' he said with dignity. 'But now I talk to you, so it is easier because you are my friend. I get to Plumshaw after I leave you that day. I find the manor, the pretty daughter Bronte answers the door, come in, come in. There I meet Mr Hugh Compton. I am taken to bedroom, which is nice, very nice.

'Then I go outside to the barn with Mr Compton. He is a nice man, the sun is shining. All is well. I am happy in my heart. The painting begins to grow inside me when I see the car. I am joyful. I wish to share this experience with the owner of this beautiful object that Hugh shows me. I do not know if it is Mr Hugh or his father who is the big boss but Mr Hugh says we will talk about that later today. It will soon be time for dinner.

'With God's sunshine upon us, we should eat outside but no, I am taken away from the sunshine into the gloom of a dining room, lit only by candles in candelabra, and we sit in silence round a large table, with silver gleaming. The food is good, and I do not drink, only coffee. But the silence, Jack. They are all there. Mr Hugh's father Peter, who I now see is the very big boss but he is old. Mr

Hugh who runs the farm is very quiet. His sister Stephanie is there, much older than Mr Hugh and older than her husband Paul too. Him I do not like. Not *simpatico*. She is more friendly, but I not think he or Mrs Stephanie like Mr Hugh. There was Mrs Hazel too, the old man's wife though she is younger, perhaps seventy-five, so she is not Mrs Stephanie's mother. Mrs Hazel is a hard one, Jack, not like my Maria. But there is the pretty one too, Miss Bronte Compton, Mr Hugh's daughter. She is very *simpatica*, very pretty.'

I thought of the long-suffering Maria and her scorn for the 'pretty ones'. I couldn't get him to tell me any more about Hugh Compton, so I decided to go easy on him and talk about the car for a while. Giovanni has a different perspective to mine on classic cars. I see them for what they are: beautiful desirable objects of the past. He sees them in terms of paint and picture and imagery. That doesn't mean his knowledge is any less than mine or any greater, but we differ in the importance we allot to each car. Over the Alfa Romeo, however, we were united. It was an extraordinary car, a thing of beauty and a joy for ever, as the poet wrote.

'Did you talk about the Alfa Romeo at dinner?' I asked.

'No, but I look forward to seeing it again. I wish to go on my own, not with Mr Hugh. How could they keep such a car and not care for it? It will take pride of place in the art of the twenty-first century, Jack, the crown of my career.' For a moment he looked his old self, but then he began to crumple again. 'They are not interested in the car, Jack.'

'What is its story? Did you ask the Comptons how they came to own it? Could they confirm it was the one that pulled out of the 1938 race?'

'It is, Jack. I was not sure before, but when I see it, I *smell* that it is right. It is the car in the photograph that I found. Mr Peter Compton say he bought it after the war in Italy, but cannot remember where or from whom he bought it. But I do not care. It is here now, and I shall still paint it.'

I had my doubts about that, but kept them to myself. To me the story didn't add up, however. Why buy a car like that and leave it to rot? If the family was strapped for cash why not sell it? They could easily find out how much it was worth. I clearly wasn't going to get any further on this issue, however, so I reverted to the main one.

'What else happened at that dinner?'

'Nothing, Jack. It was all quiet. Very formal. Even the pretty one say very little but she wink at me. I tell you, Jack, my happiness died in that silence. The seed of my picture began to wither inside me and I knew I must get back to the barn quickly and alone, so that the seed may grow again.'

'And did it?'

'No. Mr Hugh insists he will come with me. He says it is his duty as host. You English! I say I leave if I cannot go alone but he says very well, leave. How could I do that when I have a duty to paint that car? I cannot study the car with him watching me, so we have coffee, he go to change clothes, I go to get my sketchbook and we go to the barn. We do not agree about the painting, so we stand there in silence. Do they think I will run off with it, when it won't even start?

'I close my eyes to hold the image in my mind,' he continued after a moment or two. 'I try to do the best I can with Mr Hugh watching me. And then . . .' He paused and looked at me with pleading eyes. 'I wake up, Jack. I am not in the barn, I am sitting in my Daytona in a wood in a place I do not know. Night has become day. It is seven o'clock. I am alone.

'Then I see, Jack. There is dried *blood* on my jacket. There is some blood in my car on the back seat; it shows dark against the red of the upholstery. On the door there are some smears too. I do not see them at first because of the red paint, but then I do. Is it my blood? I can find no hurt on me. I am scared. I try to clean the blood off, but I cannot do so. Where am I? What has happened? I must return to Plumshaw Manor and find Mr Hugh Compton who will explain. I set my satnav but when I get to the manor they have not seen Mr Compton. *Where is he?* they shout at me. They say there is blood in the barn. They call the police, which I think is so that they can find Mr Compton, but it is not. It is to arrest *me*. I killed him, they say.'

'How are you supposed to have killed him?'

'I do not know. I tell the police there was no weapon in the car. *Where is it?* they say. There is no weapon in the barn either, but blood.' Giovanni shuddered.

'Why do the police think you would have wanted to kill him?' I pressed him. This was a crazy story and I could get no handle on it.

'I do not know. Perhaps they think Mr Compton tell me I cannot paint the car after all, which is not true. He knows nothing about painting or cars. He said that he wished it to be painted yellow, but I said no. The seed inside me did not see yellow. Now,' he added dolefully, 'that seems nothing.'

'That hardly sounds like a reason for murdering anyone,' I commented. Even for the most hot-headed Latin temperament, it would be an extreme reaction, especially for a middle-aged man like Giovanni. Nevertheless, I saw how the police must see it. Giovanni was supposed to have killed this man in red-hot passion, probably with a knife, as he was unlikely to have packed a gun in his suitcase, then taken the body and the weapon and driven away to dispose of them, and then brazened it out by coming back to the manor.

'Where did you park the Daytona when you arrived on Wednesday?' I asked, bearing in mind that bodies are heavy to move.

'Outside the barn,' he said dolefully. He'd obviously followed my reasoning.

'That's near the house?'

'Some distance. The family would not hear the car if I had driven it away or heard our quarrel even if it had been serious. But it was not, Jack.'

'But the police have let you go without charge, so they can't have a clear case.'

'My solicitor said until the blood is proved to be Hugh Compton's, there is little more they can do.'

I returned to the point again. 'Nevertheless, they did let you go.'

He shrugged. 'Like a cat with a mouse, Jack.'

He could be right. 'Did they test you for drugs?' That was the obvious explanation of his blacking out.

'I think so, Jack. But even if I was drugged they will say I killed him and then drugged myself because I am a clever person. I *am* a clever person, but I am worried, Jack. Mr Compton has been missing for three days. If he were alive, whether in hospital or anywhere else, he would have been in touch. But he has not been. They would ring his phone and he would answer.'

I tackled the problem another way. 'Did you know any of the Comptons before this?'

'No.'

'Did Hugh commission you to paint the car or did you ask them if you could paint it?'

Giovanni replied to this with dignity. 'I hear about the car from a friend. I write to Mr Compton to say I wish to paint it. With no charge. Mr Hugh invites me to come. My agent was not pleased, because he think I should take money. But for this car? No. Too beautiful. It is Italy's history.'

'And yet the Comptons don't look after the car and don't understand painting.'

'After I paint it they will. Besides, the old Mr Compton, Mr Peter, is very strange but he likes Italy and motor racing. Many of my customers do not know about painting, Jack. They ask me to paint cars because I am famous. If I don't like the car, I do not paint. I like this one and with my painting it will fetch much money for them.'

He must have realized that wasn't going to happen now, because he groaned. 'I am sorry, Jack. Let us go back to your home. I am no good company. When Maria comes it will be better.'

'*Maria?*' I queried blankly.

'She coming here. I need her, Jack.'

I was struck dumb. I like Maria very much, but having her here with Giovanni was not going to make for calm seas ahead. For whatever reason, Giovanni and Louise were hardly soulmates and having Maria here too wasn't fair on Louise. It was just as well that she had planned to be away for a few days.

Giovanni obviously read my thoughts and was amused. 'We stay in a hotel,' he told me. 'And tomorrow I will not be in your way. I go to see my friend.'

'The police won't like the hotel plan.'

I couldn't see it working with Giovanni and Maria both at Frogs Hill either, but nevertheless it looked as if our guest room was going to have another occupant.

'We go. I not stay here with that woman.'

Quick work. Maria had only been at Frogs Hill for just over an hour on Monday morning and already she had made her position clear, having passed Louise on her way out to work. Battle had commenced as soon as Maria had disengaged herself from Len's car.

She had been due to land at Gatwick airport at nine a.m., which would involve a long drive along the M25 in heavy traffic. By seven o'clock, however, Giovanni had not yet surfaced despite my bang on his door. I'd needed to remain here to keep a firm eye on him, and so Len had nobly 'volunteered' his services. He seemed to have taken to Maria, despite the long-haul drive. Hardly surprising, as I'm very fond of her myself. She's small, dark, and ultra-determined, but that doesn't stop her having a warm heart. Where Giovanni is concerned she is a tigress, the warm heart protecting him like a precious cub, except where his lady friends are concerned, naturally enough. Then battle rages. It always ends in a passionate embrace, but the going is rough. I know. I've seen it.

And that's what it was like today. She stomped after me into the house while Giovanni retreated into the Pits with Len. Maria had brushed aside my feeble offer of coffee, folded her arms in traditional style and delivered her ultimatum.

I was reeling from the onslaught. *'Louise?'* Louise was 'that woman'?

If I had a vain hope that she meant Zoe it was quickly dashed.

'Si. She no good that one.'

There was a thump between my shoulder blades as the god of jealousy landed and put a stranglehold on my throat. I'd never put myself down as a jealous man. Even when it was clear that Eva, my wife during a brief and stormy early marriage, was seeing someone else – a Mexican bandleader in fact – jealousy wasn't my uppermost emotion, only rage at her disregarding our small daughter Cara's needs. But we surprise ourselves when the unexpected strikes. I had been aware of Giovanni's amours over the years, and Maria's acceptance of the situation after the fighting was over. But *Louise?*

'Giovanni and Louise?' I struggled with this outrageous thought. Louise was quite a few years younger than me, and Giovanni was quite a few years older. Nevertheless, I had to face the fact that he was undoubtedly a very attractive man.

'Si. I no like her. Giovanni no also.'

'Why?' It was a silly question, but in the past Maria had often got on well with his light o' loves and Giovanni never harboured ill will.

'She leave him.'

'But wasn't that good for you both?' Something inside me was bleeding, haemorrhaging trust and dragging love with it.

Maria glared at me. 'Maybe yes, maybe no.'

I knew little of Louise's life before we met, apart from her public profile. I hadn't thought it mattered. The past was past. I had told Louise about Eva and of other passing ladies in the twenty-odd years in between her leaving and Louise's arrival. It hadn't been important and Louise didn't care, even when I warned her that Eva might hurtle back into my life periodically, although all seemed quiet at present. Louise had merely laughed.

Now I realized why. I'd assumed she had had unimportant relationships which, like mine (save perhaps for Eva), had come and gone, but for Louise they had not all been unimportant. She had her own past to cover up. And yet I could not see this fitting in with the Louise I thought I knew. Some time ago, I had seen Louise in Shakespeare's *Troilus and Cressida* in which she had played the faithless Cressida. When her devoted Troilus had seen her in the arms of some other chap he was a broken man. 'This is and is not Cressida,' he moaned. It is one of Shakespeare's so-called problem plays, and now I saw what that meant. I knew Louise – but I *didn't* know her, and that god of jealousy was busy sticking a dagger in my heart. What was happening to my world? My friend accused of murder and my lover turning out to be his former girlfriend.

Don't be so blasted stupid, I told myself, and tried to force myself back to 'normality'.

'But where will you go?' I asked Maria. 'I can find a hotel for you—'

'Giovanni find one.'

So it seemed I was in the doghouse too. Maria was already marching out of the door to find Giovanni and I joined her as he emerged from the Pits. He looked just the same and yet how could he now that I knew the truth about him? I hadn't been in touch with him for a while before his visit so he would not have known about Louise and me, and he had covered up his shock at seeing her so smoothly I could scarcely believe it. What else could he be covering up?

I pushed that thought away and concentrated on the present problem. At least I tried to.

'Hotel,' Maria informed him.

'No, Maria.' Giovanni was even beaming now. 'We stay with the Signora Vickers.'

He waved a hand at a blushing Len standing in the Pits doorway. 'Len ask his wife, Jack, and she say come to stay.'

I felt like a Trabant surrounded by Bentleys and Rolls-Royces. I had to get up to speed, understand what was going on here. Was I glad or sorry at the thought that Giovanni and Maria were leaving Frogs Hill? Glad, I realized, but I needed time to think this through. Louise would be back tonight and to have Giovanni and Maria lodging elsewhere would be by far the best idea since sliced bread.

I have rarely met Mrs Len, but I knew she was a practical lady who specialized in village activities and not in cars. How on earth would she cope with an Italian lady of charm but determination and the flamboyant Giovanni? The Vickers had a cottage on the outskirts of Pluckley but its size meant there would be no escape from the presence of two guests, both of whom would be in unpredictable mode.

'Yours not to reason why, Jack,' Zoe murmured at my side. She had obviously noticed my gaping mouth. 'Just let them get on with it.'

She was right and I did.

Although Len's home is not so far away that the police could object to it as a temporary residence for Giovanni, they needed to know about the switch, which gave me a good excuse to call in at Charing HQ with the details. It would be a pleasure. It gave me a mission and I wouldn't have time to brood about Louise.

Besides, DCI Dave Jennings, the academic-looking but practical head of the Kent Car Crime Unit, might know what was going on with the Giovanni case – if case it still was. He works in the same building as DCI Brandon and is therefore a useful source of information – if he feels like communicating it to me. Perhaps Hugh Compton had now turned up and, even though a missing-person case wouldn't be in Dave's pigeonhole, he might find out the situation for me.

I thought at first that Dave wasn't going to see me as I was told he was 'out' but I was wrong. He was only too eager to see me and bounded down the stairs to greet me. Unusual.

'Seen it, have you?' he asked.

I guessed he meant the Alfa Romeo.

'No, more's the pity.'

I followed him up to his office, where he plopped down at his desk and waved me to sit on the far side. I gave him the new address where Giovanni was staying and he raised an eyebrow. He too knew Len.

'I'd heard you had Donati staying with you. Fixed yourself a nice role as piggy in the middle as usual,' he commented.

Giovanni, I noted, was in police terms no longer the famous artist Giovanni, but a possible murder suspect and certainly a witness in a missing-person case.

'Brandon told me the crazy story he came up with,' Dave continued.

'If he was guilty he would have thought up a better one than that.'

'Don't agree. Could be clever planning to have a stupid story.'

'Not if other folk don't see it as such. Any chance of his being charged?' I added carefully.

Dave found it convenient to stare at his laptop. 'We may have a job for you, Jack.'

'What is it?' Usually a new job fills me with eager curiosity and excitement – not least because it's a step towards paying the mortgage on Frogs Hill. Now the idea left me cold, probably because he hadn't answered my question.

'Missing Land Rover Discovery 1989.'

'Why choose me?'

'Thought you might like it.'

'Why?' Unlike Dave to be so thoughtful.

'Reported missing by Paul Ranger. Lives at Manor Cottage, Plumshaw. Land Rover belongs to Peter Compton.'

THREE

Never had I felt less like returning to Frogs Hill. Far from being the refuge, the haven, where life had been manageable and the people I was close to were known and loved quantities, it too had become unknown territory. Today I had to face the fact that for me Louise was loved but not completely known. She would be leaving for London tomorrow but this evening she was returning to Frogs Hill. What would I say? Demand the full story of her relationship with Giovanni? Gloss over the whole sorry episode of a love affair long past? Neither seemed possible.

To make it worse, I had said I'd help Giovanni. Was I morally bound by that pledge now that he was free? Whether I was or not, it seemed I was going to be thrust right back into it. That meant I had no option but to take up Dave's job, especially since he had made it clear that it had Brandon's backing. That meant Brandon would welcome my nosing around Plumshaw on the Hugh Compton trail.

Dave had, naturally enough, thought he was doing me a favour by sending me to Plumshaw and twenty-four hours ago I would have agreed. I forced myself to consider whether the missing Land Rover had any connection with Hugh Compton's disappearance, even though Dave told me the theft had been on the Friday, two days after Hugh had gone missing. It was certain now that Hugh had been in Giovanni's car. The DNA results were still awaited but other trace evidence, including plenty of fingerprints, proved he had been in the Daytona alive or dead. Whatever my private thoughts about Giovanni, however, I couldn't see him as a murderer. An insidious voice inside me then reminded me that once I couldn't have imagined Louise being one of Giovanni's amusements.

I was still wondering what to do as I reached Pluckley and turned off for Pipers Green and Frogs Hill. The problem loomed even larger and I had a fleeting temptation to flee – maybe to Essex, where my daughter Cara lives, which is safely across the River Thames and away from this nightmare. But I couldn't do that. The long May evening was beginning to indicate that night was coming, which seemed an omen in itself. I reached the farmhouse, the security lights came on and I braced myself, still without a clue of how to tackle what must come.

No Ford Focus. Louise had either put her beloved silver-blue car away in the garage at the rear of the farmhouse, which she seldom bothered to do, or she was not yet home. It proved to be the latter. The house was dark, unwelcoming, and empty of life, but I realized that was a relief. Giovanni and Maria would be at Len's home, so at least I would not have to see them together here. No doubt Maria would be equally grateful. Which just left Louise to face. How could Giovanni have been so duplicitous as not to have told me about her? And, worse, how could Louise? I thought she had been fully aware of my friendship with him but it seemed I had been wrong.

Minutes inched by and turned themselves into half an hour. Then the landline phone rang, with Louise at the other end of the line.

'You'll be late, sweetheart?' I heard my voice ask. Odd how natural my voice sounded when inside I felt like a speedster bumping up and down in every pothole in Frogs Hill Lane – which is a great many.

'Sorry, yes, I'm in London.' Odd how natural her voice sounded too.

She's bolted there today, I thought, sinking to the bottom of a particularly large internal pothole. She couldn't face me any more than I could face her. That didn't say much for our relationship.

'Something came up unexpectedly,' she continued brightly, 'so I came here today instead of tomorrow.'

I wondered what I had done to deserve this. Our arrangement had always been that she was free to come and go as she wished and so far it had worked out splendidly. Until Giovanni had laughed his way into the picture – even though I had to admit he wasn't laughing much now.

I murmured something in reply and we talked quite normally – or so it seemed. I put the phone down with a surge of combined relief, panic and complete confusion. Was she ever coming back? Did I even want her to? And, crucially, was it because of Giovanni she was staying away? The second was the only question to which I could give an answer and it was a resounding yes, whatever the cost – although preferably not with the shadow of Giovanni hanging over us.

As I drove to Plumshaw Manor on Tuesday morning, I could not rid myself of mental images of Giovanni flashing along in his Ferrari Daytona behind my humble Polo, chatting happily to Louise sitting beside him and giving me a cheery wave as he shot past me. I was glad when I could turn right outside the imposing Georgian manor and not left towards the outbuildings. Giovanni would have left his stamp there too, even though the crime scene must now have been lifted.

I wondered why I had been told to contact Paul and Stephanie Ranger, rather than the Land Rover's owner, but realized this would be because of the worry over the missing Hugh, which overrode Peter and Hazel Compton's concern over the Land Rover's fate. The Rangers' home, Manor Cottage, was a hundred yards or so away from the manor and tucked away behind some masking trees. Hardly a cottage, I thought, as I parked outside. It was smaller than the manor but almost as impressive. It was red brick, not stone, and built somewhat later than the manor itself, I guessed. I felt some of the pressure vanish now that I was off (or could pretend I was off) Giovanni territory.

'Jack Colby?' Paul Ranger looked to be in his early sixties, greying but not particularly gracefully. In fact there was nothing very graceful about his sturdy figure. He greeted me – if that was the right word – with bland assurance, as he planted himself firmly across the doorway.

'Found the Land Rover, have you?'

'Not yet.'

'They said they'd put their best man on it.' His look suggested he had been sadly misled if I was all they could come up with.

'Perceptive of them,' I remarked. 'I need to ask a few questions. OK?'

So far there had been no sign of his inviting me into his domain, and there still wasn't as he sized me up even more keenly. If I'd been a horse, I'd be destined for the knackers' yard.

'Yes, but don't bother to ask if this business is connected to brother Hugh.'

Hugh's face was now adorning newspapers, posters and TV.

Sightings of him had come in from Cornwall, Calais and John o'
Groats, according to Dave Jennings.

'No news of him yet, I gather.'

'Never will be now they've let that Italian go.' Only Paul Ranger
added one or two more fruity words. 'He'll skip the country.'

We were at an impasse. I was still on the doorstep and he wasn't
budging. His body language suggested he thought I had plans to
rush into this dull-looking house and trash it. One can't tell much
about a home from a doorstep, but it can offer tantalizing clues.
This one didn't – not even a mat with 'Welcome' on it, which was
hardly surprising. Nevertheless, the fact that it looked dull didn't
mean that it wasn't important as the home of two of the Compton
family – which itself was as yet unknown territory. In a murder
case this would be fertile ground, so I tried the standard questions
in case the going was muddy.

'Was the Land Rover in a garage or pinched from outside the
manor – and when exactly did it disappear? I also need the year
and model.'

'Your superiors have got all that information. You should have it.'

'Bear with me,' I said, as cordially as I could manage. 'I'd like
direct information, because it helps build a picture of the crime.' I
wasn't sure what this picture could be. It was true that I flatter
myself I can tell a lot about someone from the kind of car they
drive, but the Land Rover didn't belong to the Rangers, it belonged
to Hugh. The only car in sight here was a fairly modern Jaguar.

'Friday night. Outside the manor, where it's usually left for daily
use. Colour grey. Dent on front wing.'

'When exactly did it vanish?' Patience is a virtue I have to struggle
to claim.

'Sometime in the evening,' he vouchsafed. 'We've been spending
a lot of time at the manor with this to-do over my brother-in-law.
I saw the Land Rover outside when we left about ten. Gone next
morning.'

'Does your father-in-law drive it himself or does Hugh drive it?'
Surely he was as sick as I was of this doorstep stand-off? Inside, I
might at least glean a better idea of the Compton family. I quite
saw why Giovanni had found that dinner so forbidding.

'*Does?*' he snorted. '*Did*, in my view. And forget Hugh. Off-limits.
He's dead, you mark my words.'

I would do just that, I thought. There was a great deal of satisfaction in those words. I treated him to what I hoped was the Colby charm. 'It's important for the fuller picture.'

'So that you can flog this fuller picture to the press?'

'Not my style.'

He grunted. 'More than can be said for that harpy who came sniffing round here upsetting my wife.'

That had a familiar ring. 'Pen Roxton, by any chance? From the *Graphic*?'

'A colleague of yours, I presume. In it together?'

This was going nowhere, so I would deal with Pen later. 'My job's as a classic car specialist. Could I have a look at the Alfa Romeo? The Land Rover's a classic too so the Alfa could be linked to it, even though you probably don't see it that way.'

'Too right. I don't.'

It wasn't that he was hostile to me, I decided. He just struck me as one of those people who in their working lives have not reached the pinnacle they felt they deserved, so the older they grow the more they loftily assume the trappings of missed grandeur in their everyday lives.

'Have the police discounted that theory?' I asked.

That did it. 'No, they bloody haven't!' he yelled. 'All they've done is set that murderer free.'

'In that case we can't be certain the Land Rover isn't linked to Hugh's disappearance. He could have returned and borrowed it himself.'

'He's *dead*, man.'

'Not proven. He could simply be on a mission of his own.'

Another snort. 'We'd have heard by now. Not a dickey bird.'

He then produced what he clearly thought was a killing blow. 'I still don't see how looking at the old wreck in the barn is going to help.'

'Because,' I replied calmly, 'I'm a specialist and I work with specialists in the classic car field, both the good ones and the baddies. *I need to see the car.*'

Surprisingly, he surrendered and even afforded me a wan grin. 'OK, I'll take you over.'

At last we could move away from this doorstep. He carefully shut the door behind him, perhaps in case I decided to storm in on a smash-and-grab raid, and off we walked. I felt I was walking through history along this gravelly path past the Georgian mansion with the cluster of old farm buildings that must have been here in some form for centuries. The last one was the largest and some way from the house. It was a huge tithe barn, with Kentish peg tiles and ancient wooden double doors. Despite its having been a crime scene, I could see no sign of any security measures introduced recently, although there was a strong padlock on the door that looked shiny enough to be new.

'Very trustworthy of you,' I remarked, 'given the publicity that the car might now have.'

'We've plenty of barns, and even if some blighter picked on this one he couldn't move the Alfa Romeo. Not yet.'

'You have plans for it?'

Mr Bland Face was back again. 'When we get round to it.'

'Who actually owns it?'

'If that's relevant, my father-in-law, Peter Compton.'

It was chilly and musty inside, but when my eyes were accustomed to the gloom I could see the shape of the car under a green cover and my heart began to beat faster as my anticipation grew.

'OK to touch it?' I asked.

'Please yourself. No paint left to damage after that lot went round with their crime scene paraphernalia.'

Ignoring this slur, I whipped the cover off and there she was. The Black Beauty, despite the dust of years, the dullness of the paint and brittle-looking upholstery. History sprang into life again. The Alfa Romeo 1937 8C 2900B.

That great man of cars Henry Ford once said, 'Every time I see an Alfa Romeo go past, I raise my hat.' I didn't have a hat with me, but I certainly felt I should at least bend the knee. Even in that unloved state, she deserved that with her black paint, her sleek elegant lines, the dark red upholstery, and, painted on the bonnet, the grimy but unmistakable remains of the green four-leafed clover thought to have brought the Alfa Romeo luck. Something did: Alfa Romeos won eight Mille Miglia races in the 1930s, during which a brilliant young man called Enzo Ferrari ran their racing department for much of the time.

This car shouldn't have to end its life here, so why *was* it here? What a waste. I thought of what Alfa Romeo specialist Ed

McDonough had said about one of the remaining 8C 2900Bs – that after all this time it was 'still zinging down the sweeping lanes'. That's what this one should be doing, not lying here uncherished. I forgot about the Land Rover, I forgot about the missing Hugh Compton case, I just vowed to myself that I would get to the bottom of the story that had brought the Alfa Romeo here – with which I was sure that the story of Giovanni and Hugh Compton must be entangled.

Paul was growing increasingly impatient. Just as I sensed he was at explosion point we were interrupted by a cheerful voice behind us.

'What on earth are you doing here, Paul? Trying to flog the old heap?'

This must surely be Stephanie, Paul's wife and Hugh's stepsister. As Giovanni said, she looked older than her husband, although she was giving the passing years a run for their money. She was one of those fashion-conscious ladies, who look so manicured and well-dressed that I'm always curious as to whether they appear like that at breakfast or stagger down like the rest of us to fortify themselves before they put on their armour for the day. Giovanni thought she was friendly and certainly she kept her good humour when her husband introduced me, although I received a sharp, speedy look as if life might be setting out to defraud her and I was its current emissary. Then a frown took the place of good humour.

'But aren't you a friend of that man Giovanni who murdered my brother?'

Paul's face bulged with fury. 'What the blazes are you doing here then?'

'He's been released without charge,' I pointed out, 'and I'm here on the Land Rover case which, as you assured me, is nothing to do with your brother-in-law's disappearance.'

Stephanie then took over. 'That man's a murderer,' she insisted, 'and I've been told you help the police on murder cases.'

'If commissioned to do so, but I haven't been.'

'In that case, why are you looking at the Alfa Romeo?' she enquired.

'I love classic cars and who wouldn't want to see this one?'

She ignored that. 'That's why you're here. You think this car is connected to my brother's murder. It isn't and your friend is undoubtedly his murderer.'

'Your brother is only missing at present and I hope very much that you're wrong.'

She stared at me, then glanced at Paul who nodded agreement. 'Mr Colby,' she said finally, good humour restored, 'you've seen quite enough.'

Odd, I thought, as I walked back to my car. They seemed more concerned over Giovanni than over their missing brother.

My next port of call was at Four Star Services, Martin Fisher's garage. This was a no-brainer as far as the Land Rover theft was concerned and anything I might pick up on the Comptons would be a bonus. The place looked desolate, perhaps because it was now overcast and drizzling with rain. It was a repair business, not retail, and did not sell petrol, and I thought at first that there was no one inside the large, sturdy wooden building, which looked somewhat like an overgrown Swiss chalet. When I poked my head inside though a curly-haired lad in his early twenties appeared, announced his name was Stephen and asked if he could help. He could: I would find Martin along at the Hop and Harry pub.

Leaving my car where it was, I walked back to the pub past the hotel, which was inappropriately called The Larches, as its 1990s combination of red brick and gabled mock-beamed dormers hardly conveyed the grace of the tree after which it was named. Behind it was a garden and by its side I glimpsed a children's play area, dominated, as far as I could see, by two huge plastic welcoming bears, one bearing the name Huggy, the other one Puggy.

In contrast to that, the Hop and Harry was a pleasing sight, and I liked the way it perched so confidently on the bend of the road from old Plumshaw. It was attractive, partly because the Olde English aspect had not been overdone. It was an old timbered building but the beams were stained grey, rather than the usual black, which gave it a mellow appearance, and the hanging flower baskets looked as if they were planted at home and not bought in as a job lot.

Inside I found myself in a low-ceilinged bar that looked homely in the best sense of the word. There was hardly anyone in it, however, save for a table at the rear with half a dozen people, perhaps journalists waiting for the next scoop, and for Martin sitting in front by a window and indulging in a beer and a toasted sandwich. He didn't seem surprised to see me, as he must have had a clear view of my arrival. He didn't look particularly pleased either.

'About Peter Compton's missing Land Rover, Martin,' I began, pleasantries over.

'Pull the other one,' he rejoined, as cheerfully as a man interrupted mid-sandwich could. 'You're here about the Alfa Romeo.'

'Only partly. Officially the Land Rover.'

'The other reason being your chum Giovanni.'

'Perhaps,' I replied diplomatically. 'That agreed – any idea what's going on here now that Giovanni's been released? Is that what all the press are here for? Waiting for Hugh to stroll back?'

'They'll have a long wait if so.'

'And if he doesn't, how's that going to affect the development plans you told me about?' I thought I was speaking softly enough not to be overheard, but I was wrong. A pretty woman in her early thirties emerged from behind the bar and marched over to us.

'Meet Lucy,' Martin said, clearly amused. 'She and her husband Andrew run this place. That's Andrew there, Jack.' He indicated a man of about Lucy's age in a chef's apron, currently talking to the press.

'There won't be any development plans,' Lucy told me brightly. 'We're turning the pub around successfully, aren't we, Martin?'

'You're doing a great job,' he assured her without much conviction, as she was joined by Andrew, who put a protective arm round her. Lucy was clearly the draw here, I thought. Andrew looked pleasant enough but a reluctant host. I bore in mind that he had been Pen's informer, however, so I reserved judgement on him.

'If you're here for the gossip,' he addressed me, 'Hugh's going to turn up again all right.'

'George Makepeace will be rubbing his hands with joy if he doesn't,' Lucy added, to her husband's clear annoyance.

'Is George the enemy?' I asked.

'To half the village, yes. To the other half, he's its saviour. And in between come Lucy and me,' Andrew said lightly.

'And me,' Martin offered.

Lucy and Andrew didn't comment on this, perhaps because Martin's garage stood adjacent to Makepeace land, and although I liked Martin I wouldn't care to hazard a guess as to which side he might back if push came to shove.

'We need Hugh back here,' Andrew said. 'He's the obstacle to Makepeace's deal with the developers.'

'I thought his father owned the Compton estate?'

'Hugh runs it though,' Martin replied. 'They could always sell the Alfa Romeo of course. That would keep the farm going, but the old man won't sell that either.'

'Peter Compton's our lifebelt,' Lucy chimed in. 'Paul and Stephanie wouldn't give a damn if the farm was sold and the Alfa Romeo with it.'

'He's getting on a bit to rely on him as a lifebelt,' I said.

'Ninety-five and still shouting,' Andrew said. 'Met his wife Hazel, have you?'

'I haven't had that pleasure,' I said.

'Forget the pleasure. The first wife left Plumshaw when Stephanie was a kid. Took the toddler and toddled off.' Andrew sniggered, to a reproving look from Lucy.

'Does Hugh have a son,' I asked, 'as well as his daughter Bronte?'

'No, and that means there's a succession problem if Hugh's dead.'

'Why? Because of her sex?'

Another snigger from Andrew. 'In a way. She fancies Jamie Makepeace, George's grandson.'

I whistled. 'A touch of the Romeo and Juliet?' I joked. No one laughed, which made me want to poke further. 'It would solve the feud nicely if they married.'

'Anyone seen a pig flying over?' Lucy said. 'Firstly it won't happen and even if it did, Makepeace and Compton would still be at each other's throats.'

'Hazel Compton is against development too?' I asked.

'She is, but if Hugh is dead the likelihood is that the farm would be left to Paul and Stephanie, rather than Bronte.'

'That's Peter's choice?'

'Yes, but it suits him to have Hazel as his mouthpiece. He likes to pretend he's a spent force, but no way. That's just a gambit. He was in the SAS or something like that during the Second World War and is still a raging bull. His first wife was a tornado in her own right by all accounts, and several years after she died he married Hazel. She was a nurse, I think. She's in her seventies now and there are daggers drawn between her and Stephanie if you ask me. Bronte's Mrs Compton's pet, or she'd like her to be. But Bronte has a mind of her own.'

'Suppose she and Jamie Makepeace do marry?'

'All hell will be let loose to ensure they don't.' Andrew looked almost pleased, though to me it seemed a disaster waiting to happen.

'Isn't there some way to bring peace between the two sides?' I asked. 'Don't you have a peacemaker in the village who could act as go-between?'

Martin grinned. 'Sure we do. It's an unspoken agreement that first old Plumshaw controls the parish council and then new Plumshaw does. As for a peacemaker, we do have a witch.'

'Seriously?'

I assumed it was a joke until I saw no one laughing. Instead Andrew apparently had to get back to the kitchen, Lucy to the bar, and Martin to his garage. Left alone, I finished my drink, had something to eat – which was quite good – and then I too left. Lucy had disappeared from the bar by then, and I went out through the back door to see the rest of the pub's domain. What I found was Lucy in their garden, which was not large but beautifully kept. She was hard at work digging a hole for a rose currently living in a pot, and as this witch was still intriguing me I decided to have another go at it. Lucy, rather than Andrew, seemed the better bet to me.

'It will be a great shame,' I said appreciatively, 'if the pub is pulled down and you lose this garden.'

'The Comptons won't sell,' she said shortly.

'Unless Hugh fails to return,' I commented. 'Perhaps your witch could work out a compromise if the wand method fails.'

She looked up sharply. 'I wish they wouldn't talk like that.'

'It is true, then? Covens at dead of night, that sort of thing?'

'No, it's only Nan.' She then gave her full concentration to the rose.

I tried to make sense of this but she was feverishly digging now, clearly hoping I'd go away. 'Where does this Nan live?' I asked. 'In a cottage in the dark, dark woods?'

The joke went wrong. She stood up abruptly, spade in hand.

'Nan lives in Puddledock Cottage. That enough for you?'

It was. How could I resist going in search of a witch who lived in Puddledock Cottage?

I returned to my car to check the large-scale map and my satnav for the whereabouts of Puddledock Cottage. Coming from my usual direction it lay just before I reached old Plumshaw and, sure enough, there was woodland marked all round it which ran as far as Plumshaw Manor. That suited me very well. It was time I met the Comptons. I'd call at the manor first and then take the interesting-looking track through the woods to the cottage from there. That would surely be the appropriate way to approach a witch's domain, even though with my hulking six foot I was hardly a little Red Riding Hood trotting along towards a big bad wolf.

I thought the witch had changed domains when the manor doorbell was answered. A small, elderly woman with piercing eyes – surely Hazel Compton – inspected my police identification in silence, then returned it to me.

Having ignored my condolences on her missing son, she awarded me a sweet smile and a flat 'What do you want?'

I explained. 'Did you hear anything unusual on the Friday night when the Land Rover disappeared?'

'No.' Her eyes indicated this was a game she intended to win.

'Could anyone on the estate have taken it for whatever reason?'
'No.'

'Could your son have taken it on a mission of his own?'

'Certainly not.' Another sweet smile.

'Is there anything at all that was odd about the theft?'
'No.'

I fought my irritation, and reminded myself that compared with her anxiety over her missing son a stolen car was merely an irritant. 'I'm on my way to Puddledock Cottage, but thought it polite to call here first.'

'What do you want to go there for?'

I wasn't sure I knew, so I asked for directions instead.

'Leave the car here, walk towards Manor Cottage, take the track leading off to the right just before you get there, and don't come back. Except for your car.'

Something that in happier times might have been a twinkle in her eye came and went. I went too. She was under stress, but that didn't entirely explain her attitude. I duly set off through the woods, wondering if I would need breadcrumbs to sprinkle along the path to find my way back in the best fairy-tale tradition. With my current luck the starlings would eat the lot before my return. The path was simple enough to find, and it was a peaceful if not entirely enjoyable walk through the woods. The May greenery looked attractive, but drops from a recent shower dripped from overhanging branches which, where the trees were at their thickest, blotted out the sun and gave a sinister undertone to my journey. Nevertheless the woods smelled of spring and of England at its best.

The map showed only one cottage on the far side of the wood, and only one main fork in the track. Unfortunately, there were quite a few more paths and finally I was at a loss to know which one to take. The one I chose brought me to a point where I could see a lane ahead and a cottage. With any luck it was Puddledock. It was half-buried in woodland with a rear garden surrounded by trees but with three tracks leading back into the woods. The front showed a more cheerful aspect and a neat garden with a wicket gate and a painted sign announcing that it was indeed Puddledock Cottage. There was no reply to the bell, however, nor was there any sign of life in the garden, despite the fact that there was a Ford Escort parked outside.

Blaming myself for having made this pointless and now wasted journey, I set off down a different path hoping to weave my way back to the manor. It was narrower than the one I had come by and I found myself slipping in mud. Then I turned a corner and was surprised to see a large pond with seemingly fresh enough water to support a duck population. I remember my mother calling them Puddle-ducks. This was not Puddle*duck* cottage, though, but Puddle*dock*, which means something to do with mud – as I could testify this path did. The pond was something special, however, and I stopped to admire the sheer beauty of the surroundings. Only then did I become aware that I was not alone.

On the far side of the pond stood a gigantic man whose size, muscles and shaven head would guarantee him top rates as a bodyguard. He exuded power. He was gazing down at a dark patch of undergrowth or leaves in the water, but fortunately when he looked up and saw me, he didn't begin flexing those muscles in readiness.

'Do you know where Nan is?' I called out, thinking this might be her husband or son.

'Reckon I do,' he said slowly.

'Where then?' I asked politely as he showed no signs of continuing.

'I'm Nan.'

It was only then that I looked at what had caught his attention in the pond. It wasn't a patch of dark-coloured leaves. It was a body floating face down. A very dead body.

FOUR

A ny chance that there was any life left in the body that Nan and I dragged out of the pond was rapidly discounted. This body had – at least to my lay eye – been in the water too long for that. The skin was far too wrinkled for Nan to have tipped it in himself just before my arrival. I reminded myself, however, that the first person on the scene is often the guilty party and that it wasn't beyond the bounds of possibility that he had kept the body secreted at the helpfully remote Puddledock Cottage and only recently pushed it in. I temporarily abandoned this theory because it was leaping away beyond any evidence.

Standing on the edge of a pond with even a potential murderer was, nevertheless, not my idea of a sensible thing to do. That was only a fleeting thought, especially as the police and paramedics were on their way, but it took my mind off the gruesome sight before me. There was no obvious sign of how he had died save for what were possible bloodstains on the man's shirt, jacket and trousers. The greyish skin and indications that wildlife attack had begun were not something to dwell on, however.

As to whose body it was, it was almost certainly Hugh Compton's. If so, my first thought was that this pond was miles from where Giovanni had been spotted in his car which had Hugh's blood in it. My next thought was that wouldn't matter a damn, as theoretically Giovanni could have killed him here and then driven to Challock to protest his innocence, with the result that the police concentrated on that area. No, on second thoughts they would have searched this area too.

The wood was heavy with silence while Nan and I waited. I could hear his steady hard breathing, the trees were hiding us from the afternoon sun and the claustrophobic atmosphere had to be broken.

'Had you only just spotted him when I arrived?' I forced myself to ask.

He raised his large head from the contemplation of the body, and turned to stare at me. Then he smiled slightly and nodded. It was a reassuring smile, not the sort that suggested I keep my mouth shut.

'It's him, isn't it?' I continued.

'Yes. Mr Compton.'

I liked the way he afforded him some dignity. Corpses have a right to a personality.

'Did you hear or see anything going on here recently?'

'No.'

That seemed to end it, but I didn't want our stilted conversation to end. I'd have to look at the corpse again if I did. 'So you're Nan,' I said fatuously. 'I came here to find you.'

That slow smile again as he picked up my unspoken query. 'Full name Nantucket Brown, sir.'

My attention was well and truly on him now. What a name!

'My grandad,' he told me, 'was a whaler. In his time,' he added reflectively.

Ah! All was explained. '*Moby Dick*,' I said. One of my father's favourite novels. There was a Gregory Peck film made in the fifties which I knew Dad watched whenever it came on TV and so I had bought him the DVD not long before he died. The original, he demanded, not the remake. Nan must have acquired his name from the island off the Massachusetts shore, as Nantucket was a big whaling centre.

Nan nodded. 'They maybe told you in the village I was a witch. That why you came?'

This man would expect a truthful answer. 'Yes,' I replied. 'I'm curious to know what they meant by that.'

A long pause for consideration. 'What they means is me just looking, just seeing.'

'Did you foresee this?' I looked briefly at the corpse.

The English language is complex; it can convey meaning with precision because it bends and accommodates it in the most simple of words. The hitch, as Humpty Dumpty pointed out to Alice, is that some words can mean just what one chooses them to mean, but which isn't obvious to other people. In what sense, I wondered, did Nan want 'seeing' to be interpreted: understanding or observing?

'There'll be work for me to do here,' he replied – if this could be termed a reply.

I could hear police sirens now and cars drawing up nearby. We stopped talking, Nan and I, as we watched the police approaching through the hundred yards of woodland towards us, calling out to us. Then they were with us. Two at first, then more.

Whatever work Nan had in mind, it wasn't yet needed as the police went into action and we withdrew as indicated to the far side of the pond, as they put up their cordon. It didn't take long for the whole caboodle to assemble at the distant roadside, judging by the row of vans I heard drive up, crime scene officers, forensic personnel, paramedics and more. It was obvious this was a suspected major crime incident, as the proximity to Plumshaw Manor would have been obvious.

And so it all began. The invasion that a death such as this brings in its wake seemed all the more incongruous in its woodland setting. We were ushered back into the trees with the cordon taping off the path I had travelled along, but we could still see the tent over the body, and the white-suited forensic team moving around. As I had expected, DCI Brandon was very much in charge as the Senior Investigating Officer. He and I are well acquainted, verging on being cautious and temporary partners when it suits him, and if we need a bridge between us, Dave Jennings in the Car Crime Unit supplies it.

The question was, assuming this was indeed Hugh Compton's body: was his death one of those cases for partnership or not? At the moment I sincerely hoped not, but the issue hadn't yet arisen and in any case my personal friendship with Giovanni (although currently wavering) would rule it out.

Nan and I remained onlookers until the PC guarding us was detailed to detach himself along with Nan. They were replaced by Brandon. He's quiet, of medium height and size, in fact a medium everything sort of man, until he turns his policeman's eyes on you. They didn't seem to be on me yet, thankfully, as he spoke professional to professional. Once upon a time it would have been a suspicious 'You again?'

'Here on Dave's case, are you?' is what he in fact asked me.

'Yes. Just begun. Nothing of relevance to this – yet. Could well be though. One strange thing, don't you think?' I'd refrained from discussing this with Nan, but it had struck me immediately.

Brandon glanced thoughtfully at me. 'The clothes?'

He doesn't miss much. 'Yes. Hugh Compton went missing immediately after a formal dinner, so the Comptons' statements read. Corduroys unlikely then.'

'Slow down, Jack. Early days. He could have changed before he went to the barn.' He looked over at Nan. 'Did he find the body or did you?'

'He did. Just before I came up that path. He was on the opposite side of the pond.'

'Did you hear anything as you approached?'

'No.'

'What were you doing here?'

'Looking for Nan. He's a village character.' I decided to keep the word 'witch' to myself.

Brandon doesn't do characters, only witnesses. 'Right. Later, Jack. Both of you. Can you hang on here?' It wasn't really a question and I hoped it was leading to a request to keep on poking my nose in, but report to him.

I nodded. 'Hugh Compton, I presume?'

'Looks like it. I'm going to the manor now.'

Nan and I were detailed to be fitted out with scene shoes, give our details for the scene attendance log, and then to return to his cottage with his faithful PC, to await our turn for official interview. To my relief, the PC indicated he'd stay outside Puddledock Cottage although he hinted that a cup of coffee would go down nicely. I welcomed the chance to talk to Nan alone.

It was as weird walking with this six footer rippling with muscles under the black T-shirt and heading for a fairy-tale cottage as it had been to see a corpse in that peaceful little duck pond, a calm now vanished amidst the paraphernalia of suspicious death.

The cordon took in all the paths leading to and from the pond, so we crunched our way through the woodland itself. What was Nan's story? I wondered, to take my mind off that body. And why was Nan deemed a witch? This business of looking and seeing didn't quite add up to witchcraft. The outside of the cottage and garden were immaculate and that didn't sit easily with the abode of a wicked witch in the wood. Early roses were coming into bloom, clinging to the walls of the house with lattice windows peeping in their midst. Once, the cottage would probably have been thatched, but now it had a well-weathered tiled roof.

Nan carefully removed his boots as I did my loafers for shoe-printing and we padded our way in scene shoes into his cottage. The door was unlocked, and there was probably no need to lock anything with a reputation and physique such as his. Inside, the house was as neat as a shiny pin, although it struck me as empty of atmosphere, which suggested he lived here alone. I followed him into the kitchen, where he proceeded to make ground coffee in a jug, which smelled wonderful. This task accomplished and a mug duly delivered to the PC, Nan brought our two mugs into the 'parlour'. Its comfortable chairs, sofa and watercolour landscapes adorning the walls demanded the use of this old-fashioned word. It told me nothing of the man, however. I could see only one photograph and that was of a middle-aged woman smiling somewhat grimly at the onlooker. The style of her hair and clothes suggested she would now be in her eighties.

'My mum,' Nan told me, as I looked at it. 'Died three years back.'

'Did she come from the States or was that your grandparents' origin?'

He shrugged. 'British as far as I know.'

'You were born here?'

I had had a vision of a birth aboard a whaling ship, owned by his grandparents. It was a big jump from whaling to Puddledock Cottage.

'Lived here fifteen years or so. Mr Compton said they had this place going. Dad and Mum liked it. Puddledock, see? House by a muddy pool.' He didn't seem disposed to go on talking and we sat quietly for a while. This wasn't the time to question him further about his family. He'd have enough to face from Brandon.

He eventually broke the silence himself. 'How come that body got in the pool, eh? What would Mr Compton be doing there? I'm up to date with my rent, so he weren't coming here.'

I had no idea how much was generally known about Hugh Compton's disappearance or Giovanni's part in it, but I had to produce some kind of answer to keep the conversation alive. 'Tripped and fell, perhaps.'

This was deservedly dismissed. 'Water not deep enough. Not in Puddledock pond. Two, three feet maybe. I'd have seen him there.'

'When did you last go by it?'

'Policeman asked me that. Maybe four days back. Been too busy at work.'

As a witch did he mean? 'What line are you in?'

'Handyman. Work at The Larches Hotel. And at the pub. And at the church. I like that.'

'Both Makepeace and Compton territory. A foot in both camps,' I observed.

He looked at me as though I had disappointed him. 'I can do a lot that way. Make . . . peace,' he added. 'That's my other job.'

He then cut off my instinctive reply of 'how do you do that' by asking, 'What else are you here for, mister?'

Fair enough. 'I'm a classic car restorer and do odd jobs for the Kent Car Crime Unit. Peter Compton's Land Rover has been stolen from the manor.'

'Police,' he said to himself more than to me, I thought. 'What can they do, eh?'

'They try.'

'Can't see inside a man, they can't.' He didn't seem hostile but added abruptly, 'I'm good at putting things right.'

Careful, Jack, I thought. 'Inside people or outside?' I kept it as matter of fact as I could.

'Mum was more outside. I'm best inside or maybe they're both the same. Unless you see inside how can you deal with outside? I can do my bit outside too though. Want to see?'

See? Was I going to be a guinea pig? Hypnotized? I followed him uneasily but I went – partly through curiosity and partly because it would take my mind off Hugh Compton.

He led me back through the kitchen, opened a door to an adjoining room and I followed him inside. Once again I was taken by surprise. This could have been a pharmacy with its white cupboards, worktops, spotless jars all neatly labelled, and distilling apparatus.

'Mum's still room,' he said matter-of-factly. 'I do a bit now and then. When wanted. I'm good at rosemary bruise ointment and itches and things. Mum was keen on freckle remover and honey face cream so I picked up a lot of that too.'

I decided not to press too far into this. The idea of Nan dabbling in facial products fascinated me though. 'Did your father help?'

'Years back, maybe. He liked it here. Safe in Puddledock, he said, and then he died. Just Mum and me then,' he added.

The son looking after the widowed mother. It was a familiar pattern, and yet something wasn't familiar about it. This gentle giant must have seen the battle between the Makepeaces and the Comptons at close quarters and must be tough himself. He worked for a living, so what had he been doing out by the pond in mid afternoon on a working day?

I walked back to the crime scene when Brandon's sergeant arrived to interview Nan and to tell me I was wanted there. I had a connection with this case on three counts: first, because I had been so early on the scene; secondly because of the Dave Jennings job and thirdly because of Giovanni. It was the last that made me want to run like hell. If, however, the clothes Hugh Compton had been wearing had not been those he had on in the barn, that was surely a big plus in Giovanni's favour.

When I arrived, there was no sign of Brandon, only the forensic operators going about their work. I announced myself to the PC in charge of the scene attendance log and, by the time I was properly equipped with a scene suit, I could see Brandon walking back with a woman PC, but not with Paul Ranger, as I had expected. Instead, Hazel Compton was with him. I was appalled. She was Hugh's mother, so was this identification task by her choice? I couldn't believe it would be Brandon's. Underneath the wooden face he's reasonably sensitive.

Brandon indicated that I should join them, and reluctantly I did so. It was not a time for conversation. Hazel Compton didn't even register my arrival and looked glassy-eyed with shock.

'It's some mistake,' she kept repeating. 'It can't be Hugh. It can't.'

She seemed to regain some composure as she went into the tent with Brandon and the PC, but that quickly changed.

Everyone heard that scream. It must have chilled more than me to the bone. Then there was another one, and another. I stepped away as she was supported out of the tent and the first-aider rushed over to help. He was pushed aside as she clung to Brandon, partly for support but it seemed more like an attack as she pummelled him with her fists.

'It's *him*,' she was screaming. '*Hugh!*'

'She insisted on coming,' Brandon explained, when eventually he was free to talk to me. 'She didn't want anyone else with her, not the stepdaughter and not the husband.'

'It's natural enough for her to take it badly.' Badly, yes, I thought, but even so there was something unexpected about her collapse that I couldn't define. I wasn't going to forget that scream for a long, long time.

'He's been missing for nearly a week, but it's the shock,' Brandon said soberly. 'People don't conform to the norm under pressure.' He looked shaken himself.

'Do you know yet how long the body had been in the water? All the time he'd been missing?'

Brandon shot me a look, as it must have been clear that I had Giovanni on my mind. 'The provisional verdict is about two to three days, judging by the skin condition. Beginning to detach itself. He'd been stabbed several times in a fairly frenzied attack, although there wasn't much blood left on the clothes.'

'Giovanni's been free since Saturday afternoon.' I knew he wouldn't have spent time carting bodies around but Brandon wasn't going to think that way.

'Staying with you, is he?' He looked sympathetic.

'Only until yesterday morning; he's now in the village with Len Vickers. His wife's come over to keep him company.'

Brandon said nothing. No better way to rile me.

'Is the theory,' I asked, 'that Giovanni hid the body, then crept over on Saturday or Sunday by dead of night to remove the body from its hiding place and plonk it in the pond? Not possible.'

Then I remembered Giovanni had told me he was going out on Sunday – and that I hadn't told Brandon that, so I had to add, 'He has the use of a BMW rental car. He picked it up before he came to Frogs Hill on Saturday and used it on Sunday.'

'So that line's possible,' he said. 'Too risky where the body was and there are no signs yet of a struggle here.'

He was wrong – I was struggling hard. 'And a darn sight more risky to lug bodies around. Pointless too, since it eluded your searches the first time.'

He let me off lightly. 'Not looking good for Donati, Jack. The DNA results of the blood on the front and back seating and the car door, as well as in the barn, show it's Compton's all right and there's plenty of it. That plus the trace evidence looks more than enough. He was drugged, certainly, but easy enough to do that himself.'

Just as Giovanni had predicted. I tried another tack. 'But the clothes. Giovanni wouldn't have had a change of clothes ready for Hugh. Have you checked them yet?'

Brandon looked even more sympathetic. 'Sorry. Mrs Compton says the family saw him after he changed his clothes that night and he has the same shirt on now. Seems to have dressed in a hurry though.'

My last hope snapped in two. Brandon was right. It wasn't looking good for Giovanni.

'This Land Rover job for Dave,' I managed to say more reasonably. 'Are you going to tell him he'll have to fire me?' To me it was a foregone conclusion.

'I've been thinking about it. You're personally involved: black mark. On the other hand, I've known you long enough to know you'll turn in *anything* you find out impartially. You've just told me about that rental car for a start. Sometimes you turn up results, so I'm willing to give you a long leash, *if* you keep a low profile.'

I handed in my scene suit and walked through the woods towards my car, still parked at the manor. I was mentally reeling from what had happened and what might happen now that the body had been discovered. Add the super-heavy layer of my personal turmoil about Giovanni and Louise and I was completely thrown. Did I want Brandon's 'long leash'? Think of it another way. Did I think Giovanni guilty? No. I clung to the fact that Giovanni could have no possible motive for killing Compton. Sudden row? What row could have broken out that was so serious as to demand physical attack? At least Louise was not part of that conundrum. She had never met the Comptons as far as I knew. It began to dawn on me, however, that perhaps as far as I knew was not as far as I had hitherto believed.

I forced myself to concentrate on the situation itself, not to think about Louise. Put that way, I'd no choice. I was going on with the case, whose ingredients were:

One dead body.

A grieving family – which for nearly a week had had to face the fact that Hugh might be dead. Nevertheless some of that family might have their own reasons for wanting Hugh dead.

Feuding villagers with their own reasons for wanting Hugh out of the way.

One Italian who had never met Hugh until the day he died.

Which out of the latter three was the most likely to be behind

Hugh's death? On statistics alone, the family. But in this case? And if it was a family-based murder was it just coincidence that Giovanni's visit had been timed for the day it happened? It would be an elaborate murder plan, involving drugging Giovanni, putting Hugh's body in Giovanni's car, and driving him off to wake up without a clue as to what was going on. The rear seat of that Ferrari Daytona is hardly big enough for a third person to fit in both a deadweight Giovanni and a dead body, yet to drive them separately would require the use of another car. Too cumbersome a scenario.

Next: why the need to make another journey to pick up the body and transport it to the duck pond? Why such an elaborate plot to frame Giovanni when, if Hugh's death was the object, he could have been killed at any time and in a much less risky way? Would any guest have served their purpose or was it Giovanni in particular? He was a stranger to them so perhaps he filled the role of unsuspecting visitor. No way, I realized. As a celeb, he would be a very bad choice in that role because the eyes of the world press would be focused on the case.

Or, I wondered, was I looking at this pyramid the wrong way up? Was the central factor not Hugh or the family but the Alfa Romeo? With Hugh's murder it would attract world attention and would be worth way over a million, if not several. Could that be a linchpin factor?

Great thinking, Jack, I told myself crossly. How could it be? Hugh Compton didn't own the car. His father did. I felt there was something to this theory, unsatisfactory though it was overall, but I couldn't quite shake it into working.

Then an insidious little voice inside me asked: are you trying to get away from seeing Giovanni as the central factor? That's how the police doubtless saw it.

I knew I should get back to Frogs Hill, find Len and then break the news of Hugh's death to Giovanni, but I realized I was manufacturing reasons not to return until forced to do so. I knew all too well what the central core of *that* problem was: Louise. She was colouring every aspect of Frogs Hill, including its now problematic visitor, Giovanni.

I convinced myself that there was work to do here in Plumshaw village before I returned, as Hugh's death could equally be down to the status quo of the feud, one side of which I had never met

– the Makepeaces. First, I gave way to temptation when I saw the barn door was open. My mission could wait.

Inside the air was cool. The Alfa Romeo sat there without her cover looking sublime. It was hard to believe that this car, which had taken part in what is called the 'most beautiful race in the world', had anything to do with murder. It had not been driven for decades, but why did Peter Compton leave such a treasure here untended and unloved? Plenty of cars have been discovered in barns such as this one but there is usually a reason for the neglect. Often, their owners had died, the next generation often honoured a beloved car but left it to rot, and by the time the succeeding generation came along there was no interest at all and its provenance was forgotten. Only when someone took up its cause would interest be aroused in its value. But in the case of this Alfa Romeo the owner was still alive and, it seemed, very much a power to be reckoned with. I was looking forward to meeting him, but today was not the day. He had his son's death to cope with. All the same, as I looked at the Alfa Romeo I thought what a crying shame it was to see it so unloved. Was Peter Compton missing a trick?

I drove my Polo out of the manor gates with a feeling of relief, and made straight for the pub, hoping I might find Martin there. It was five-thirty and his garage closed usually at seven p.m. Today, however, the news about Hugh would have spread.

Parked on the forecourt of the Hop and Harry was a white van with the legend 'Manning and Thompson Limited: Surveyors'. That might mean nothing, but on the other hand it could be a provocative move on the Makepeaces' part if they were planning to put in a development plan to the council to get approval before the land was sold to them.

The pub was full and I hardly recognized anyone there. Then at a large table I spotted Martin, and standing plumb in front of me, back to the bar and with arms folded, was Nan. No one took any notice of me, even Nan.

I made my way to the bar, listening to the continuous babble of voices as Lucy served me with a shandy and a whispered: 'Careful where you sit.'

I hadn't been planning on sitting anywhere so far, but I would defend my right to do so. 'Why's that?'

'The Comptons are sitting over there—' she indicated the area

to the right of me – 'and the Makepeaces there.' That was to the
left, and where Martin was sitting. 'You should be OK,' Lucy added,
'because they're just talking about what it will mean for the village.'

'Suppose they don't like where I'm sitting?' I meant it as a joke
but she treated it seriously.

'Nan will deal with it,' she told me.

I glanced at him but he showed no sign of wishing to continue
our earlier acquaintanceship, so I decided I'd join Martin. I was an
outsider, after all, so I took my glass and strolled over to the table.
Outsider or not, I was in no doubt that my choice had been noted.

There was a murmur of appreciation from the Makepeace table,
and Martin greeted me, looking self-conscious. The pub seemed
more and more like a kids' playground – with Nan playing the same
role as The Larches' Huggy and Puggy bears: an imposing welcome
that no one could miss. A sour-looking man in his sixties, opposite
me, seemed disposed to fight my claim to a seat at the table.

'Heard you'd been at the manor,' he grunted.

'Jack Colby,' Martin quickly introduced me. 'He's been on a job
there.'

The tension relaxed. 'George Makepeace,' Martin continued,
introducing me to Mr Sour Face. 'And this is his grandson, Jamie.'

Ah. The Romeo of the pair, who had designs on Hugh's daughter.
Jamie, a good-looking lad in his early twenties, grinned at me.

'We heard you were up there this afternoon, Jack,' Martin
continued awkwardly.

This information must have been courtesy of Nan, I presumed.
The eyes round the table were fixed on me expectantly.

'I was at the pond when Hugh Compton's body was found. Or
rather the body presumed to be his. Not officially published yet.'

'It's him all right. And you can give the old bastard my compli-
ments next time you're at the manor,' grunted good old George.

'No need to take that line, Grandad,' Jamie muttered.

'Where them Comptons are concerned, there's every need, son,'
he retorted. 'All this toadying, yessir, nosir. Them days are over.
And you're as bad, Martin. Up there like a flash when they crook
their crooked fingers.'

'Business, George,' Martin replied mildly.

'All of you, boot lickers,' George continued. 'Still, I'll say no
more today, in respect, like. Lost his son, but we'll soon see the

manor taking a different turn now, eh? No more of this beating the bounds of Plumshaw in his Land Rover as though he owns the lot of us.'

There was the scraping of a chair and one of the men – a retired businessman perhaps – came over from the Compton camp. 'Suppose for once you keep your mouth shut, Mr Makepeace?'

'It's a free world.'

'You'd never know it the way you grab every penny you can.' Another Compton supporter had joined him. There was a further scraping of chairs and the Makepeace table (save for me and Jamie) rose as one. They made their way east, as the Comptons promptly edged west.

The atmosphere was turning ugly, and Nan slowly uncoiled himself from the bar.

'A man died in my pond today,' he said quietly. 'I'll not hear ill of him till the mourning's over.'

To my amazement this had a remarkable effect. The Comptons simply melted back to their own side without a word and the Makepeaces to theirs. Although this stand-off had lasted perhaps half a minute, it was a sign to me that, even with Nan as umpire, this was a village that would carry on the infighting. It would be firm in the knowledge that it could only go so far in public. But in private? What went on there?

Eventually I had to drive home. I was still shaken by the events of the day and the thought of what I might find when I reached home made it worse. It *was* worse. It was seven-thirty, long after the time when Len and Zoe might be found in the Pits and any hope that Louise might be there was dashed. I had to face whatever might be happening at the Vickers' home. Had they heard the news or not? Rather than ring first, I drove straight to Pluckley, aware that I was breaking unspoken taboos. Crazy though it might sound, although Len has worked for my family for many years, I have never been inside his home. The doorstep, yes, but no further. It riled me that Giovanni had entered it without even earning the privilege. Today however I had to break bad news to him.

It was Len who came to the door and he let me in without a word, which set my alarm bells ringing. They rang even louder when in the living room, a friendly looking place crowded with family photos and souvenirs, I saw Mrs Len, Zoe, and Maria. There was a gap.

'Where's Giovanni?' I asked, though I hardly needed telling.

'They arrest him for murder, Jack!' Maria screamed at me, leaping up from her chair.

'It's serious,' Zoe told me. 'Looks as if they're going to charge him this time. There's a body been found. We heard it on the news.'

Maria rushed over to me, throwing her arms round me. 'He want you help him, Jack. He say Jack will save him.'

FIVE

I pulled into a lay-by in the lane to Frogs Hill. There is a good view from this point down over to the Weald far below and it's good for thinking, whether idly or seriously. It was the latter I needed. It was hardly a surprise that Giovanni had been rearrested and could very well be charged this time, but that Brandon should have acted so quickly took me aback. It suggested that even his hotshot solicitor wouldn't be able to do much for Giovanni at this stage, save to find him a good barrister. If charged, would he get bail after the first hearing? This might be a side issue, but it would be important for Maria. As Italy is an EU country, there wouldn't be much danger of his skipping the country to evade justice, but even so bail restrictions might include his staying here – if it was granted at all.

I put this issue aside in view of the much larger one facing me. Giovanni was expecting me to save him. Brandon was expecting me to help either way. Around me dusk was falling, the air was fresh and peaceful. Everything was preparing for the restful night, and metaphorically so was I – except I'd delete the 'restful'. The die was now cast and I had to sort out what to do. I wrestled with the core of the problem again: did I believe Giovanni to be a killer? No, except possibly by accident, if for instance he had hit Hugh Compton who had then fallen on something that caused his death. As he had died by stab wounds that probably ruled this out. So I was still left with a question mark: could anything after so short a time together have caused such an outbreak of rage on both their parts that it led to murder? Surely nothing could. It's true Giovanni doesn't like people criticizing his work – but who does? True, he doesn't like being told what to do – but who does? True, he doesn't suffer fools gladly – but a great many people don't. In my experience of the man, however – I struggled to be objective – he bore such everyday matters with equanimity, usually laughing them off.

I was going to need a fuller account from him as to what had happened between him and Hugh than I had so far received, including what he remembered of the time before he blanked out, exactly when that must have been and what Hugh was wearing. Assuming his basic story to be true, had he blanked out because of the sheer shock of seeing blood around him, with or without remembering the awfulness of what had happened? The alternative was that someone had drugged him. But that didn't add up in practical terms. This 'someone' – who could be one of the family – would have had to be sure that Giovanni was well and truly out, killed Hugh, put him in the rear seat of the Ferrari, driven the car to the woods in Challock and then walked back to Plumshaw, a theory I had already dismissed. I had also ruled out the possible accident-on-the-spur-of-the-moment scenario, and so even the cool air of the Downs wasn't inspiring any sensible alternative to the version the police were obviously going by. Which was that Giovanni killed Hugh either by plan or on the spur of the moment, panicked and drove away to find somewhere to hide the body.

There was no alternative to my next step. I had to talk to Giovanni again as soon as I could, but I'd have to separate the Giovanni I thought I'd known from the new one who had emerged on this visit. If the latter was the real man, I reasoned, then my instinctive opinion that Giovanni wasn't a killer might not be worth the paper it wasn't written on. To my frustration, I couldn't go far down that line. My father had been dead for over five years, but even so I sometimes sense his reproving eye glaring down at me. Giovanni was his friend long before he met me. Letting him down would be letting Dad down too.

Wrong, I eventually decided after a tussle. I'd bear that in mind, but I had to start from scratch and look at this case objectively, with no Dad and no Louise in mind. I waved goodbye to the placid scene in front of me, started the Polo and drove the remaining way to Frogs Hill. At least I had come back to the same decision. I would go ahead. If I could help, I should do so and with no holds barred. The past had to be ignored – however tough that was.

The lights were on. I pulled up on the forecourt of Frogs Hill and took stock of the situation. Had I left the hall light on? No. And that meant either I had a burglar waiting for me or that Louise had unexpectedly returned. Then I saw her car tucked round the corner of the Pits. At first sheer pleasure coupled with relief uplifted me,

but less pleasant thoughts soon followed. Had she heard about
Giovanni and come flying to his rescue?

'Jack!' She came running downstairs as soon as I was in the
house. 'I thought I heard you crunching your way in.' The gravel
on the drive is useful both as a deterrent and a warning. 'Have you
brought supper?' she continued practically.

Had I brought supper? What wonderfully normal words to hear.
I hugged her and it felt good. 'How could I? I didn't know you
were coming. I had a sandwich on the way home.' That was true;
it had been a delaying tactic on my way back from Plumshaw. 'I'll
cook you up something though.'

'I'll do it myself. I'll get a ready meal out of the freezer. What
kept you? Work I presume?'

Now for it. 'Well, in view of the news . . .' I began awkwardly.
Louise seemed remarkably composed, which was good.

'What news? World War Three?'

I steeled myself. 'About Giovanni.'

Her face fell. 'Is he still here?' She was trying to sound casual.

I remembered I hadn't told her that Giovanni had moved in with
Len. I explained the situation and that he wasn't there now, of
course.

'Why of course?' she asked carefully.

So she didn't know what had happened, which was, I supposed,
hardly surprising and made me ashamed of having attributed him
as her reason for being here. Maria was not going to put her at the
top of the list of those to be informed about his arrest. I tried to
make my answer sound deadpan.

'Giovanni has been arrested again and this time he'll probably
be charged with murder.'

'*Charged?* Oh, Jack!' She unwound herself from my arms, either
through her choice or because mine were already loosening their
hold. 'But he's not a murderer. How could anyone think that? This
means I—'

'Means what?' A cold feeling came over me as she broke off.

She shook her head impatiently. 'Nothing. Nothing at all. Is Maria
coming back here?'

Was Louise so nervous of Maria because of her affair with
Giovanni? Was she . . .? Stop, I commanded myself.

'It's not yet settled,' I told her. 'I'll have to suggest it. It isn't fair on Len otherwise, especially if Giovanni gets bail again after the initial hearing.' I hesitated, but realized it was no good holding back. I had to know, so I took the plunge.

'Tell me what's wrong, Louise. What's with you and Giovanni?'

Her face had a mulish expression that I had never seen on it before. 'That's not important. Giovanni *isn't* a murderer, Jack. He couldn't have done it.'

However important it was to *me*, I could see I would get no further. The matter was dropped. She ate some supper while I watched and a polite silence reigned. When we went to bed her back was turned to me. Worse, at that moment, I didn't care.

I needed a break from this avalanche that was smothering me, but I could see no way through it. Louise had left the next day and apparently the short run she was doing in London had been extended so she might be staying at the flat even longer. My wandering star arrangement with her hadn't been meant to cover this sort of situation. Under it she was free to come and go – because of her career, though, or so I had assumed. Never in my wildest nightmares had I thought that this would apply to our relationship as well. After all, nothing – it had seemed – could ever go wrong with that. Her flight today, however, was to escape from Frogs Hill, not the call of her own special star.

In the Pits, Zoe took one look at me as I approached – I had thought I appeared at least reasonably normal – and decided she had an urgent call to make outside. Len didn't even glance at me. I realized that without being conscious of it I was sending out signals set at danger.

After a while Len suddenly stood up. 'What's to happen to Maria?' he asked me belligerently. 'Up all night with her, my missus was.'

I was aghast. This long speech (for Len) meant things were really serious. 'I'm sorry, Len. She's naturally upset.'

'Me too. Can't go on, it can't.'

'I'll sort something out for Maria,' I said wearily. I knew very well, knowing Maria, that it *would* go on and on and I wasn't sure I could cope either. The idea of her coming to Frogs Hill now Louise had left again didn't attract me, but I had no choice. 'She'd better stay with me.'

'What about—?'

'Louise will be staying in London,' I said through gritted teeth.

'*Women!*' Len muttered darkly as Zoe came back to join us.

She took the slur on her gender amiss. '*Some* women!' she yelled at Len.

Len glared at her. I glared at them both. Frogs Hill was not in for a good day, and my best plan was to get out of it. But where to? I couldn't go to Plumshaw so soon after yesterday's trauma. My association with Giovanni was hardly going to go down well and nor would irrelevant questions about a stolen car. I'd tackle the Maria question later. For now, the Glory Boot was my immediate haven provided that Dad, whose memory is stamped everywhere there, didn't kick me out. Luckily he didn't bother to turn up today.

I was only on the starting grid of this case, I reasoned, but the Alfa Romeo was a great starting point. Its 'home' in the barn was where Giovanni and Hugh had been on the night it all happened. I needed to understand this car. There was no doubt it was a very special one, as it had been Giulio Santoro's own.

Dad didn't believe in filing systems, although he did believe in occasionally captioning photographs on their rear. I managed to find several more taken of the 1938 Mille Miglia race at various stages, including the one Giovanni had rhapsodized over, which was lying on the top of the pile. At least he'd had the grace to leave it there, but that didn't make me feel any better about this case.

I stared at this handful of pictures, one by one, and wondered what relevance they could possibly have to a murder almost eighty years later. From my iPad, I checked my memory about the 1938 race. Coming in first in a 2900B were Clementi Biondetti and Aldo Stefani, with a time for the 1600 km drive of eleven hours fifty-eight minutes twenty-nine seconds. Coming in only about two minutes behind them and also in a 2900B were Pintacuda and Mambelli. The third Alfa came in thirty-seven minutes later in a 2900A. These three had not been the only Alfa Romeos in the race, of course – one of the others was Giulio Santoro's.

So far so good, but where next? Those were the statistics, and anyway Peter Compton's wreck hadn't been one of the three winners, but the one that dropped out when nearing the end of the race. According to the press, that story had captured the hearts of the people. In 1938 its driver Giulio Santoro was twenty-three and married with a young daughter. He and his co-driver Enrico di

Secchio were the celebs of the day because of Giulio's compassionate act. He had been well positioned for winning the race until the final stages, when Enrico had been taken ill and Santoro insisted on diverting from the race to stop at the nearest hospital, where a burst appendix was treated just in time.

A great story and Santoro was undoubtedly a good guy, but it was still a long step from being a popular racing driver to a car ending up in England over seven decades later. I followed up with an online search and after many false starts (when aren't there?) discovered that Enrico, whose life he had saved, had bought the car for Santoro after the race and that, as Giovanni had found out, Santoro had republican sympathies (not a brilliant life plan under Mussolini's fascist dictatorship and the complacent monarchy). Nothing more seemed to be known about him. Interesting, but not helpful.

And then at eleven o'clock fate stepped in with a lucky break in the form of Dave Jennings on the phone.

'You're on the move, Jack.'

'Anywhere in particular?'

'Plumshaw. Peter Compton's Land Rover's back.'

'Good grief!' At the very least this proved that it hadn't been a straightforward theft for cash – unless of course the thief had a kind heart and returned it because of the owner's bereavement. I had to tread on eggshells here, however. 'What about Brandon?' I asked.

'It was he who told me about it. The Comptons rang him and for some crazy reason he wants you out there soonest. He's got his team checking it out and probably taking it away with them, so get your skates on.'

Suited me. 'Any no-go areas?' I didn't want to barge in on the Comptons without his approval.

'None. When there's something fishy in the pie, he wants the stink removed forthwith, and this stinks. And incidentally, he says to tell you it's fairly certain Compton wasn't killed there – no weapon was found in the pond or the barn, and the pathologist says he was dead when he went into the water. It could have been an ordinary sharp kitchen knife or,' he added cheerily, 'perhaps it wasn't.'

'Good news in a way, considering Giovanni would hardly have been carrying a kitchen knife away from the dinner table.'

'Make the most of it. It may be the only good news you get.'
Dave rang off with this consoling thought.

Never had I been so glad to get away from Frogs Hill. Even the
Glory Boot, normally a retreat, had become oppressive and the
image of Louise met me round every corner of the house. It was
straight to Plumshaw, therefore, with a brief diversion to Pluckley
and the Vickers' home to tell Maria how eager I was for her to
come to Frogs Hill. She howled on my shoulder and I felt a heel
for my insincerity, but at least I was in Mrs Len's good books for
ever. I hoped Maria's sobs were in gratitude to me, but I couldn't
stop to enquire.

When I arrived at Plumshaw Manor two members of the forensic
management team were indeed going over the Land Rover with a
fine-tooth comb, so it was obvious that Brandon believed that it
could be tied up with the murder. Dave was wrong. This was surely
more good news as I couldn't see how it could be part of his case
against Giovanni. That's one of the things I respect about Brandon
though. He investigates everything, not just potential evidence
against one suspect, no matter how convinced he is of their guilt.

I rang the bell and this time it was a girl who opened the door,
her eyes red with lack of sleep or weeping or both. It must surely
be Hugh's daughter Bronte, the young Juliet to Jamie Makepeace's
Romeo. She was, as Giovanni had said, pretty and I hoped she at
any rate fell outside the general impression that the Comptons were
all weirdos. She brushed aside my apologies and self-introduction
as 'half a policeman sent by the Car Crime Unit'.

'Don't worry about intruding,' she said wearily. 'We want to get
this awful business sorted out and if the Land Rover theft is anything
to do with it, we need to know. And even more important,' she
added wryly, '*you* need to know.'

Inside the manor it felt depressingly like Frogs Hill, as though
it too were weeping with loss. Even the graciousness of the albeit
dilapidated Georgian house could not mask that.

'Let's go in here,' Bronte said, turning into a room immediately
by the front entrance. 'Once the morning room, but now a dump.'

Not quite, but I could see what she meant. Gracious spindly chairs,
elegant tables with daily newspapers laid neatly upon them for the
visitors awaiting their turn were not what this room now boasted.
Instead I saw a utilitarian table, chairs, a cupboard or two and an

array of walking boots adorning the floor. It had a charm all its own, though, which suggested that visitors took it as they found it.

It only remained for me to be sure of what I *was* finding in the manor. 'Did you hear the Land Rover being returned?'

'No. It happened during the night, and the family bedrooms are at the back. We just don't understand it. It's not fair so close to Dad's death.'

'No notes left? Hot engines? Petrol consumption?'

'Your job, Mr Semi-Policeman. The key was in the lock if that's any help. It's weird, isn't it? Did that man who murdered my father do it? No,' she instantly corrected herself, 'he's been arrested again, so he can't have been around last night. He must have had an accomplice who returned the car.'

'Whoa,' I said gently. This girl was suffering badly. 'Even if Giovanni Donati is charged, that doesn't mean he's guilty.'

'But he is. We all know that.' She looked at me pleadingly as if longing for me to agree. 'He seemed such a nice man that night at dinner.'

'Did anything happen then that could explain the attack on your father?'

'No,' she answered immediately, but then added, 'Everyone was rather quiet, but that's all.'

'We have to look at everything.' I tried to be tactful. 'And as regards the Land Rover, it couldn't have been Giovanni who stole it in the first place or returned it. He was with the police on both occasions. Why would he have stolen it anyway?'

Stupid of me, because Bronte's voice became unsteady. 'To put my father's body in that pond. How could anyone *do* that?'

I waited while she regained some composure. 'It can't have been Giovanni who took the Land Rover,' I repeated.

She sighed. 'No, and Grandad is so pleased to have it back. He wants to start his daily trips round the village again to show the stiff upper lip, he says. The Land Rover's so good for that. With the top down, he looks splendid riding around in it, so having it back is at least a little comfort for him. Not for me, though.'

I waited again while she recovered and then she said brightly, 'Jamie knows Zoe Grant. He says she works for you.'

'She does. Jamie's your boyfriend, isn't he?'

'Fiancé,' she said firmly.

'The Romeo and Juliet of Plumshaw.'

'You'd think so.' She grimaced. 'But it would take more than our marriage to unite our two families. Make it worse probably. Good luck to them. Why should we care? We're getting married as soon as we can. I can't stick this place without Dad.'

'Will you live in the village or move away?'

'No choice. My grandparents won't have me anywhere round here, even though Dad told me they had a vacant cottage. I'll move to Makepeace territory which will please them even more. Jamie might look for a job somewhere else though so that we can move away. Plumshaw's going to be a building site for the next umpteen years or so, and I shan't be sorry to leave.'

'Is development certain? Your grandfather won't sell, I'm told.'

'Perhaps he will now, with Dad gone.'

'Are you already a Makepeace in your loyalties?'

'Not really. I can see why my father and grandparents want to stay here though. I think Paul and Stephanie would go like a flash if you greased their palm with a million quid or so.'

'Is that likely?'

'They'll get the farm and estate once I'm going to be out of the picture by marrying Jamie, and probably Grandpa will leave them the Alfa Romeo too. It must be worth a bob or two and they may be counting on getting the loot from it. Once they get all that I wouldn't mind betting they'll sell up and move, and to hell with all their pretence of keeping the old estate going.'

I decided to keep her talking, if only to keep her mind off her father. 'It sounds as if only your grandparents are keeping old Plumshaw's interests alive.'

She looked surprised. 'You're wrong there. There are heaps of old codgers round here who don't want anything to change and, to be fair, not just old codgers either. Anyone with a brain can see what will happen if the Makepeaces' plan goes through the way they want. We'd be living in a town not a village and one that's all made of concrete. No room for green grass or cricket pitches in the Makepeace plans for the future. They're all idiots.'

She had the grace to blush when she realized what she'd said. 'Except for Jamie, of course. Anyway the Comptons will put up a good fight with their supporters behind them. The manor gives them a figurehead.'

'A strong one though.'

'Grandpa and Grandma make a formidable team,' she agreed. 'Grandma was an incomer to Plumshaw which makes her even more determined that nothing should change. Except,' she added, 'as regards her granddaughter's choice of marrying into the opposition.' She managed a grin. 'I know you've met her. Do you want to meet my grandfather? He's keen to meet you.'

I leapt at the chance. 'I would. Is he up to it?'

'No, but it will take his mind off my father for a while. He likes classic cars, you see.'

Even odder then, I thought, that he had left his Alfa Romeo alone and unloved all these years. Now I could ask him why.

I was over-hopeful. Bronte left me to check on her grandfather but it was Hazel who swept back in. No twinkle in the eye today. She looked drained and older, but she wanted it to be known by her body language that she was still the tigress in charge of the gateway, not Bronte.

'I hear you want to meet my husband.'

'At his wish. And only for as long as he wants to see me.'

'Quite. Bear in mind that he is over ninety and our son . . .' Her voice cracked, and I hurried to assure her that I would.

She looked mollified. 'No doubt you'll do your best to prove your friend innocent but I suppose the police know what they are doing in sending you along over this extraordinary Land Rover business. Or whatever else you may wish to know.' A keen look here. 'I expressed my views, but my husband is insistent that he wants to meet you.'

She led me to a room at the back of the house, where Peter Compton was sitting by the window in a splendidly old-fashioned wing armchair. Immediately I could see why he was still such a dominant figure in Plumshaw. A shock of grey hair, no thinning there. Keen eyes, and strong hands gripping the arms of his chair as though he were contemplating leaping out to attack me. I remembered he had been in the SAS during the war, and hoped he had forgotten his old methods of dispensing with opposition – which after all might be what he asked to see me for.

I was entirely wrong, to my surprise. As I approached him, he welcomed me, looking more Pickwickian than aggressive and certainly not like a lion scenting his prey. 'There,' he said loudly, as if addressing the troops. 'Sit there, so I can see the whites of your eyes.'

'To shoot me?' I sat down opposite him as he indicated.

'Probably not today.' A belly laugh as he patted Hazel's hand. She had protectively taken the upright chair at his side.

'It's good of you to see me in the circumstances,' I told him.

'You know what we did in the war with friends falling all round us? We went out twice as strong the next time to take our revenge. It keeps you going, Mr Colby.' He switched subjects. 'Martin tells me all about the cars you restore at Frogs Hill. It keeps me going, car talk.'

'You own that fantastic Alfa Romeo. Do you have other classic cars?'

'My dear chap, I'm ninety-five. There have been quite a few in my life.' He embarked on a rambling account of the classic cars he had once owned, from a Brough Superior to a Gordon-Keeble. This elegant sports rarity gave us something in common because of the one I had inherited from Dad. Then we came to the Alfa Romeo again.

'I heard you bought the Alfa Romeo in Italy. When was that?'

There might have been a hesitation before he spoke or perhaps I was mistaken for he answered readily enough. 'I did. In 1946.'

'And it used to belong to the racing driver who had to fall out of the Mille Miglia in 1938.' Peter Compton had not been so forthcoming with Giovanni about its early history, I noted.

'You've been doing your homework, Mr Colby. You're right. I believe the owner died during the war and I picked it up afterwards about the time I married my first wife. Sofia was Italian.'

All this was flowing surprisingly well in the circumstances although Hazel was looking at him anxiously. 'Is this relevant?' she snapped at me.

'Forgive me,' I replied. 'Car talk is second nature to me. No, it's not relevant, but a lovely car to talk about. The Corto wheelbase, I noticed.'

'Good man,' Peter said approvingly. 'And you know your stuff.'

'Did you race it when you brought it back here?'

'Not my style. Drove it a bit.'

'On these English lanes or on a track?'

He roared with laughter. 'Tried the lanes once. Then I brought it straight back here and drove it round the estate. No, never raced it, except round here. Like the Land Rover. Good now that it's back. I hear the village has missed my little jaunts out in it. I'll be starting again now. Stephanie or Paul will drive me.'

'*I'll* drive you,' Hazel informed him.

Poor Plumshaw, I thought. The stately appearances would continue, with the stiff upper lip on display. Never admit defeat. Even so, even with this indomitable man, signs of his age were becoming apparent the longer I stayed. The shoulders had dropped a little and the lines of tiredness on his face had become more obvious. A tired soldier, a tired Pickwick too.

'How could you resist the temptation not to drive the Alfa Romeo more often?' I asked him, still curious about it.

'No temptation, my dear fellow. One hangs an Old Master painting on the wall. One doesn't move it around, one venerates it.'

'But cars decay,' I said gently.

'I knew it was there. That was what was important. After what I had suffered—'

At this point Hazel rose to her feet. 'Thank you, Mr Colby. We won't detain you any longer.'

I took the hint and thanked them. There was clearly more to this story, but to my annoyance I knew I wasn't going to hear it now. I couldn't resist taking one risk before I left. 'The car must be worth a lot of money now.'

He looked at me steadily. 'Don't be a fool, man. I'll never sell it.'

No longer the eccentric squire. This was the former soldier speaking. I turned round to close the door behind me, however, and saw them off guard. No roaring tigress, no patriarch. Only two old but very determined people whose agenda remained a puzzle. It would be easy to underestimate them. And that might be just what they wanted. They were the victims in this murder case, and yet perhaps it was not as clear cut as that. Something, as Shakespeare wrote, was rotten in this state of Denmark. And for Denmark read Plumshaw.

'Tough, was it?' Bronte caught me up as I walked to my car.

'You could say that,' I agreed. 'Your grandparents are unusual people.'

'Don't I know it. Come down to the pub?' she suggested.

'For more battering?'

'No. I need to get away from this house, just to forget for a while, and Jamie can't come here so I have to go there. Tonight I need company.'

We went together. I was aware of eyes watching me from inside the pub as I got out of the Polo, eyes that then swivelled to the other side of the car where I held the door open for Bronte to disembark.

'Won't Jamie be here?' I asked as we walked up to the door.

'I doubt it. He's at work.'

There was silence as we went in, although not an inimical one. I could see Andrew behind the bar, and the Makepeaces including George well in control here. It occurred to me that they must be wondering how to play this one. George finally broke the silence.

'Have a drink on me, both of you,' he said loudly.

'Thank you, George,' Bronte said calmly, and I thanked him too.

That relaxed the tension and temporarily the Hop and Harry seemed a normal pub.

SIX

The visits hall at Chelmsford, or indeed at any other prison, is not my idea of a great afternoon out, no matter the prisoner concerned. In fact it hadn't been my idea. Maria, now installed at Frogs Hill, had stomped up to me on Friday with a grim look on her face.

'Giovanni not want to see me Sunday. He want to see *you*.'

She had been here some days now, and this was the first major glitch. She loved my pasta, I admired her way with tuna – in short, she and I had come to a working arrangement at Frogs Hill, which now seemed in jeopardy. She had just visited Giovanni and the result had clearly not been an overwhelming success. He wanted her to return to Italy, she wanted to find board and lodging right next door to the prison.

No bail had been granted to Giovanni. This could perhaps have been because his solicitor's approach had put backs up. Apparently this had been on the grounds that Giovanni was far too important a person to be imprisoned even on remand. As he could hardly be seen as a threat to the community at large, the reason was more likely the risk that such an important person would disappear back to Italy with consequent delay in retrieving him.

It was clear why Giovanni wanted to see me. His solicitor must be in despair faced with the evidence Brandon was holding. Giovanni was obviously pinning his hopes on me, leaving me with no option but to get involved. I ran it by Brandon, who was dubious but somewhat to my surprise finally okayed the visit. As Giovanni had been remanded for trial, there was in theory no case to be explored as far as Brandon was concerned. Hugh Compton had been thrown into the water two or three days before he was found; Giovanni had been freed on Saturday, three days before the discovery of the body, and could not satisfactorily account for all his movements. As Hugh had not died during the night of the barn episode, their theory had to be that he had been dying of wounds while Giovanni was in custody. I just could not go with this line. The murder had not taken place at the pond itself and the body therefore had to have been transported along the track through the woods, or from a car at the roadside by Puddledock Cottage (or, I had to consider, from the cottage itself). Perhaps there was a lingering doubt in Brandon's mind also, because he had sanctioned my presence at the scene and my visit to Giovanni.

Despite my mixed feelings about Giovanni, seeing him now was pitiful. I felt like a convict myself after the rigorous security I'd been put through. I'd put all my worldly goods inside a locked locker, passed all the inspections, produced identification, been searched and finally conducted to the visits hall, which was plentifully supplied with watching security eyes and, as it was a Sunday on a holiday weekend, also packed full of visitors of all ages.

His face looked thinner, older, with no sign of the bravado I was so used to seeing. I only hoped he had a reasonable cell-mate. When I asked, he shrugged, which I took to mean it wasn't a problem. The old Giovanni who would have waxed volubly on the subject for good or bad had vanished. What, I wondered painfully, would Louise make of him in this state? I heard from her only sporadically and it was tacitly understood that while Maria stayed at Frogs Hill, Louise would not be joining me, even for the weekend. She was visiting her father, she said. I was in a crazy situation, but for the life of me I couldn't see how I could have done otherwise.

I tried to put all thoughts of Louise out of my mind as I braced myself to sound cheerful for Giovanni.

'How's the *spaghetti pescatore* here?' I joked.

Wrong move. He wasn't into light-hearted banter. 'You know I kill no one, Jack. You help me, please.' He put out his hands towards me and a dozen pairs of security eyes fixed on us. He withdrew them.

I had to play it his way. 'What line are your solicitors taking?'

'To them I am already dead.' A touch of the old dramatic Giovanni. That was something at least. 'They do not believe my story, or if they do they think I killed him and do not remember doing so. That I thought Mr Hugh owned the Alfa Romeo, that I wanted it and he refused to give it to me.'

Weak as a motive, thankfully. 'What do they think you planned to do with it? Tuck it under your arm and walk away?'

'I do not know. Perhaps they think I am conspiring with you, Jack.'

'*Me?*'

Even Giovanni realized he had gone too far. 'Because you have a classic car business,' he explained. 'You could have taken the body for me from Challock to Plumshaw, looked after Hugh while I was with the police and then put him in the pond. Your fingerprints are in my car.'

'Thanks, Giovanni,' I said bluntly. 'So are Len's, come to that. Your story is hard to believe anyway, without dragging me or anyone else into it.'

'But you know me.' He looked hurt. 'You know I could not kill a man. Why kill a man I have only just met?'

'I can't answer that. But if I'm to help you—' I was fighting my desire to get out of this as soon as I could – 'I'll need some help from you.'

He looked pained. 'Of course I help, Jack. I want my life, not to take Mr Hugh Compton's.'

Remembering your life with Louise? was what I immediately thought, and made an enormous effort to forget. 'Then you must tell me a better tale than you did last time,' I told him firmly.

'I tell you the truth last time.'

'Then tell me *again*. Tell me everything Hugh Compton said. Everything that took place at dinner. Hugh's daughter Bronte confirmed that everyone was on the quiet side.'

'That is how the English are at dinner,' he muttered. He seemed unwilling to continue and so I tried the yes and no method.

'You told me it was your idea to go to the barn after dinner. Is that so, or was it Hugh's suggestion? Yours?'

The method failed. 'His, mine. I do not know which.'

'*Think*, Giovanni.'

He sighed. 'Mr Compton say in the afternoon that we talk later today about the car. I say at dinner I want to see the car again today. He say we go together and then we can talk. Mrs Compton say: Begin tonight. You both go. She's a very forceful lady, so I agree. I do not wish this, but we go.'

'No question of Peter Compton going?'

'No. The old man say Mr Hugh will inherit the car as he is the firstborn son and he is too tired to go himself.'

'Although he sat through the dinner?'

'Yes, but he say little. He just stare at me. The other man, Paul, he there too, with his wife, the sister of Hugh. And the pretty Bronte of course. I not mind if she come to the barn.'

My exasperation hit new heights. *I bet you wouldn't*, I thought. Any pretty girl and you think she's yours. *Like Louise* . . . Stop, I warned myself again and did my best not to react.

'Hugh change clothes and come with me to the barn. I want to think car and that is hard with someone there, so I am cross. But I look at the car and try to think how to paint it. How to understand it. Hugh wants to talk, but I am thinking.'

'He talked about the car?'

'He tried, but I tell him not to do so, because that changes things in my mind.'

Surely there must be something I could grasp here that would help his case? I persevered. 'What clothes was Hugh wearing?'

Giovanni looked at me blankly. 'I do not put Hugh in the painting, so my eyes would not be on his clothes.'

I held back from telling him exactly why he should be trying to remember. 'Did you get the impression he was interested in the Alfa Romeo?' I asked instead.

'No. He did not see its beauty covered in the dust of past times.'

'Why did he bother to come with you then?'

A shrug. 'He want the job done quickly perhaps. I do not know. Does this matter?'

'Yes.' *Anything* might matter. 'What were your ideas for the painting?'

'I cannot tell you.'

I tried to be patient. Artistic temperament was irrelevant. 'You can, Giovanni. You won't be painting the Alfa Romeo now.'

That roused him. 'If I still wish to, I will,' he said indignantly. 'No one can stop me painting an Alfa Romeo 8C 2900B. This one is in my head and I have copyright on my head.'

I couldn't bear it. For all my reservations about him, I only hoped he'd have the chance to do it. Giovanni's paintings reveal the character or soul of a car and I'm all for that. No such thing for an inanimate object? A viewer's reaction to it can confirm there is. Giovanni's painting of a Lancia Aurelia consoling a weeping woman in a storm of rose petals proves it.

'But,' he continued, 'do not worry. I do *not* wish to paint it now, Jack. Never.'

I was surprised at that. 'Why not? It is still a beautiful car.'

'Because I look at a lovely car as a lovely woman. It give me good thoughts.'

I dismissed the desire to punch him in the nose. Hardly advisable in these surroundings. 'So why not this lovely car?' I pressed on.

'I cannot say.'

'*Say* it, Giovanni.' It must have been obvious I was running out of patience, because he shot me a scared look.

'No sunshine there, Jack. No light. Cold beauty only. What came to me, as I sat by that car, was something not good.'

I had a feeling I wasn't going to like this. 'What was it?'

'Sadness.' He glanced at me nervously to see how I took this. There was obviously more. 'Go on,' I told him.

'You will say I killed Hugh if I tell you,' he pleaded. 'They will hang me for it.'

'*Tell* me, Giovanni.'

'I smelled death.'

I'd never put Giovanni down as someone with psychic powers, even though his surreal art must stem from some intuitive reaction to auras. Death had most certainly been around in that barn, whenever and wherever Hugh had actually been killed. What troubled me even more was that I had asked Giovanni what he had been doing after his return from the police HQ and before Hugh's body was found. On the Monday, I was fairly sure he remained with Maria all day. He was curiously vague about the Saturday afternoon when he picked up the BMW after he was freed, and was definitely mulish on his movements on Sunday. All he would say was, 'I drive to see my friend, that is all.' I hoped he was right and that Brandon had the same story. I couldn't help remembering that he must have come home very late that night, for I had been sound asleep.

Did I believe Giovanni over the death aura? He isn't in the habit of covering his emotions with light jests. He's more in the habit of conveying them to all and sundry as they happen. Where did this get me, though? No one was denying death was around with his scythe and skeletal skull in the barn that night. What seemed odd to me was that although they had agreed to Giovanni's request to paint the car, the Comptons seemed to have no other interest in it. True, they had left it in the barn unrestored for many years, but a famous artist's request to paint it would surely have evoked more interest in it, if not for itself then for its potential value.

Missing Louise, I prowled around on the Bank Holiday Monday thinking about the Alfa Romeo, which I was certain was a focal point of interest in the case. I got no further, however, so when Dave Jennings rang me on the Tuesday morning to suggest I took the Land Rover back to the manor after its final search in the police pound, I jumped at the chance.

Kent was looking its best and the Land Rover was just the sort of vehicle in which to enjoy it. I felt like a Yeoman of Kent, owner of all I could see. If it wasn't for the unhappy cloud hanging over Frogs Hill and the equally unhappy situation I was heading for, I would have been a contented man. Even so, today felt like a respite.

As I turned into the manor drive, however, the cloud enveloped me again. Something about Plumshaw still didn't smell right to me, any more than it had to Giovanni, and the tragedy of Hugh's death seemed more of a symptom of this than its cause. I deliberately parked the Land Rover by the barn so that I could have an excuse to stroll idly into it for a spot of solo Alfa Romeo admiration.

It wasn't solo, however. When I walked in, I saw Peter Compton sitting by the car on a bale of hay. He was gazing fixedly at the Alfa Romeo but didn't look surprised to see me as I joined him.

'I heard you were coming,' was his greeting. 'Any more news on Donati? Heard he'd been charged. Open and shut case, of course.'

I held back my views on this in consideration of his years. 'Strong evidence, I agree, but not quite open and shut.'

The keen eyes swivelled back to the car. 'If he didn't kill my son, who did?'

'He may have had other enemies.' It was a risk but worth taking, and Peter Compton was well able to cope. His brain if not his body ignored the years. 'The Comptons have been at Plumshaw for three hundred years, Mr Colby. They have always had enemies. We have them now close at hand. They have taken my granddaughter from my side – why not my son too?'

This was hopeful. 'Do you think that Giovanni might be falsely accused?'

'I do not.' The answer was very firm. 'But there are those who

would applaud the result of his action, not condemn it. George
Makepeace and others. All those who see their fortunes in bricks
and mortar, not in the land that nurtures us to which we have a
duty. We are only caretakers of the land, not the owners.' An abrupt
switch. 'You saw my son's body, didn't you?'

'Yes.'

'I saw many dead bodies during my army days, but I could not
look on his.'

I saw my opportunity. 'I was told you were in the SAS.'

'I was. In Italy. Winter of forty-four to 'five. It was a crazy time,
the Partisans fighting both the Germans and the Italian Fascists, but
almost as ready to fight amongst themselves. The communists, the
Christian Democrats, republicans – all Partisans waiting for their
chance to further their own cause when the war ended. We British
had to coordinate their efforts with our own to drive the enemy out
of Italy. After the armistice with the Allies in forty-three, the Italians
opened up their POW camps and the prisoners they'd been holding
were either shipped off on trains to German camps or made their
escape hoping to reach the British lines to rejoin the fight as their
army moved slowly up the Italian peninsula. Not easy, when we
were fighting the Germans back through the peninsula, village by
village and street by street, in the north of the country as they poured
more and more troops in. SOE was coordinating all the British
special forces working in the north behind the German lines and a
big job it was in the mountains. The Partisans were carrying out
pinprick raids from there, with what limited supplies they had, but
when we parachuted in to join them in December forty-four, supplies
came with us.'

'It was a tough time,' I replied. My father had been an avid reader
of Second World War memoirs and histories so I'd grown up with
them. 'That gave you your love of Italy?'

'We did our job. It made me hate war. This wasn't country against
country; it was man against man and the enemy against women and
children. We had to fight back. The need for vengeance doesn't die
until it's accomplished; it just festers. Do you believe in revenge,
Jack?'

'I believe in justice. Not the same thing.'

'No.' He sighed. 'Not a fashionable word, revenge, but that doesn't
wipe it out.'

'Wanting revenge against your son's murderer is a natural emotion – once it's known for certain who that was. And I don't believe it was Giovanni Donati.'

'We must differ then. I'm getting old, Jack. But I'll live to see him get his deserts.'

Time to change gear if I was to get to the end of this journey. The Alfa Romeo was crying out for attention. This, after all, was where the story began. 'The driver of this car, Giulio Santoro, died in the war. Do you know whether he was a Partisan, or had he died earlier during the war when Italy was still allied to Germany?'

Silence. 'It was all a very long time ago,' he said at last.

'But a time that must be vivid in your memory,' I said.

'It never fades, the loss of friends. The loss of loved ones. The loss of enemies. But he was none of these.'

I was getting nearer, I sensed. Peter seemed to be indicating he had had enough, but I had to push. 'What took you back to Italy after the war?'

'I met Sofia,' he told me after a while, 'while I was still in Italy after the war ended. We married in 1946 and came back to England to live.'

'Many happy marriages came about that way.'

'Mine was not one of them,' he said shortly. 'She was not happy in England, but my life was here. She returned to Italy and died a few years later.'

'Is that why you lost interest in this car?' I asked. 'Because it reminds you of her?'

'Perhaps,' he replied, and I thought what cold eyes he had. 'There are always stories, Jack. Always. Many old scores left to settle after the war. The Mesola family, to which Sofia belonged, was prominent in the resistance, helping the Partisans. You are right about the car. It speaks of Sofia. Most stories die with time, and most of them change. But cars remain as they are. Isn't that strange? There's love, there's betrayal and there's revenge. War memories die hardest of all.'

'Many bad ones get forgiven with time.'

'Many do not. I believe in justice too, Jack. And that is why I need to know what happened after my son was attacked by Donati. His body—' his voice trembled, the first sign of personal emotion

I had seen – 'was only placed in that pond a few days before it was found. Where had it been?'

'That's what the police are looking into, so far without result.'

'If they failed to find him in the first four days, they will query why the painter would have moved it to somewhere where it would be more easily found.'

'That's true and a big point in his favour,' I agreed. This was a sharp man. Hazel might often be his mouthpiece to the world, but that was clearly through choice and not incapability on his part. 'After all,' I continued, 'Giovanni had no motive for wanting to kill your son. He only came here to paint a picture.'

Those cold eyes again. 'Can you be sure of that?'

Before I could reply, Gatekeeper Hazel arrived on the scene, together with Stephanie. They'd clearly spotted the Land Rover and guessed whom they might find inside the barn. They were an odd couple, Hazel in her jeans and T-shirt and Stephanie looking as though she were about to open the village fête.

'Are you rattling on about the war again, Peter?' Hazel spoke lightly, but the message was clear. She was displeased to find us together.

I could be reading too much into a fleeting impression, because Peter replied good-humouredly, 'Jack is a good listener.'

'No doubt he is also taking his opportunity to admire the car,' Stephanie said drily.

'Not entirely,' I replied. 'I've heard some interesting stories as well about the Partisans and your mother's family.'

Nothing like throwing a cat among the pigeons in a conversation and seeing those feathers bristle. Not Peter's though.

'Ancient history,' snapped Hazel.

'Not that long,' Stephanie retorted.

An inimical look passed between them, as I said, 'You must be proud of your heritage, Mrs Ranger.'

Stephanie unbent a little – perhaps because Hazel was still looking furious. 'My uncles were Partisans. My mother and sister too. Many young men avoided conscription by the Germans by fleeing to the hills to join the resistance, but they needed support from the villages to survive. That's what my family organized.'

'This is a long way from my son's death, Mr Colby,' Hazel said coldly. As Giovanni had observed, there seemed little love lost between her and her stepdaughter. 'I am glad to see the Land Rover is back with us. However, I presume you are also here with the fruitless task of proving this Italian murderer innocent.'

'I'm attempting to find out what happened,' I replied.

'The police have already discovered exactly what happened.'

'There may be unanswered questions, Hazel,' Peter put in sharply.

'Only in your mind, Peter. Mine is quite clear on the matter. There is talk of the village being involved, but no one would go to such lengths as murder to achieve their aim of so-called progress.'

'Where money is involved people are inclined to go to any lengths,' I pointed out.

The glint in Hazel's eye suggested I would not be invited back to the house. I'd arranged with Martin to give me a lift back to Frogs Hill as he had to pick up a magneto from Len, and so I took a footpath through the fields to his garage, reflecting that soon these pleasant meadows could be covered in housing. What of Plumshaw then? Just how strong was the desire – and need – for expansion and to what length would its supporters go?

By the time I reached Frogs Hill farmhouse, having left Martin in the Pits with Len and Zoe, I was beginning to dread facing Maria because of the inquisition she would immediately put me through. I wanted to avoid a repetition of the Sunday evening after I had returned from seeing Giovanni. Maria had insisted on cooking me a superb pasta which took three hours to simmer to perfection. As a result, we were eating it as midnight struck and then came the inevitable dissection of my visit to him. His current plight had taken us way into the small hours. Finally I had reassured her that British justice would see Giovanni cleared and went to bed. I was by no means sure of this myself, given the facts, and Giovanni's reluctance to tell me (and presumably also the police) about his exact movements after he had been released from custody, particularly on the Sunday, added to my doubts. There had been no point in my telling Maria this. She needed reassurance, whether baseless or not. Without it she could not keep going and would be of no comfort to her husband.

Now as I walked over to the farmhouse, summoning up my courage to undergo another such endurance test, the pit of my stomach dropped even further. There was Louise's Ford Focus. Delight was immediately mingled with even more apprehension.

What on earth was she doing here? Had she thrown Maria out? I might find a blood-curdling battle going on inside. Had Len taken Maria back to stay with him again? Both Zoe and Len were in the Pits, but Len could have driven over to Pluckley with Maria. Please, please, let that have happened, I thought. Otherwise Jack's Return Home, to quote the old melodrama, would be far from pleasant.

Cautiously I opened the door and crept in, but I could hear no signals of battle and silence reigned. Perhaps the confrontation had already taken place and both combatants had retired to their rooms? I might sound facetious about this deadly serious matter, but I was very shaken. For Louise to find Maria still installed would be an unpleasant shock. I would have expected her to turn round and leave right away, so perhaps, I comforted myself, Maria had indeed returned to Len's home.

Confident that this was the explanation, I headed for the kitchen. The first sound I heard was a chuckle and then a laugh. I found Louise and Maria ensconced in the living room each with a large glass of wine before them, as matey as salt and pepper.

'Jack!' Louise leapt up and came over to kiss me. 'Maria told me you had gone to Plumshaw. Any further news on Giovanni?'

I tried to pull myself together. After all, Maria in the past had befriended one or two of Giovanni's girlfriends, so perhaps it had happened again in the interests of his welfare.

Louise read my expression correctly and giggled.

'I rang Maria, Jack,' Louise told me. 'We've talked our problem over, and now we're friends again.'

Just like that. *Women!* I thought. No one seemed to care whether *I* was OK with my beloved being on happy terms with her ex-lover's wife, not to mention the ex-lover himself.

'For Giovanni's sake,' Maria said eagerly. 'He like it we friends.'

Now I was really dazed with shock. 'Well, that's great,' is all I could manage to say. It sounded lukewarm even to me, so I added another 'Great' to help it along.

Apparently I was expected to join the happy party, and Louise was looking at me encouragingly.

'My Giovanni will be safe now,' Maria assured me. 'I tell Ricardo Louise here. Ricardo not happy, but if it help Giovanni I not mind.'

Help *Giovanni*? What about helping *me*? 'Who's Ricardo?' I asked weakly. Maybe in this crazy new world he would turn out to be Maria's lover.

The two women looked at me in amazement. '*My* Ricardo, of course,' Maria failed to explain.

Louise began to look worried. 'Ricardo is Maria and Giovanni's son. You must have known that.'

'*Son?*' I did a ninety-degree turn and landed up flat on my mental back. 'Why must I have known about him?' I threw at them belligerently. I had vaguely known Maria and Giovanni had a family but not the details. By the time I came to know Giovanni myself I was an adult, his children had left home and we seldom talked about anything save the here and now.

Louise seemed bewildered. 'Because you've had a face like a grumpy old bear for the last week or two, after you deduced that I had an affair with him. Which I did. I lived with him for two years.'

'With *him?*' I wrestled with this. '*Ricardo?*'

'Yes,' Maria told me crossly. 'She broke my Ricardo's heart. Giovanni not happy. He not like Louise but now it will be all right.'

'Me not happy then either,' Louise told me levelly. 'Ricardo wanted me to give up the stage, Jack. It wasn't that I didn't want to have a family, but he insisted I gave up acting altogether for ever. I had to be what he called a real wife and mother.'

I was still staring at them both, dumbstruck. I felt like crying. I felt like leaping into the air with joy. All I actually did choke out was: 'I thought your lover was Giovanni.'

Shock. '*Giovanni?*'

I don't know which of them squeaked this out. Or which of them laughed first. But suddenly we were all doing so. Another glass of wine was brought. That evening we ate, we drank and we were merry.

Except for one thing. My friend Giovanni was on remand for murder and I had to clear his name.

SEVEN

I spent the next two days living alternately in the Glory Boot or glued to my bookshelves. The Glory Boot provided such information as I could glean on the Alfa Romeo and its owner. Fascinating though it was, I didn't learn much more, save that Giulio Santoro's co-driver Enrico di Secchio was the son of the Count di Secchio – which was ultimately to prove unfortunate for him. Mussolini and the compliant monarchy had smiled benignly on this wealthy aristocratic family from the north of Italy, which explained how Enrico could afford to buy the Alfa Romeo for his friend and saviour Giulio. Come the armistice, the rise of the Partisans and in 1946 the republicans' victory in the constitutional referendum leading to the end of the monarchy, the fortunes of the di Secchio family declined.

As for Giulio himself, I could find nothing about his war record, which I supposed was not surprising given that it would be fifty years before the Internet began to spread its web all over the world.

I was back to considering Giovanni and Peter Compton, the two people at the centre of this case. Hugh had arranged Giovanni's visit, but Peter was the real power here. The two men had never met each other before, so their common ground was the Alfa Romeo and the proposed painting. If, as I believed, Giovanni was innocent, the battle between the two Plumshaws also had to be taken into account. I wasn't getting the full story on either front, either deliberately or because I had not asked the right questions.

Six days had elapsed between the attack in the barn and the discovery of the body, and probably four between the attack and Hugh's death. My stumbling block was that at present Giovanni could be linked to both. He had claimed that he had visited a friend on the Sunday, but he was hardly forthcoming on the subject.

Giovanni was only allowed a certain number of visits per week and their time was limited. Maria was using up a great deal of it, not to mention his lawyers, and so I decided not to visit him again myself until I had something more concrete to latch on to. Besides,

I felt somewhat shamefaced over my mistaken assumption about Louise; he might laugh about it – in due course – with Maria but he might not be so pleased with me. Given his current situation perhaps that was not important.

Instead, therefore, I tackled Maria. Louise was rehearsing most days but Maria was all too present at Frogs Hill, to Len and Zoe's despair. Her frequent visits to the Pits were distracting them from what they considered the real business of life, which currently was tuning a Lanchester. I'd had the happy idea of giving Maria a free rein in my garden, but I found her there removing a stone statue of Venus (a present from Louise) to a position where her nudity could not offend – behind the runner beans and close to the compost heap. I wisely did not comment. Instead, I asked:

'Was the friend whom Giovanni visited on the Sunday before you arrived the same one who told him about the Alfa Romeo being in Plumshaw?'

She stopped rearranging the beans and gave much thought to this. '*Si.*' She began her rearrangement again.

'Where does he live?'

'I do not know. I ask Giovanni. This look better, eh?' She stood back to admire her work.

She and Giovanni live in the northern half of Italy near Bologna and the Apennine mountains. Peter Compton had been parachuted into that region during the war. No great coincidence there. It was a huge area and there were thousands upon thousands of soldiers and Partisans fighting there. Giovanni was now only in his late fifties, so the two could not have met. Nevertheless, bearing in mind Peter's comments on long memories it was worth digging further.

'Was your family caught up in the Second World War, Maria? And Giovanni's?'

She took a long time over pulling up the bindweed that had dared climb up the beans. 'Every Italian family in war, Jack,' she said at last. 'Every English family in war. Like every family in the world.'

She wasn't getting away with that. 'How were yours and Giovanni's involved?'

She straightened up again and proceeded to tell me a very long and horrifying tale of poverty, conscription, enemy brutality and Italian suffering. Maria is a very astute woman once the drama queen is stripped away. But then I'm pretty determined too.

'And Giovanni's family?' I asked when she finally ground to a halt.

'Not know.'

'You must know *something*,' I persisted.

She went back to the bindweed. 'Perhaps yes, perhaps no.'

'Was his a Fascist family? Pro-Mussolini?' This might be the reason for her obstinacy.

She was genuinely shocked. '*Fascisti?* No, no, no. His family Partisans.'

'In the north of Italy?'

'*Si.*' She looked uncomfortable now.

'Could his family have had anything to do with Peter Compton?'

'I not know about his family and Giovanni only same age as me. Peter Compton old man, I think.' She had her mulish look on.

I can be stubborn too. 'Could Giovanni's father have met him?'

She had no problem with this question because she replied immediately. 'Luigi. Good papa. Lived in Florence. But only child during war.'

'OK, then. Luigi's father. Giovanni's grandfather.'

She had no problem with this either. 'Yes. He in war. With ships.'

A naval man. So that ruled that line out. After the armistice, wherever he was, he was unlikely to have been up in the mountains with Peter Compton.

She smiled at me happily. 'I ask Giovanni about him when I see him. Now I garden.'

Maria had relaxed, so where had I gone wrong? I must be missing something.

I was missing more than one 'something'. Before I tackled Giovanni about this 'friend' who was his alibi for the Sunday on which Hugh had probably died and been thrown in the pond, I needed to talk to Brandon again. This was easier said than done. I left a message but it was early on Friday evening before he called back.

'Giovanni's alibi for that Sunday,' I began tentatively. Brandon usually rebuffs questions on his evidence. 'He told me he went to see a friend of his.'

This time Brandon was again surprisingly helpful. He actually chortled. 'That's what he told us too. Drove there in his hired car.'

'So who's the friend?'

'The name is Umberto Monti. Runs a restaurant in the Eynsford area.'

'Any reason I shouldn't go to see him?'

'No reason at all, Jack.' Brandon was too obliging. 'Only one thing you should know. The restaurant was closed all day and the friend didn't see hide nor hair of Giovanni. In fact he went to France for the day.'

Brandon picked up on my horror and added compassionately. 'Sorry, Jack.'

I was going to have to work hard and quickly if I still thought Giovanni innocent. I put that to one side – it was too tough to face at present. Anyway, first I had to find out what had happened that night and in the six days after it. And for that I needed to follow up the undoubted fact that the Comptons had enemies in the village, and Martin Fisher had to be my first port of call.

Owning an independent garage he could – as he had pointed out – sit comfortably between the two rival sides and wasn't reliant on either side for his future. I wouldn't have thought he was making a fortune out of Four Star Services, but at least independence gives you security in one way – no one can tell you what to do (except the bank and taxman of course). Nevertheless, restoring classic cars is an up and down business as we know all too well at Frogs Hill, and I'd noted that Martin now had only the one mechanic working for him instead of the two I recalled in the past. Not that that means a lot, as we do it for the love of the job, although we do have to make ends meet. Martin was single – divorced I think – so unless he had heavy maintenance costs he could afford to follow his heart. At the moment that must be divided between the Makepeaces and Comptons, as both sides of the village depended on his services. Although classics were his main love, he handled any sort of car.

It was a Saturday and Martin was working there alone.

'Care for a quickie lunch?' I suggested.

'Not today, thanks. Got a job to deliver. You should enjoy it though. The grapevine's already humming. George Makepeace put in a way-over-the-top offer to Compton for the freehold of the Hop and Harry. Bold move.'

'Not the most considerate one with Hugh so recently dead.'

'Could be a good time for George though. Catch the enemy when he's weak.'

'Good if cold-blooded,' I observed.

'George *is* cold-blooded – over the Comptons at least. He's a grand old chap provided you see things from his point of view. Without his heir, Peter Compton could decide to throw in the towel over the Hop and Harry. And once that's settled, the way would be open for Makepeace all the way to the bank.'

'Would the family go with that?'

'The Rangers would.'

'And Bronte?'

'She'll be a Makepeace soon and out of the picture. Not a penny to her. Compton and Makepeace will stick to their guns over that and neither will budge.'

'Why did this feud start? Over land or something more personal?'

'All sorts of stories. But the one most people believe is that way back when the Comptons first came to Plumshaw in the 1880s they bought a piece of land from the Makepeaces down around the church. It was a symbolic purchase only, because one of the Compton sons married a Makepeace and it was a gift to her. But the husband died before the wife so the Comptons said it was still their land when the Makepeaces tried to claim it.'

'Bronte going over to the Makepeace side must seem a double betrayal?'

'Yup.'

'If the Hop and Harry goes and development forges ahead, the whole village will change.'

'Yup to that too. To outside planners, this battle isn't over that, it's only about a pub that's old, decaying, not listed, and with a landlord who's all but skint. We're all fond of it, but that won't win the day, however many protesters there are winding up the media and preservation societies. The pub's doomed. I don't want to see it go, but pretty pictures don't make money.'

Could this be the reason for Hugh's murder? That someone wanted Hugh off the playing field? Removing Peter would achieve nothing because Hugh would inherit and take the same view as his father. There was a lot at stake and I needed to be in the picture. Quite how I was going to catch a murderer in the Hop and Harry I wasn't sure, but the pub would be one sure source of information. Everyone would gravitate there to find out if there was any news on the Makepeace offer.

The first thing I registered was that Nan's Ford Escort was outside the Hop and Harry from which I deduced he was probably inside. If so, his usual powers of peacemaking were failing. The noise of angry voices reached me even before I got out of my car. It was a fine day and some customers had retreated to the garden, but the battle was raging inside. The main entrance door was standing open so I made straight for it.

Too quickly for my own good. As I ran up the steps to the door a man came staggering out, reeling under the force of a blow. He overbalanced straight into me, sending us both tumbling down the steps together. I painfully picked myself up and hauled my assailant to his feet. I didn't recognize him, but I did recognize some of the group that spilled out after us.

The formidable Nan came rushing to the fore – not to my rescue, I noted, but to separate the contenders who were intent on continuing the fight outside. One of them was Jamie Makepeace. The man he'd assaulted was older than Jamie, maybe in his mid twenties, and must, I assumed, be one of the anti-development protesters. He was certainly protesting now and very vocally. He made a sudden rush at Jamie, but was fielded expertly by Nan. While they were still sorting themselves out, I slipped inside to assess the situation.

'What happened?' I asked Lucy, who had emerged beaming with pleasure from behind the bar with Andrew, still wearing his apron.

'Good news, for us,' she said. 'Mr Compton's turned down George Makepeace's offer. Mr Ranger brought in a letter from him and a few minutes later the Makepeaces arrived in force to back George up.'

Andrew was very quiet, I noticed, as I congratulated Lucy. 'That's really good news,' I said to her.

'What's good about it?' Andrew muttered.

Lucy looked horrified. 'That's what we wanted. It means we can stay here.'

'But face it, Lucy. This place is a dump.' Andrew seemed torn between anger and tears. 'What are you staring at?' he yelled at me. 'Nothing to do with you.'

'As I've just been knocked down your steps by one of your customers, the Hop and Harry is very much to do with me.'

To this, Andrew had no reply and marched off leaving me puzzled and Lucy completely flummoxed. 'He's just having a bad day. He gets dispirited,' she told me bravely, 'but perhaps he got the wrong end of the stick.'

It seemed to me that Andrew had got very much the right end of the stick – it just happened to be a different stick to Lucy's. She went to talk to Nan who seemed to have done a good peacemaking job, as for the time being the warring parties had called a truce. The noise level dropped and people began to move back inside. I went with them and Paul and Stephanie Ranger came to check that I was in one piece.

'You seem to be everywhere, Mr Colby,' Paul said.

'I am. I enjoy being knocked about.'

'What are you here for?' Stephanie demanded.

'A quiet Saturday lunchtime drink.'

'Nonsense, you're still convinced that Mafioso friend of yours is innocent.'

I wasn't amused. '*Mafioso?* Giovanni? You have to be joking.' But I could see she wasn't and it wasn't a joke.

'His family then,' Stephanie said dismissively.

'Stephanie!' Paul said sharply, with the result that she stopped the attack and turned back into jolly mood.

'I'm sorry, Jack. I know he's a friend of yours. Only a figure of speech.'

Paul switched subjects. 'You've heard that the Hop and Harry is safe now?'

'I have. That's good news. Is it final?'

'While Peter is alive, yes.'

That might not be long, judging by the look on Jamie Makepeace's face as he overheard this exchange. He moved towards us, hotly pursued by Bronte who could obviously see trouble coming. Paul speedily took his wife's arm and shepherded her to the bar to order drinks.

'Upper-class twits,' Jamie hurled after them. 'Don't care a damn about the rest of us working to make something of this village. You and that father of yours, Mrs Ranger.'

Bronte flushed. 'Don't you dare, Jamie. My grandfather does what he thinks right. Which is what your grandfather does too.'

'He does what any sensible person would. You have to admit it, Bron. Peter Compton's a dog in a manger.'

'Only because yours is set on ruining this village, Jamie. A lot of people will stand by Grandpa when push comes to shove.'

Jamie bristled. 'Including you, Bron?'

In a trice the situation had turned from disagreement to crisis, a position from which neither could retreat. Certainly not Bronte. 'Yes, Jamie. Including me,' she hurled back at him.

The turkey cock forgot his common sense. 'That's it then, Bron. The wedding's off.'

I hoped Nan would step in but he was nowhere to be seen. The turkey cock folded his arms, waiting for an apology or retraction, but it never came.

'No problem, Jamie,' Bronte cried loud and clear.

Still no sign of Nan, so I intervened. I had to, because as Bronte walked away Jamie grabbed her arm to yank her back. I quickly detached him, saying firmly, 'Leave it, both of you. Sort it out later, when you've calmed down.'

They took no notice. Jamie gave a sort of howl, while Bronte ran out of the pub. I thought he'd go after her, but he didn't. He just stood there.

'Do it, Jamie,' I urged him. 'Run after her. Hug her.'

But he just went on standing there with folded arms to show what a big gun he was, poor lad.

At last George came up to him and put his hand on Jamie's shoulder. I'd noticed he had been watching what was going on and hadn't looked pleased. It would have suited his book much better to have Bronte as a bargaining point in the feud, but the row must have its good side for him. His objective now would be to make hay while the sun temporarily shone in that direction.

He fixed Paul and Stephanie in his sights. 'And you two banking on young Bronte being cast off without a penny. Ten to one that young madam has her eye on the farm.'

'More to the point,' Paul retaliated drily, 'what do you do now the pub is safe?'

'Safe?' George snarled. 'This pub's coming down to make way for the new road. Never doubt that.'

'But it won't, George, not now,' Lucy said happily.

'Won't it? You talk to your husband about that, young lady.'

Having scored this point, to Lucy's distress and general bewilderment, George surveyed the rest of his audience. 'There's already been mischief done in Plumshaw. They think he's locked up good

and proper and it's over. But there'll be more. I can promise you
that.'

I was bemused. A pub brawl is never an edifying event, whether it
be physical or verbal. I felt I had been battered by both. I had no
stake in the fight between old and new Plumshaw, unless it had
something to do with the murder of Hugh Compton. Were Jamie
and Bronte really going to let the rest of their lives be swayed by
squabbles over land issues? It seemed to me they were indeed
trapped between the two sides.

The struggle for the Hop and Harry would not be the end of the
matter. Battle lines were definitely being drawn. Without the consent
of the Comptons to the sale of the Hop and Harry, I'd assumed that
there would be no point in the Makepeace applications for planning
permission for the new road being submitted, but there I was wrong.
Martin had turned up just as I was leaving and when I told him
what had happened he grimaced.

'They'll steamroller ahead whatever Compton says. You'll see.
Either George will put in an application for roads round the side
and rear of the pub so that it's marooned between major roads or
something else will happen to change Peter Compton's mind.'

'The murder of his son hasn't changed anything,' I pointed out.

'Things are moving, Jack, whether we like it or not. The housing
development can still go ahead, whether or not the industrial site
and road do. Plenty of people need the houses with or without the
jobs on the doorstep. Nothing to stop the odd shop going up with
it. Every development could do with a convenience store.'

'Unless the protesters win their battle against any
development.'

'I'd like to think you're right, but I don't see it.'

Driving home I began to feel sorry for the Comptons. They were
stuck in their way of life, true, but then so were their opponents in
that they could only see progress in terms of bricks and mortar.
Somewhere in the middle of this battle, however, Hugh Compton
had lost his life, and Jamie and Bronte had their marriage plans
ruined. Nan, the peacemaker, had failed for once.

I ran through it once more in my head as I turned off the A20
on to the Pluckley road. Nothing in Hugh Compton's murder made
sense. If Giovanni was guilty – though I couldn't believe he was

– why on earth would he have bothered to return to the scene of the crime in order to lug Hugh, dead or alive, somewhere else? On the other hand, if he was innocent, how could the blood in the car be explained?

When I reached Frogs Hill there was no comfort to be found. No sign of Louise and, being a weekend, no Zoe or Len. There was no sign of Maria either. At this stage, I'd have been grateful to see her pottering around in the garden despite the drawbacks of her presence. There was, however, a message from Dave asking me to ring him. In fact he had rung yesterday and in the excitement of Louise's return I hadn't checked either the mobile or landline.

'Took your time, didn't you?' he asked sourly, by which I deduced he was at home.

'Busy on your Land Rover case.'

'Ah. Well, since you're nosing around Plumshaw, you'd better take into account what Brandon authorized me to tell you.'

'What's that?' I didn't like the sound of this.

'Update of the path report,' Dave replied. 'It's confirmed Hugh Compton had been in the water about two days, and he probably died not long before he went in. A day at the most. And, in case you're feeling sorry for the poor bloke, he'd eaten a good meal before he met his end.'

'That's good news for Giovanni then. It takes him out of the picture.'

'Not according to Brandon's way of thinking. Your chum could have hidden the body and come out to dispose of it later—'

'You said he died not long before he went in.'

'Could have died of wounds received earlier, Jack. And Giovanni being a good-natured chap fed him a nice meal before he died.'

'That,' I said flatly, 'is crazy.'

'Not so. Theory goes they had a fight, which no one in the house would have heard. Too far away. Giovanni panics because he's stabbed his host, gets him in the car, intending to take him to hospital, changes his mind, hides him, feeds him—'

'Giovanni was in custody,' I howled down the phone. 'How could he have fed him?'

'He was released at three o'clock on Saturday afternoon, according to Brandon's log. What time did he reach you?'

I thought back. 'About five-thirty.'

'He had the use of a car?'

'Yes,' I had to admit. 'He arrived in Frogs Hill in the hired BMW,
courtesy of his agent.' I did a quick calculation. Twenty minutes at
the most from Charing to Frogs Hill, allow time for collecting his
gear and finding the car, possibly having to wait a while for it . . .
I froze. There might still be an hour or so free.

'Finds Hugh Compton where he left him. Compton has died.
Panic. Drives him to that pond. Tips him in. Ticks all the boxes,
Jack.'

'Except the glaringly obvious,' I retorted. 'If Giovanni was guilty
he'd leave the body right where he had hidden it, whether that was
Challock or anywhere else. He wouldn't risk moving it.'

'People do crazy things when they're scared. Blood in the car.
Blood on Giovanni and no doubt it was Compton's. You can't get
round that and nor can Brandon.'

I noted the 'nor can Brandon'. Did that imply Brandon himself
might want to get round it because he was beginning to have doubts,
as I had suspected? That might account for his unusually cooper-
ative attitude towards me. 'The forensic boys would demolish that
theory. Can't they be more precise on how old the stab wounds
are?' I asked hopefully.

'Water complicates things. And it doesn't get round the blood
evidence.'

He was right. I could find no explanation for that. I fantasized
that Hugh had been wounded slightly by Giovanni, then someone
took advantage of the situation and finished him off. No, that
wouldn't work. The 'somebody' wouldn't have taken the body
anywhere, but left it right where it was.

Or did Giovanni have an accomplice? I wondered. Remembering
Giovanni's 'joke' and excluding myself and Len, this unwelcome
thought had to be considered. The sheer impracticality of it, however,
made me dismiss it. How would Giovanni arrange to have an accomplice when he had only just arrived in the country and was a stranger
to the Compton family. Maria? No way. His agent? No way again.

I had returned home bruised in body and mind, both of which
had taken unexpected blows. By the time Louise returned, however,
the bruising had improved considerably. Physically anyway. When
I cautiously enquired after her day, she told me it had been bad,
but redeemed by the news of a role she had always wanted to play,

although it meant she would be away in the autumn . . . This was for real, I could tell that, so was within the rules of our arrangement. How could I object – provided she came back?

'You look as if you've had a rough day too,' she said as we adjourned to the garden for the last of the sunshine, and she saw me limping to the bench to rest my battered body.

'People have been playing rough with me.' I explained what had happened and Dave's information.

She fussed over me in a most satisfactory manner and finally returned to what Dave had told me. 'I really can't see Giovanni either as a murderer or as a master planner – it's far more likely he just wandered into something that someone else had planned.'

'If someone else planned the murder, though, it would be very unlikely that Giovanni just walked into it. It's not as if this drama had happened during the day when other people than the family might be around the barn. Nor can I believe a stray murderer would be hovering outside it at that time of night on the off chance that Hugh Compton would stroll out of the house to visit the barn *and* that he would have a handy companion who could be blamed for Hugh's murder.'

'What you're saying,' Louise pointed out, 'is that if Giovanni is innocent the family must be involved.'

I looked at her blankly. 'I suppose I am.'

'But if anyone in the family – or the whole family together – planned to murder Hugh and to put the blame on someone else, whether Giovanni or not, why not kill Hugh outright at the barn, rather than leave him alive and wounded for some days before killing him? Fairly sadistic.'

'Damn,' I said. 'You're right. Would you like to take over this case from me?'

'No thanks. Maybe it was fake blood,' she added after a moment or two. 'We use it all the time on stage.'

'It had Hugh's DNA in it.' The evidence against Giovanni was beginning to look too strong, even to me.

Nevertheless I fastened on what she had said about fake blood. As a result, my brain produced one of those ideas that pop out of their own accord without going through the usual deselection process.

'Maybe it was a fake murder?'

EIGHT

ake murder? What on earth did I mean by that? Was there such a thing in real life? I had a vague memory of a Golden Age mystery with a suicide faked to look like murder, but it hardly fitted this situation. Louise was gazing at me as though I'd arrived from another planet, and I could understand why.

'Explain, O great detective,' she suggested.

'I can't.'

'You must have had something in mind or the words wouldn't have come out.'

Perhaps she was right, so I thought my way carefully through the maze. 'I suppose that night in the barn seemed stagey from the way Giovanni described it – the silent dinner party and then Hugh's insistence on accompanying him to the barn afterwards. True, he was Giovanni's host, but . . .' Yes, this was what had been nagging at me . . . 'Hugh wasn't that crazy about the Alfa Romeo, and he'd already been to the barn that afternoon to show it to Giovanni.'

This was a very tentative peg on which to hang a theory, but I began to warm up to it. 'This idea that Hugh had been badly wounded and died of wounds days later – I can't believe Giovanni would leave a badly wounded man untended. Granted he was in jail for two days, but most of the human race would have done something to indicate a wounded man's whereabouts.'

'He said he'd been drugged,' she pointed out, 'and couldn't remember what had happened in the barn so he might not know where Hugh was.'

I wasn't to be thrown off so lightly. 'That would mean Giovanni is innocent and *that* means someone else knew what had happened, left Hugh for two days or so, then killed him, threw him in the water and—'

Louise regarded me with pity as she interrupted me. 'Jack, if I were asked to play that scenario on stage, I'd refuse. I know when I see a flop heading my way. I'd be booed off stage and rightly so.'

'Thank you, my darling. What do *you* suggest?'

'Nothing, my sweetheart. I'm only a player on stage, I don't scribble *Macbeth*s in my spare time. Over to you.'

I instantly thought of *Macbeth*'s three witches, which brought me uncomfortably back to Nan and his possibly black arts. I'd only seen his white arts side, because that was what he would have wanted me to see. No, this was the wrong turning. Once off the track and I would miss something vital – which could be this notion of a fake murder.

I took another shot. 'OK. Suppose Giovanni was framed with this fake murder. Somebody, knowing where Hugh was and therefore safe in the knowledge that Giovanni had been fitted up, killed Hugh several days later and put the body in the pond right away.'

'Much better,' Louise said approvingly. 'That I could play. It could run and run. Except that—'

'Giovanni was free again by then,' I said, my spirits sinking faster than a rowing boat with a hole in it.

'Bullseye. Take your magnifying glass, Sherlock, and see what Giovanni has in the way of an alibi for the Sunday. I hope it's good.' Bullseye for Louise too. Straight to the weak point.

'He can't have been in bed with Maria . . .' Sherlock began.

'Not all day unless she was very lucky. Where is she now, by the way?'

'No idea. She must have gone back to Pluckley with Len. Anyway,' I continued doggedly, 'she didn't arrive here until Monday and then she would have stuck to him like glue. So Sunday is probably the vital day. Giovanni's clear for most of Saturday as he was still in the loving arms of the police. There could have been a free hour, when theoretically he could have made a detour to deal with Hugh's dead body, but Sunday is mostly unaccounted for.'

'What's his story for that?'

'He went to see a friend near Eynsford.'

'Really?' She thought for a moment or too. 'Yes, I think I remember something about Eynsford but I can't remember what it was.'

'Only one problem, dearest. The friend says he never saw Giovanni that day, and Giovanni was very late in returning to Frogs Hill. I didn't hear him come in.'

'This,' she said gloomily, 'is not looking good.'

'Someone else could have been involved. Giovanni isn't my idea of a subtle game player,' I tried to reassure her, 'so he wouldn't see a set-up if it hit him in the face. Someone could have faked the murder in the barn *and* carried out the real murder. Or perhaps someone else did that,' I added, aware that I was hardly convincing myself, let alone her. I was trussed up tighter than a turkey at Christmas.

'A plot with a hole. Difficult to play, Jack,' Louise warned me. I groaned. 'Time to rewrite the scene.'

How though? I looked round the garden and thought how peaceful it was, with Louise at my side, summer roses leaping into bloom and every flower that could squeeze an inch or two of space looking its bountiful best. It was a scene far removed from the world of the Alfa Romeo, so lovingly built by Enzo Ferrari and his team over seventy years ago.

'How about this, Madame?' I continued. 'Someone set up the fake, someone else the murder. Neither of them Giovanni.'

'A Moriarty pulling the strings, do you mean?'

'Could be. He'd have to be close at hand.'

'George Makepeace organizing his troops?'

'I don't see it. He might have come in after the barn episode, but for the barn set-up the Comptons must surely have been involved.'

'Agreed. Shouldn't you begin with where Hugh was during those few days, wounded or not? Off on a cruise maybe?'

'He was probably not far away, despite the wide search.'

She nodded. 'If – and *only* if – there was a fake set-up, Hugh must have known about it.'

My turn to gaze at her as I speedily leapt on to this promising bandwagon. 'And someone – not necessarily one of the Compton family – knew where he was hiding and stepped in to murder him. Louise, if you ever get sick of the stage we'll have to become one of those private sleuth partnerships.'

'No,' she retorted.

We were both content. Light-heartedness is a good balm for bad times, even though it cures nothing. Even here in the garden at twilight, with the sweet smell of lavender and roses in the air, I was fully aware that tomorrow life would become all too real once again. I had a role to play in that, but at least I had an inkling of where it might be leading me.

Once I'd recovered from the sheer shock of having to take my own words seriously, I began to think them through. If there was a grain of truth in this fantastic notion, then surely the Comptons must be its originators. But why on earth would they set such a thing up? Just give me one good reason, I told myself. The part of my brain responsible for producing rational thought, however, seemed to be taking a temporary holiday at the moment. It might be Sunday and the beginning of June but that didn't mean it was licensed to have time off. I tried again.

Was a fake murder a double bluff on the Comptons' part, so that a few days later they could really murder Hugh? That was surely out because Hugh had to be part of the conspiracy if it was going to work. If Hugh had been their intended victim and they had planned to entrap Giovanni, how could they be sure that he would be released from custody in time for him to apparently commit the real murder – unless of course they had hoped to kill him in earnest that same night and something had gone wrong? No, I couldn't go with that. On the other hand, if they didn't plan to entrap Giovanni, why on earth bother with such an elaborate hoax?

Nonsense. I realized this was sheer fantasy. Hugh was Peter and Hazel's son, Bronte's father and Stephanie's brother. Passionate feelings might be involved, but not calm, calculated murder.

'Hoax, Louise,' I demanded of her at breakfast. 'What does that mean to you?' I'd feared that, Sunday or not, she might be rushing off in the small hours to dance in the dawn dew on a film set, but blessedly she was still here.

Unlike Maria. I realized I had not heard her return last night, and she was usually down in the kitchen at her post before anyone else. She must still be with Len, but I would ring after breakfast to check.

'Weren't hoaxes quite a thing in the early 1900s?' Louise replied. 'Virginia Woolf? She had this friend – Horace something? – who specialized in hoaxes. They travelled to Weymouth masquerading as Abyssinian royalty for a formal inspection of His Majesty's Ship *Dreadnought*. Everyone fell for it.'

'What made them do it?' I asked curiously.

'To see if they could fool everyone.'

Would anyone fake a murder just to see if it worked? Hardly. For a start, in this case Hugh would have to be involved in it as his blood was going to be used. One can't fake that. Back to square one then, as the only alternative would be that he had been wounded and left to die. No way. Hugh appeared to have been a decent enough man, not one who would stir up such antagonism that it led to murder – not by design at least. Now *that* was a good line of thinking. Was he killed for *who* he was, not *what* he was?

I clung on to that as I scooped half a banana on to my muesli. His family knew *who* he was, as well as *what*, so why initiate his murder either faked or real at this particular time? Because of the Alfa Romeo and Giovanni? Was the family united over the Alfa Romeo? Stephanie and Paul stood to gain from Hugh's death if Bronte was excluded. Could Bronte have her own agenda? And what about Hazel? Something clicked neatly into place. Blood, I thought, and Hazel had been a nurse. Nurses knew how to take blood, how much and which drugs to knock someone out. Then the theory clicked right out again. Hazel was Hugh's mother. No way would she have connived at his murder. If that had been planned, it looked as if I was back at the village development issue as a motive.

'Why are you staring at that banana?' Louise enquired politely, reaching for the coffee.

'Thinking.'

'Breakfast comes between waking up and thinking,' Louise said. 'I emphasize the *between*.'

I obediently took the point. Nevertheless, I went on thinking. I only had half the banana in this story. No point grabbing at the other half until I had eaten this piece. Another half-eaten banana was Maria and her whereabouts and so after breakfast I duly rang Len. Maria wasn't there.

'Said she was going to some friend of Giovanni's,' he told me. 'Up near Eynsford somewhere.'

This friend near Eynsford was beginning to sound like Oscar Wilde's fictional sick friend Bunbury. Anyway, Maria would have to wait, now I had satisfied myself that she had left Frogs Hill.

More trouble promptly arrived on Monday morning. I had just turned round from waving Louise goodbye in her silver-blue Focus when an ancient jalopy roared through the gates, narrowly missing her. What had I done to deserve Pen Roxton so early in the morning?

'Time to come clean, Jack!' she yelled out at me.

'Time your engine did too, Pen,' I retorted savagely.

'I'll get round to it. More important things.'

'Such as?' I asked warily.

'I'm on the trail. We're mates, remember? Brother Giovanni, man of honour. Look into it.'

'Pen, what are you on about? You make him sound like a member of the brotherhood.'

'So?'

'It's far too early for daft theories.' Even as I said it, I remembered Stephanie's reference to Mafioso Giovanni. If I wasn't careful this absurdity would be round the world in no time, courtesy of social media and Pen. Think quickly.

'I've a sensible line that won't land you in court,' I offered.

She made a face. 'Pity. What is it? Not the old village witch story?'

Pen was good, I'll say that for her. 'No, not Nan,' I cried in mock alarm. That would instantly get Pen on her toes. 'Much better. The Comptons have turned down the development offer.' I'd misplayed my hand. Even to my ears it sounded a dud story for Pen. She agreed.

'What are you hiding, Jack?' she asked suspiciously.

Thank heavens for my usual get-out line – my work for the police. 'Can't say. You'll be the first to know.'

'One-sided so far, Jack, this collaboration of ours. What have you *really* got for me?'

I was reasonably safe with this. 'Two things, Pen. Where was Hugh Compton between Wednesday night and that weekend? Close to home in my view.'

A nose twitched. 'At the manor?' she asked eagerly.

'The police searched the whole estate.' But perhaps not *again*.

'So?' Pen was still suspicious.

'He was close. Perhaps he was injured and tried to find help. Escape his attacker.'

'Sanctuary,' she breathed, clearly seeing the headline. 'Missing man sought sanctuary in the church.'

'Something like that, perhaps,' I said encouragingly.

'Second point?'

'Ask the white witch to look in her crystal ball.'

I'd meant it as a joke, but she was on to it.

'*His* crystal ball, Jack.'

Poor Nan. I reckoned he could cope though.

Half an hour later I was well on my way to Plumshaw with the church on my list. Pen wouldn't be heading there today as she had another story to follow up and press day was tomorrow, for Wednesday publication. I didn't really think there was much mileage in 'sanctuary' but I needed some idea of where Hugh might have been hiding, whether in captivity or of his own volition, assuming he hadn't died on the Wednesday night. It had to be a good place because of the police search.

Every village used to have an ancient ritual whereby all those fit enough beat the bounds of the parish according to the established markers, following them through every stream, field, bog and wood-land, thus establishing their right to their territory for another year. Maybe some villages still do, and I certainly felt I was beating the bounds as I toured both halves of Plumshaw.

I reasoned that if Hugh had hidden of his own free will, he wouldn't have chosen new Plumshaw, but if in captivity he would have had no choice. That meant he could have been in one of perhaps 200 houses. Just walking round new Plumshaw wasn't going to give me any answers, but at least it might kindle ideas. The Larches Hotel would hardly prove a good hideaway and neither did Martin's garage offer a solution. George Makepeace and his wife lived in a large modern house not far from the garage and Jamie lived with his parents further back in the estate. None of them was likely to have held Hugh captive. Short of demanding entry to the rest of the homes, I was no further forward.

Immediately after I crossed the road into the narrow lane leading back to the church and into old Plumshaw I grew more hopeful. The lane, although tarmacked, was little more than a farm track, which suggested less populated areas. I passed a farm entrance, then cottages, an all-purpose shop and the church. Any one of them might have sheltered Hugh Compton, as the larger gardens and the screening trees meant no one was too close to his neighbour.

St Michael's church was an impressive medieval building which gave no sign that its influence over the village was lessening. Mindful of Pen's sanctuary quip, I went into the porch to see if the church was open. It wasn't but as I turned back, a polite female voice asked if she could be of assistance. Although clad in tunic and jeans, she was clearly connected with the church so I explained that I was beating the bounds of both parts of Plumshaw and had heard about the rift between the two sections.

'God hasn't quite decided which side he's on,' she replied cheerfully, 'so we keep impartial in St Michael's. As his mere vicar, I couldn't possibly speak for him anyway.'

I then showed her my police ID and asked her whether there was any chance that Hugh had been hiding out anywhere near here, including in the church.

'Ah, that is a terrible business. We had the police round here several times, but I doubt if he was here. He wasn't hiding in the bell tower or the vestry or the vicarage if that's what you're thinking. There's something weird about the whole story, though.' She smiled at me. 'I'm glad I'm not a detective. I deal in certainties.'

'Did you know Hugh?'

'Everyone did. He was squire to all intents and purposes, given his father's age.'

'Popular?'

'Yes, except for his views on Plumshaw.'

She urged me to attend the coming village fête and then I carried on down the lane until it reached the main village road. On the corner was a cottage advertising teas and, realizing I was close to Puddledock Cottage, I wondered again whether Hugh had been hiding there for those few days. The Comptons were his landlords, so it was possible Nan might have obliged by sheltering him. The cottage was far enough away for Hugh to have escaped notice and the woods were close enough to provide an escape route if there was a search.

The pond was near Nan's cottage. I couldn't get away from that. Had Hugh's murderer found him there and Nan returned to find him missing? No, that would not work. He had been in the water for two or three days, and Nan would have raised the alarm. As for Nan himself, I still could think of no reason that he would have wanted to kill Hugh.

It was with a sense of unease, however, that I continued beating my own particular bounds through the woods to the manor and then to the Hop and Harry. The pub was not yet open so I wandered round to the car park at its side, which stretched back some way. Behind Lucy's garden, I could see a number of chalets set in a strip of woodland with fields beyond.

There, I thought, was a real possibility. They weren't much overlooked from the fields and would escape attention from the car park.

This was Compton territory, near enough to be accessible to the manor and secluded enough to escape too much attention. Provided Hugh kept himself to himself (and was fed from time to time) he could have stayed here unobserved. Cleaners? Easy enough to avoid given notice. The chalets would undoubtedly have been searched when Hugh was declared missing but with prior notice he could have hidden himself elsewhere. Andrew and Lucy must have been involved of course. Lucy would have looked after him well, although I bore in mind that Andrew was ambivalent about the Comptons despite the fact that Peter was his landlord.

'We're not open yet.' Andrew appeared as if in a puff of smoke from the kitchens facing the car park and he didn't look pleased.

'Get many visitors here, do you?' I nodded towards the line of chalets.

'Thinking of making an offer for the place?'

'Do you need one? I thought you were doing well.'

That stopped him. 'We are,' he snapped.

'You seemed sorry that the Comptons won't sell though.'

He glared at me. 'All the same to me. Doing well here, but I can get a job anywhere.'

I doubted that. The food I'd had here was good, but hardly Michelin standard. 'But Lucy seems happy here,' I commented.

He didn't reply. He seemed to have an urgent call on his mobile to answer – at least he clasped the phone to his ear as a subtle hint and strode off. I returned to my Polo to put through a call to Brandon's team to see if they had checked the chalets. They had. They'd searched all of them on the Thursday morning and all had been empty of signs of occupancy. But they hadn't checked them *again*.

With the manor being so close and probably accessible through the fields, these chalets were a real possibility. I had to be careful not to overplay my hand, though. The Comptons were determined people and were not going to give the game away without being convinced that I had winning cards in my hand – and that I was prepared to play them.

In fact I had precious few cards at all. Nevertheless I thought through my line of attack and prepared to tackle the manor. The days of magisterial butlers being over, Hazel answered the doorbell again. I couldn't have been her favourite visitor but she betrayed no signs of that, just waited for my first move.

Should that be as pawn or queen on this particular chessboard? Queen, I decided. 'Where was your son hiding after his *faked* murder, Mrs Compton?'

Hazel had style. She studied me for a moment, and merely said, 'Come in.'

Without another word, she led me to the same room as before. Peter was sitting in the same armchair with Paul at his side and Stephanie opposite. There was no sign of Bronte, however. Whatever it was that the family meeting was discussing, Hazel's announcement changed it.

'Jack,' she declared, 'has some strange idea that Hugh was not murdered on the night that Italian artist dined with us, but concealed himself locally while the police were searching high and low all around Challock and Plumshaw village.'

No one seemed surprised and no one commented. They only looked at me as though I were an interesting specimen of insect life. Obviously the news of my presence had already travelled round the village, and thus the subject of the family meeting was now clear.

'I should make it plain,' I began more confidently than I felt, 'that either I hear the full story now or the police will be fully primed and request your presence at Charing HQ. If you tell me the story first, I might – just might – see angles that could mean they take a more lenient view, especially with the loss of your son so recent.'

No one spoke.

At last Peter took the lead, looking even more Pickwickian than at our first meeting and surprisingly unruffled. 'Hugh was concealed in the grounds of the Hop and Harry.'

'The chalets at the rear?'

'Yes,' Hazel replied for him. 'You refer to a faked murder, Jack. Might I point out that our son *was* murdered?'

'But not at the time or in the way the police believe Giovanni Donati killed him.' I was appalled at the comparative calm with which they were taking this.

'Immaterial,' Stephanie shot back. 'He did murder my brother, albeit later than the police believed at first.'

'My daughter is right. There has been no miscarriage of justice, Jack.' Peter was looking tired now.

So that was their line. 'Your theory is therefore that although you faked Hugh's murder in the barn, Giovanni realized what had happened, deduced where Hugh was hiding and killed him for real.'

Peter flinched – but I had to press on.

'Yes,' Paul barked at me.

'Why should he have done so?' I threw back.

'That too is immaterial,' Hazel said coldly. 'Can you prove that he did not? Were you with that man every minute of the day and night after his release?'

'You forget,' I said, ignoring this, 'that without the blood found on the car and his clothes there is no evidence whatsoever against Giovanni either on the Wednesday night or later.' I then played my last card with as much flair as I could muster. 'Andrew and Lucy Lee would have been involved in your plan, and the police will be interviewing them too.'

It won my case. There was a tense silence, and then Peter surrendered. 'Jack, it is time to explain our position.'

A great relief flooded over me, but I had to steel myself not to relax to the point of letting the Comptons fool me yet again. 'It's understood,' I said firmly, 'that everything you tell me will be passed on to the police.'

'I'm sure you'll be most eager to do so,' Hazel said drily.

There followed some family friction as Stephanie and Paul did their best to persuade Peter that there was no 'position' that could possibly affect Hugh's murder. Hazel kept silent, however, and again I wondered where Bronte was.

Peter was not swayed. 'The disappearance of Hugh was, as you deduced,' he told me steadily, 'a plan that went tragically awry. Our purpose was for Donati to be discovered miles from Plumshaw after recovering from the sedative that we had administered in his wine. The blood had been taken from Hugh earlier by Hazel and of course with Hugh's full cooperation.' His dry recital continued, and I wondered if he had any idea how chillingly this was coming over to me.

'Once in the barn,' Peter continued, 'and with Donati unconscious Hugh drove the Ferrari himself while Paul took his own car to bring him back to Plumshaw, where Hugh remained quite happily at the pub, moving while the police search was in progress and on one occasion returning to the manor over the fields by night in order to discuss the situation.'

'Which night?' I asked sharply.

'Friday.'

'You saw him after that?'

'We did not, but Lucy did on Saturday morning and evening. We had all heard the news that Donati had been released, and Hugh told Lucy that he might move somewhere safer. Therefore, we did not worry overmuch when she reported that he was not at the chalet on Sunday morning.'

'How long had you intended that your son should remain in captivity?' I'd take this step by step and tried to sound as detached as Peter – which included holding back on the pressing question of why on earth they had thought up this crazy idea. At least this meant Giovanni was in the clear for Saturday afternoon. Only Sunday remained a mystery.

'I prefer the word hiding. Hugh was as much part of the scheme as the rest of us. The answer to your question is a few days only, after which he would simply return home with a most convincing story of where he had been.'

Breathtakingly facile! 'How could that explain the blood in Giovanni's Ferrari?'

'It takes time for forensic testing. We planned for him to be home on the Monday evening before it became relevant. It was, you must understand, a joke, albeit one that went tragically wrong. When he did not arrive that evening, we were worried but assumed he would return during the cover of darkness and would be with us for break-fast. He was not, and we were very concerned. Then came the news of his death. We could not have foreseen that terrible outcome.'

I wondered if any of these Comptons knew what the real world is like. I might be judging too much from external appear-ances, of course. The shock to this family, especially to Hazel and Peter, must have been immense if their story was true. The bereavement must have been doubly hard as they themselves had been responsible for lighting the touchpaper that set it off. Nevertheless, I couldn't lose sight of the fact that one or all of them might have used the hoax as a cover for murder. Looking at their impassive faces, how could I tell what churning thoughts lay behind them? At present they were looking at me like span-iels expecting to be patted and told what to do next.

I didn't pat anyone.

I went to the heart of the matter. '*Why*,' I asked, 'play such a ghastly joke? And why Giovanni?'

'Old scores, Jack,' Paul answered almost laconically. He was out of tune, however, because Peter promptly came in with his version.

'The Alfa Romeo is the reason. Donati came here under false pretences, pretending he wished to paint the car.'

'Pretending? He was passionate about painting it.' My head really was spinning now. This just could not be true.

'He was passionate about claiming its ownership. Ever since Hugh received his request to come here, we have known that.'

'You're completely wrong,' I argued. 'How could he be the owner?' Even if Giovanni had had such a nonsensical idea in his mind, he would have told me that. Laughed about it.

'To his way of thinking, very easily,' Peter replied. 'Giulio Santoro, the original owner of the Alfa Romeo, was his grandfather.'

I was knocked sideways once again. 'His family name is Donati.'

'His mother was Giulio Santoro's daughter. His only child.'

He sounded so certain that I took this seriously. I remembered Maria's reticence when I had asked her about Giovanni's family. She spoke only of his father – and I had not followed up with questions about his mother. I had some hard work to do here, but meanwhile I must struggle not to be distracted from the basic story. Whoever Giovanni was, he had been framed.

'Why the hoax? A cruel way of telling him he wasn't going to be able either to own or paint the car.'

'Revenge, Jack, and fully justified. The hoax was intended to teach him what captivity on a false charge can be like.'

Another knockout blow? 'Why, for heaven's sake?'

'Because as a result of the Santoro family's actions, I once found myself in captivity in Italy on a charge of having stolen the Alfa Romeo and collusion with an illegal regime.'

The Comptons had told me enough to convince me I needed a complete reassessment of the case – and so would Brandon. Unless the story was without any foundation at all, Giovanni had been keeping me in the dark. Why? He wasn't stupid. He had been charged with murder. I needed time to get to grips with it. Nothing more could happen today, surely, or so I thought as I reached Frogs Hill.

I was wrong. Pen was waiting for me in her car.

'Your witch,' she yelled as she scrambled out to accost me.

'Cast a spell on you, has he?' I asked wearily.

'No, on *you*. Peacemaker, my foot. Nantucket Brown served eight of a fifteen-year sentence for murdering his wife.'

NINE

After a night's sleep, I was better prepared to face the bombshells thrown my way. The vital one had been Giovanni's alleged connection with the Alfa Romeo through his ancestor, of which he had given me no inkling whatsoever. The second was also troubling. Nan the peacemaker now had a question mark over him, given his violent background; there was, however, a wide gulf between killing a wife over twenty years ago in a crime of passion and killing his landlord as the result of the careful plan there must have been behind Hugh's murder.

Giovanni, whom I was struggling to save from his murder charge, had, it seemed, been as economical with the truth as he was uneconomical with flowing wine. There was little doubt about that and my best route would be through Maria who, when she abandoned her drama queen role, was a practical, no-nonsense woman. She had to be to have remained married to Giovanni for so long.

Tracking down Maria should not be too difficult, and tackling her was more urgent than following up a possible Nan link. Assuming this 'friend' was the one Giovanni had hopefully cited as an alibi, I could call Brandon's team for information on this restaurant in the Eynsford area. The back history between Peter Compton and the Santoro family meant that the prosecution might be able to produce a much stronger motive for Giovanni wanting to kill Hugh Compton. I remembered Peter Compton's mention of 'revenge' and, coupled with Pen's clearly ridiculous 'Mafioso' reference, it could mean there were even darker angles to this case than had so far been apparent. And somewhere in the middle of them was the Alfa Romeo.

Brandon's team, after some huffing and puffing, supplied me with the restaurant's name – La Casa. It was in a hamlet called Castleford, between Swanley and Eynsford and Umberto Monti was its owner. It was situated conveniently near the M20 and its junction with the M25, the motorway that girdles London (usually slowly due to heavy traffic), so it was also convenient for reaching Colchester and Giovanni.

I had feared Maria would do a runner when I rang to tell her I was coming and was now on my way to her early on the Tuesday evening. She had agreed to see me, even if somewhat reluctantly. When I arrived at five thirty before the restaurant opened for the evening, she had obviously decided on battle, judging by her expression. That suited me, because this time I would take no prisoners. Unfortunately, I could not play the ace in my hand. Brandon had naturally flatly refused any mention of the fake murder – at least until he had worked it through. He had been the nearest I had ever heard to incandescent when I rang him with the news, although he had grudgingly agreed that I'd done a good job in forcing the issue.

I let Maria finish her seafood linguine – either a belated lunch or early supper – and then fired my opening shot. 'How come neither you nor Giovanni mentioned that Santoro was his grandfather – *and*,' I added, seeing she was about to let forth a torrent of denials, 'therefore the first owner of the Comptons' Alfa Romeo?'

The torrent was stopped in its tracks. She looked puzzled, then apparently enlightenment came followed by an expression of great wisdom. 'You must ask Giovanni about his family. He will tell you.'

She then proceeded to study the dessert menu, always a favourite with her. I gently removed it.

'I shall ask him, Maria, and so will the police – far from politely.'

She reached out for the menu again. 'Why?' she asked aggressively.

I could play games too. 'Because it's connected to the murder of which he's accused.'

'It is not,' she snapped.

'How would you know?'

'Giovanni care only about painting – and me,' she added defiantly. 'He do not want to own cars, only paint.'

'He likes owning his Ferrari Daytona.' I moved the menu slightly towards her but kept my hand on it.

She brushed this comment aside. 'Giovanni is great artist. Only that is important.'

I was not going to get any further on that score, so I pushed the menu further towards her, keeping my hand firmly on it. 'The police will be asking him, Maria, so you might want to warn him of that.'

She remained stony-faced, so I began on another track. 'Giovanni told me and the police that he came to see a friend at this restaurant. Is he here now?'

'No.'

I pulled the menu back again.

'*No.*' She could see I was not going to give up, however, because she graciously added, 'Umberto's family friends of the Santoro family, friend of Giulio's sister Floria – no, that was Lucia – and friends of Donati family.'

'You're sure he's not here?'

'No. Not here. Day off.'

This was like getting petrol out of a dry pump. I had made some impression on her, however, so we concluded the festivities with a zabaglione each, which restored her to happiness – until it occurred to her that Giovanni might not be fed zabaglione in prison.

Encouraged that at least she had admitted the family connection, I pondered on the case against Nan again on the way home. I still could see no motive, however. Whoever killed him must have known Hugh's hiding place in the chalet. That could still leave Giovanni in the frame and it also put Andrew into it as well. Andrew had no driving motive for the murder either, despite his ambivalence over the development plans. He might have passed on Hugh's whereabouts to the Makepeace clan though. Where, I wondered, was the safer hiding place that Hugh had apparently found for what was to be the last day of his captivity before his planned return home?

It's not often I'm honoured by a visit from DCI Brandon himself – it's usually a summons over to Charing HQ and must be a sign that he was becoming worried over this case. He asked me, greatly to my surprise, if he could see the Pits. As he has no great interest in cars, this must be counted a tribute of some sort.

Brandon can be an affable man, when he's not nose-to-grindstone, and Zoe was impressed at his interest in the Lanchester. Len was less so, I suspect because he thought he was going to be implicated in the Giovanni story. I noticed the glint in his eye which suggested the visitor would get short shrift if he interrupted his work schedule unnecessarily.

He need not have worried. Brandon did not even mention Giovanni, only told a story about his grandfather's Javelin in the 1950s. I guessed that he had been satisfied that Len was in the clear and had no more to offer in the way of information on Giovanni's movements.

When Brandon finally returned to the farmhouse he came straight to the point.

'This crazy fake murder – do you believe the Comptons?'

'Risky, but yes.'

'I'm on my way to see them. We'll have to consider charges. More police time wasted, no doubt.'

'Will it clear Giovanni?'

'Not if he hasn't a damned good alibi for Sunday the eighteenth.'

'I didn't see the famous friend, but he does seem to exist at least.' I knew what I had to ask next. 'OK if I go to see Giovanni?'

'I won't stop you. But the fake murder is off limits.'

'I'll concentrate on the grandfather and Peter Compton's captivity.'

He was more grudging this time. 'Tread on eggshells, Jack.'

Fate then stepped in. It chose to do so in the middle of the night via a phone call.

Louise shot up in bed and by the time I had struggled out of the land of Nod she had already picked up.

'For you,' she said, handing the phone over. 'It's Martin Fisher.'

Even my sleepy eyes could see from the alarm clock that it was 2.05 a.m. and not even the earliest bird had as yet opened its beak to greet the day. Martin was calling from his mobile, so something was up and it wasn't the birds.

'Thought you'd want to know, Jack.'

'Know what?' I slurred.

'The Hop and Harry. It's burning down.'

I didn't take it in at first. Then I rearranged the jumble of my first thoughts. 'Burning down' sounded no mere small blaze. This was bad. 'I'm on my way,' I told him.

'What on earth for?' Louise said wearily as I swung my legs to the floor. 'What can you do about a fire? Nothing.'

'Perhaps I can. It's my case anyway.'

'Whether it burns down or not, your being there won't solve anything,' she pointed out reasonably enough.

She was right, but I still knew I had to go. 'It seems the right thing to do.' I pulled on the nearest clothes at top speed.

'Correction. The wrong thing even if for the right reasons. Need me along?'

'If you weren't so beautiful already, I'd say you needed your beauty sleep.'

She threw a pillow at me, flopped down into bed again and was instantly back in Nod. Nothing is more beautiful than the sight of a beautiful woman sleeping, especially when it's my bed. I kissed her and tore myself away.

I could see the glow in the distance, as I drove along the Canterbury Road to the Plumshaw turning. Fire has an emotional effect on those who view it, whether or not they are directly involved. Fear is only one of those emotions, but it's a powerful one. Fire is man's friend and his enemy, but tonight it would be solely enemy.

I parked some way from the pub – or what might be left of it. As I hastily locked the car I could smell the stifling smoke in the air as I ran along the road to join the crowd watching outside. All the way I passed open doors with people standing with their eyes fixed on the pub. I could see the occasional flame, although the fire must already have been well under way when Martin had called me. I began to think Louise had been right and there was no place for me here, and yet with what seemed most of the village gathered I knew I'd been right to come. For whatever reason I was temporarily part of this village – for good or ill.

I briefly wondered how this would affect the case. It would certainly affect the Compton/Makepeace battle. With no pub many of the protesters upholding the rights of the old village would see their hopes as doomed and only the Comptons might be left to deal with the Makepeace clan.

When I reached the corner of the road where the pub stood, flames were still licking one end. The familiar gabled outline of the roof had changed, almost vanished. I could smell charred wood and see that the roof seemed partly to have fallen in, taking with it the top storey of the building at one end. The fight seemed to be more successful on the other end, where it had only just begun to eat its remorseless way through the timber and walls. I could see not only fire engines and the usual police car but three of the latter which meant there must be a crime scene investigator here, plus the Fire Investigation Team. I saw one of the fire fighters taking off his helmet briefly to wipe the sweat from his face and I recognized him. It was Nan, who must include this amongst his many other jobs. Almost immediately he put his helmet on and disappeared back into the burning building.

At last I spotted Martin in the crowd and went over to join him. He was bright-eyed with tiredness, his eyes fixed on the burning pub.

'Was anyone inside?' I asked him.

'Only Andrew and Lucy. Their son was over with her parents. It was Andrew who called the fire brigade and so he and Lucy got out quickly.'

That at least was good news. 'Is it known yet how the fire started?' *With someone's help* was my immediate thought and must surely be on most people's minds.

'Don't think so. Someone said it began in the snug. Then it must have been forced upwards plus spreading out around the rest of the ground floor. The alcohol around can't have helped.'

I could see clearly the burnt-out left side of the building, now a smoking ruin although the walls and ground floor were still standing.

'Foul play? A little bit of help from their non-friends?' I asked.

'Could be accident, but a coincidence.'

'The police must think so. There's plenty of them here.'

I walked over to take a closer look at the pitiful sight. Fire takes lives in more ways than one. As well as physical life it can sweep away the whole basis of everyday life and destroy emotional life through the loss of the memorabilia and other irreplaceable posses-sions that define individuals' existences. For Andrew and Lucy it was an extra hard blow after their struggle to build up the pub. I could see them standing close together for comfort, hypnotized by the sight of their lives being destroyed in front of them.

'Do you have somewhere to stay?' I asked Lucy when they moved closer to me.

'My mother's.' She didn't even look at me. She was staring at the ruins of the Hop and Harry as though even now she could not believe what was happening. 'They won't let us in,' she said abruptly.

'Tomorrow they will,' I said in a vain attempt at comfort. 'They have to ensure it's safe first.' I could see that was optimistic to say the least. The majority of their possessions, both private and the pub's, would either have been burnt beyond salvage or at the least damaged, as would the fixtures and fittings, both their own and anything belonging to the Comptons.

'We won't let this get us down, Luce,' Andrew said without conviction. 'Bloody Makepeaces,' he added.

'You think this is down to them?' I asked.

'Who else?'

'Even a stray match could have caused it.'

He didn't bother to reply and I could see why. George Makepeace had threatened further action and perhaps this was it, whether by his hand or another's. I too could not believe that this was an accident. I could see Jamie Makepeace in the crowd but there was no sign of George, something that the crowd seemed to be taking as evidence of his guilt. Jamie was staggering around – whether through drink or overwrought emotions – and had his eye on Bronte who was comforting Lucy. Although clearly aware of his presence, she was ignoring him.

'This'll put paid to the bloody Comptons,' Jamie declared loudly. 'Can't use the pub as an excuse any more.' There was a roar of disapproval from the crowd at such ungraciousness, and even Jamie's smarting youth could not make this forgivable. Certainly Bronte didn't think so.

'We still own the land, Jamie Makepeace,' she yelled at him. 'And we have some respect for others' feelings, not like you. Lucy and Andrew have lost their home.'

He looked shamefaced, but didn't heed the voice of caution that Martin was urging on him. 'The future and jobs are all that's important.'

'Maybe thinking about Miss Bronte is too,' Andrew yelled at him.

That infuriated Jamie even more. He lowered his head and charged at Andrew. Time for me to intervene. I grabbed Jamie, just managing to swing him away from Andrew before contact. I received a punch in the face as a result from Master Jamie. I'd had enough, so I treated him to a couple of quick judo moves, pinioning him by both arms.

'Sober up,' I told him sharply. 'Bronte needs you. But you won't get her by behaving like a complete jerk. *Or* by punching me,' I added.

'Oh yeah? Want another one?' he tried feebly.

This time he found himself on the floor, by which time two police officers had arrived. I showed them my ID card to prevent myself being arrested. Jamie was still groaning on the ground and, at a nod from me, the police decided to turn a blind eye as I dragged him to his feet and sent him on his way – which was not towards Bronte.

Depressing, I thought. A young couple so much in love, so unable to talk it through. If it was meant to be, I supposed, they would get together again, but now there were more pressing problems.

'Arson?' I enquired of the police.

'Too soon. Maybe. Wads of burnt paper at a possible seat of the fire.'

The sight of the old building in such a state was sobering, even for me who didn't live in Plumshaw. No one was going to class this wreck as a safe house to enter for a while.

The mutterings about Makepeaces and Comptons were subdued now. First light had come and the birds had the nerve to begin their cheerful racket to tell us what a nice day it was going to be.

As the crowd began to disperse, I could see no further sign of Andrew and Lucy, and Martin and I adjourned to his house for a restorative coffee. His home was next to the garage, a small detached modern house, tidy and somewhat soulless inside, although I glimpsed a model railway in one room. I asked him if it was his hobby, and was told it was his son's who liked playing with it on his visits, from which I deduced that Martin was indeed divorced.

'A shock for old Peter Compton,' he said, handing me the coffee. 'He doesn't deserve this.'

'You look fairly shaken,' I said. 'Not the best way out of the village problem.'

'Don't jump to conclusions. I've never known the Makepeaces go this far before.'

'It might be their last throw of the dice, now their offer has been turned down, although burning down the pub doesn't mean that Peter Compton will sell.'

'He'll have to. The estate needs the cash. It's struggling.'

'Selling the Alfa Romeo would keep a few wolves from the door,' I pointed out. Provided, of course, that Peter Compton had the right to sell it. As there had once been a dispute over the ownership that might not be straightforward. Peter had accused Giovanni of coming

here to claim it for himself. Were there grounds for that? Did
Giovanni have a legitimate claim on behalf of the Santoro family?
If so, the ownership might be tied up in litigation for years to come.

That brought me back to the pressing need for another visit to
Giovanni. I could foresee a battle ahead, and this one would not be
settled by withholding the dessert menu.

More than charity has to begin at home. The next morning I needed
to do some preliminary work before I saw Giovanni. Louise had
left me to sleep, thankfully, so it was eleven o'clock before I staggered into the Pits, even then not at my brightest. Len pretended
he hadn't seen me and began polishing the Lanchester very
vigorously.

I gave no quarter but planted myself directly in front of him.
'Giovanni stayed with you on the Monday after his release from
prison. You went to Gatwick to pick up Maria and then took them
back to your home. What did they do all day?'

'Nothing much. The wife said they sat in the garden, though they
took her out to lunch at the pub.'

'Giovanni didn't leave Maria on her own? Drive anywhere else?'

He fixed me with a glare. 'Ask the wife. She says no. And I
reckon she'd have noticed if he nipped off to murder that bloke.'

Point taken. Well, at least I knew what questions to ask Giovanni
once I had arranged my visit. That took a while and it was Monday
before I got to see him.

My first impression was that he was avoiding my eye. I interpreted
that as meaning Maria had relayed the content of my visit to her,
so I had a clear run on the grandfather angle.

'Your grandfather Giulio Santoro. Why didn't you tell me about
him?'

Giovanni attempted a lofty disdain. 'I did not know he was my
grandfather.'

'I'm told that you did know. Maria did. And now so do the police.'

He began to crumple. 'I did not want the Comptons to know
about Giulio. They think bad things maybe, but all I wished to do
was paint.'

'They knew as soon as you sent your letter to them asking to
paint the car. But why did you not tell me, Giovanni?'

His head went up again. 'This is a matter of family, Jack. You would not understand. We settle such matters within the family. Outsiders know nothing.'

'Then how did your friend at La Casa come to know about it?'

Giovanni looked trapped. 'From a customer.'

'How did the customer . . .?' I stopped. Ten to one the customer was one of the Comptons and probably Hugh. This hoax had been better planned than I had realized.

'Are you sure the Compton family knew about my grandfather?' Giovanni asked me. 'They said nothing to me. How could they have known?'

My lips had to be sealed on the hoax issue and on Peter's past, so I switched subjects. 'The car, Giovanni. Do you really believe it still belongs to your family?'

He glared at me. 'It was stolen by Fascists when my grandfather died.'

Could I be getting some cooperation at last? At least he was opening up. 'At some point after the war it was sold to Peter Compton.' Then I remembered this was not strictly correct. 'Sold to him through his first wife, Sofia Mesola, who arranged the sale. Your family disputed ownership and he was imprisoned.'

He thumped his fists on the table which brought two warders smartly to their feet. 'I not born until 1957, Jack. How could I know?'

'How could you not? It's your family history.'

He looked sulky. 'Italy, my family, *every* family want to forget after the war. A new country, a new republic.'

'A split country, half monarchist, half republican, some of them communists, some Christian Democrats. That's why the car's ownership could be disputed?'

'Yes,' he agreed sulkily.

'Your friend at La Casa told you about the rumour of the Alfa Romeo because he knew your family had a claim to it.'

'Perhaps that is so.' He was very grudging about it. 'I do not want the car, Jack. I went to *paint* the car,' he repeated. 'It is my right.'

Knowing Giovanni of old, I was reasonably satisfied with this, so I moved on to the vital point.

'Tell me what you were doing on the Sunday after you were discharged from the police station, Giovanni. You didn't see your friend at La Casa, did you? The restaurant was closed and he was away that day.' (I hoped Brandon would excuse me one bit of evidence revealed.)

He took a very dignified stance. 'That is not your business, Jack. I am an important man. I have places to go.'

'Is that what you're telling the police? They know your story is not true.'

Silence.

I sighed. 'Tell me, Giovanni.'

'I was not in Plumshaw. That is all I say. This is all you need to know. I was not murdering Hugh Compton.'

'Tell me, Giovanni.'

'You will not like this, Jack.'

'*Tell* me.'

One glance at my face and he surrendered. 'I went to see my son Ricardo.'

I'd walked right into it. One never sees the blow that fells you. 'He's in England?'

'Yes. He is living here.'

A dozen fearful scenarios shot through my mind. 'Has Louise seen him?'

'I do not know. She would not come on that Sunday.'

The world tipped back into balance again. That was a relief. Or was it? Perhaps she was having tête-à-têtes with Ricardo? Perhaps she wanted to go back to him and had sworn Giovanni to silence?

'Does Ricardo have a new partner?' I asked hopefully.

'Partner?'

'Wife, girlfriend,' I said impatiently, aware that he was stalling for time.

'Of course. He is a Donati,' Giovanni said proudly. 'But Louise is a very special lady.'

Pride would not let me ask: 'Does he want her back?' Would she go if he did? Was she still in love with him? I wanted to hurl all these questions at Giovanni but I managed to restrain myself – just. Instead I asked the obvious question.

'Why did you not *tell* me you were with Ricardo on Sunday?'

'If you knew about Louise and my son, you would not have liked it, Jack.'

He had me there. I wouldn't have done. 'Why not tell the police?'

The head went back again. 'It is family matter.'

'As it will be if you are found guilty,' I said grimly.

He glared at me. 'If the police know about my family they could discover I am Santoro's grandson. Then they think I lie when I told them I only wish to paint it. And if I tell them I go to see Ricardo they would not believe me. He is my son.'

He was right. 'Not a strong alibi in police terms,' I agreed.

'It is the truth.' He sat back and folded his arms. I got the message but ignored it.

'You also have a motive for Hugh Compton's murder.'

'Why?' Giovanni said indignantly. 'The car belongs to his father, so if I was to kill anyone I kill Peter.'

'Not,' I pointed out, 'if you had a row with Hugh about it and lost your temper.'

Giovanni looked puzzled. 'But my lawyer tell me he not die until the next weekend. So if the quarrel in the barn was over who owns the car, I would not wait a week to kill him.'

The hoax. He didn't know about it and I couldn't tell him.

TEN

The great thing about cars is that what you see is what you get. That sounds trite, but underlying car problems can be stripped away layer by layer to find the root cause of the trouble. Unfortunately, it's more tricky with human beings. I can't just diagnose the fault, send away for the spare part and have him or her on the road again, waving happily at the rest of humankind. With human beings you have to be very sure what spare part the fault requires before you press their accelerator pedal to full speed ahead.

With Giovanni I was far from sure I had the right spare part. He had admitted what I needed to hear – the family connection with Santoro – which meant I had stripped away to what must surely be the root cause. The complex story it revealed, however, still did not fully explain his present predicament. It had rung true that the painting rather than the car itself might have been uppermost in his mind, not the possibility of claiming back the Alfa Romeo. I just couldn't see Giovanni (or the Giovanni I thought I knew) going berserk over a family incident dating back seventy years. He is a man who lives in the present, however much he admires classic cars. Furthermore, I couldn't believe he was either lying or holding something back about the Alfa Romeo. I now had both Peter Compton's and Giovanni's pitches on the car and they more or less dovetailed. What more could I want? Goodness knows. Perhaps nothing. The burning down of the Hop and Harry at this particular time almost surely was more than coincidence however.

I couldn't tackle Louise on the Giovanni angle with the shadow of Ricardo still hanging over us, and so when she picked up on my preoccupation at breakfast the next day I took the plunge into the deep end and hit a pool full of cold water for my pains.

'Did Ricardo ever talk about his family—?'

She cast a scathing glance at me. 'I don't talk about Ricardo.'

A shadow over the day already. 'You should.'

'My business.'

'Mine too. Otherwise I'm living with you both.'

She slammed down the marmalade pot – by which I deduced I had won a point, and was quick to capitalize on it.

'If you talk, you normalize. If you suppress, it festers.'

'It's past, it's gone.' She had her obstinate look on.

'If it's gone, you *can* talk about it.'

'Oh, *Jack*. Keep clear, *please*.'

We were at an impasse so I risked a leap into darkness. 'Let's both go and see Ricardo. Clear the air.'

'Whatever for?' The portcullis stayed where it was.

Keep your voice deadpan, I counselled myself. 'I can talk to him about his family history. It could help Giovanni and Ricardo's his son.'

'Unfair pressure,' she whipped back. 'And you're in too deep, Jack.' At least she hadn't rejected the idea outright.

'Do it, Louise,' I said more gently.

'I'll think about it.'

Perhaps she did. She certainly wasn't talking to me through the rest of breakfast. When we'd finished, however, she grudgingly conceded a point. 'Tell me what Giovanni told you.'

I didn't want to prejudice my case by overplaying my cards, so I told her without comment that he had admitted to knowing who his grandfather was and about the Alfa Romeo but that he claimed he only wanted to paint it.

'That fits,' she commented. 'What worries you?'

I couldn't analyse that myself at first, but I had to do it somehow. 'The facts that a brutal murder took place, preceded by an almost unbelievable hoax, that ownership of the car is disputed, that its sale could bring in what would be a fortune to most people and that the village pub has burnt down. Nothing seems to link up.'

She began to come round. 'Does that matter? What certainly does matter is whether Giovanni is guilty of murder. And that's going to be decided by what's happening now, not by an old car from seventy years back. It will be settled by forensic and trace evidence, which isn't your province.'

'I agree, but I have a valid province too: if Giovanni is innocent then someone else killed Hugh Compton. Unless someone works out who could have done it and why, then even in these DNA days my province is useful. That's what I'm here for,' I added unwisely.

'You're also here to do the washing up,' she informed me.

I kissed her. 'A pleasure. Your turn tomorrow.'

Only three words – but they brought contentment. Tomorrow we would still be together, and I thought of all the tomorrows when we hadn't been. Then Ricardo slunk back into my mind. *Get out*, I warned him, and then belatedly took the advice that I had handed out to Louise. I wouldn't keep ignoring his existence. I'd let him come in, which was much more sensible. Well, I'd try anyway, especially since Louise seemed in a mood for compromise.

'If the story's out of balance,' she reflected, 'maybe it's the story that's wrong.'

'I can't believe both Peter and Giovanni are lying.'

Then I saw what she meant. That the Alfa Romeo and the fire seemed out of balance in comparison with the crime of Hugh's murder. I examined this angle for a moment or two.

'Not necessarily,' I said. 'The strength of the car's monetary value as a motive would be measured by how much the killer needs, not what's available. In this case Giovanni wants the car, but most certainly money is not the objective, and neither Hugh nor Peter planned to sell it. Both Peter and Giovanni seem to value the Alfa Romeo as an object, not for itself. For Peter it has memories of a bitter time and for Giovanni it's the prospect of a wonderful painting with family connections. And if Hugh did have plans for its sale, he kept them very quiet.'

'Then when – how – did Giovanni or anyone else hear about it?' she asked reasonably enough.

'My theory is that Hugh was a customer at La Casa and talked about it to this friend of Giovanni's who passed it on.'

Her eyebrows shot up. 'Well, well. Bit of a coincidence that a casual comment over a plate of pasta hit so big a target.'

'OK. I surrender,' I told her. 'It was engineered by the Comptons. Set on wanting vengeance, Peter Compton worked out this way of luring Giovanni here through leaking the news that the Alfa Romeo was in his barn. If it failed, no harm done. If it worked, the hoax could go ahead.'

'And they just happened to know that the owner of La Casa was a chum of Giovanni's?'

'Could well have. Giovanni's a well-known name in this country;

this Umberto could have been boasting about him and that's why they set up The Mousetrap. How would that one work on stage?'

She laughed. 'It would run and run.'

The former Hop and Harry was a desolate sight when I went over to Plumshaw later that day. It had obviously been made safe in the five days since I was last here, for the cordon had been lifted and the front, albeit charred, was open. I could see Andrew inside. There were a pile of black bags and a stack of boxes outside and two vans parked in the road. Andrew was staggering out with another one and managed to give me a wave, albeit a lacklustre one. I went over to talk to him.

'Christopher's Lego set,' he said, indicating a bag put to one side. 'At least he'll be happy.'

'How is your son?' I asked. 'Where's he staying?'

'We're still with my mother-in-law in Ashford.'

'Has any of your kitchen survived?' I doubted it as it was near the side of the building that had suffered most.

'I rescued my knife,' he said, almost cheerfully despite the circumstances. 'Just as well. It's my lucky talisman. With that in my hand I could cook for the Queen, so I take its rescue as a sign that I'm on my way to fame and fortune.'

Looking at the Hop and Harry I couldn't see much hope of his achieving that here. 'Are the Comptons going to rebuild?'

'Not known. The place is on the borderline for being demolished, as it would cost the insurance companies – Peter's and mine – a fortune to restore it. If it goes, my job goes with it. I don't see him rebuilding. What with Hugh's death and all that he'll surely sell up now.'

I wasn't sure that would be the case, but if it helped Andrew to believe it, who was I to contradict him? 'What will you do next if he doesn't?' I asked.

'I'll pick up a job somewhere,' he said laconically. 'I'm good.'

I wasn't as convinced as he was about that, but confidence carries one forward a long way.

'Here in Plumshaw?' I asked, more for the sake of keeping the conversation going than for information. He seemed reluctant to leave me and as the alternative would be plunging back into that sad building I could understand why.

He shot a look at me. 'Where would I get that then? In the village tea-rooms?'

I thought of the small tea-shop in the cottage on the corner of Church Lane, and I had to admit that I didn't see Andrew in that context, even though his ambition seemed somewhat to overweigh his capabilities. When did that ever stop anyone rising to the top, though? I couldn't see another pub opening in the village unless one went up in the new development – *if* it went ahead.

'No,' I said. 'I don't see Lucy in a tea shop either.'

'She deserves the best,' he said simply. 'She's upset about her garden. Mess all over it. Flowers trampled down, veggies gone for a burton.'

'Is she here now?' I asked. I could see someone moving around on the ground floor. I would have thought the top floor must be fairly uninviting, even though it had obviously been made safe.

'No. She's over at her mum's moving stuff around. We're having to ferry Christopher to school and back, so we're hoping we'll be settled by next term.'

The question of who was within was quickly solved when another two black bags arrived through the door. All I could see was a pair of jeans transporting them, but as the bags were offloaded, Jamie Makepeace materialized from behind them. A surprising place to find him, I thought, given that the obvious suspects for an arson attack would be the Makepeaces.

One of the bags split open so I obligingly went to help pick the stuff up – and what a heartbreaking job this was, even though it wasn't my family. The bag contained photos, no doubt going back years to a time when photos only existed as printouts and not stored in a computer. Many of them were charred round the edges, some curled up and partly burnt.

'Look at them,' Andrew said bitterly, coming to have a look and then quickly turning away. 'That's our life burnt up.'

'You can take many more,' I said. 'You're young.'

He ignored me, perhaps rightly. 'When I find out who did this lot—'

'It wasn't an accident then? It was deliberate?'

'You bet it was. Mr Compton thinks I left something burning in the kitchen. I didn't, and the police don't think so neither. They found newspapers and stuff and a paraffin can which wasn't mine, I can tell you that.'

'The accelerants,' I said.

'Whatever, but it's done for us.'

He seemed to have forgotten his earlier confidence that a new and better life lay ahead, as he went back into the pub. This left me with Jamie, who seemed embarrassed at my presence, which was hardly surprising since not that long ago he'd punched me in the jaw, plus been the cause of sending me flying down the steps of the pub to gather a few painful bruises. He kindly acknowledged the fact.

'Look, about that punch-up – sorry and all that,' he managed to say, blushing to the roots of his sandy-coloured mop of hair. 'Been under pressure, see?'

'Let's forget it,' I said nobly. 'You could stand me a drink, but I doubt if there's a glass to be found. Did all the bottles go?'

'Most of them. Wouldn't fancy drinking out of the rest.'

'Nor me. You're a chum of Andrew's?'

'Sort of.'

I noted the touch of wariness there, and wondered how he would react to Bronte's name.

'Are you still at odds with Bronte?'

His face crumpled. 'Can't do nothing about it. She's gone right off me.'

'I doubt that,' I said robustly. 'It's just the stress of what she's going through.'

'No, it ain't. She's gone right over to the Compton way of thinking. Got to stand by her grandfather now that her dad's not there. That sort of thing. I tell her he's got a wife to do that. And he's got a daughter. Bronte's got her own life to lead – or so she reckons, and it's not with me.'

'That might be the problem. What happens after Peter's death now that her father is no longer alive to inherit?' This might be a painful subject for him, but that was too bad.

'I dunno. Bronte says she's got to do what her grandad wants. I tell her it's the twenty-first century and we do what *we* want. We had it all planned. A cottage too and all.'

'How about a compromise?'

He looked blank and then shrugged. 'No such word between Makepeaces and Comptons. My grandad says it's a fight to the death.' A pause as he realized his choice of words was unfortunate and shuffled his feet. 'Not that Grandad would have gone that far. Not to burn down the pub, nor kill off those Comptons. Not really. But it's what those bastards deserve. Think they can rule other folks' lives.'

'What will happen to your family's development plans now? Stalled until the pub situation is sorted out?'

A touch of his old aggression returned. 'Grandad will go ahead. Course he will. Still got the homes to build, even without the road and industrial site, but he wants the lot, does Grandad. And he's going to get it.'

'Can't the road skirt the Hop and Harry?'

'Been into that. No way at all. But now,' Jamie said with satisfaction, 'there ain't no Hop and Harry. That should hurry things along. Maybe Bronte will come round when it's a done deal.' He looked at me hopefully.

'I hope she will,' was all I could say. I also hoped that it wasn't for that reason. They needed a fresh start, as did Andrew and Lucy, although none of them saw it that way at present.

We were interrupted by the slam of a car door behind us, followed by Stephanie making her way up the path. She nodded to me as though it was normal to see me here, as perhaps it was. Jamie didn't seem to be on her list, however, as she swept by to find Andrew, murmuring to us en route. She must have failed because out she came again, wrinkling her patrician nose.

'Not good in there,' she commented, as Jamie made a hurried escape. She sounded friendly enough, and she looked younger too, as the set mouth and hard eyes seemed to have softened. I bore in mind, however, that setting aside her brother's death, fortune was now favouring her. She stood next in line for taking over the estate – or the cash from it in due course – not to mention the Alfa Romeo. If Bronte came back on to the scene, however, it could be a different story.

All this was speculation, however, and in front of the ruins of the Hop and Harry it seemed out of place. We were spectators at a private tragedy in which a young couple's livelihood had disappeared and with it the Comptons' dreams of keeping the estate intact.

'How is Peter coping?' I asked her. 'After your brother's death this must be one more blow at a time when he can least face it.'

'He hasn't taken it in. He's dwelling in the past just now. Hugh's death changes a lot of things. Paul and I are running the farm between us at present.'

'And Bronte?'

'Not her, nor my stepmother who's rushing around intent on planning the funeral – whenever the police deign to let us know when we can hold it. Bronte's still brooding over her father's death.'

'And her love trouble, of course.'

'I doubt whether that's the case. For all his solicitous help over clearing up the mess of the pub, who's the most likely person to have burnt it down? The Makepeaces – and Jamie is their front man. I noticed you were happily hobnobbing with him just now.'

I ignored that. 'The arson attack could have been by someone who stood to gain from the Makepeace plans.'

Stephanie stiffened, which was interesting. Did she include herself and Paul amongst them?

'What will happen to the Alfa Romeo now?' I continued casually.

I thought she was going to cut me off with a curt 'mind your own business' but she didn't. 'It stays,' she said. 'Hugh wanted to sell it, but my father wouldn't allow it and he still won't.' She smiled, which made me warm to her. 'I'm not sure why I'm telling you all this.'

'Talking helps shock.'

'The shock of Hugh's death? Or this?' She stared at the Hop and Harry.

'Both, I'm sure. As it must be for Bronte. Will she continue to live at the manor?'

'She says she will. She's a changeable creature though. First she riles my father by announcing she's marrying a Makepeace, now she's dropped him. I sometimes wonder what is behind that.'

So did I. Cutting out Paul and Stephanie perhaps? 'Maybe she wants to live with her grandparents, now she's not going to live with Jamie in new Plumshaw.'

'Nonsense. Hugh had promised them Puddledock Cottage.'

'*What?*' How many more surprises were in store from this manipulative family? 'But that's Nan's cottage. Is he moving out?'

'Who knows, now that Hugh is dead. He'd told him to leave, offered him a cottage by the church, but he simply spat in Hugh's face.'

'Literally?'

She shrugged. 'Perhaps not,' she conceded, 'but as good as.'

'He's still in Puddledock.' This sounded an odd story to say the least, almost sinister. 'He said nothing to me about leaving, and presumably he has rights as a long-standing tenant.'

'If he'd ever had a contract he might. He more or less squats there,' she replied. 'He pays a hundred quid a year. Less than ten pounds a month. His parents did odd jobs in return for the small rent charge and when they died my father felt sorry for him. Now he works for everybody else but us. Brings us a load of useless medicines now and then.'

She laughed at my astounded expression. 'Rather unfair of me. He's our vet too, if there's anything wrong with the dogs or cats. Still a cheap rent, don't you think? He has to go.'

I murmured something as I thought of all the pots, the gardens, the animals, and of the carefully tended gardens. That cottage was Nan's life. It had been his mother's life. He wouldn't have taken Hugh's news lightly. I thought of his criminal record, of that pond, and of a secret hiding place that could so easily have been no secret to those used to striding the fields behind the chalets or those to whom Andrew could have confided their secret. I thought of the night and Nan's strong arms around the body of Hugh Compton. Nan the peacemaker, Nan the reformed murderer.

ELEVEN

'd thought Plumshaw Wood a peaceful place when I first saw it. Now it seemed full of secrets; it was a kingdom of its own, and one that didn't welcome intruders. Before it had seemed to beckon to me, but no longer. The mind can play odd tricks. This was the same place, but that first impression had been blanketed over by what had happened since. I had slept on it, but I knew I had no choice. I had to draw a deep breath and confront the witch, wicked or otherwise.

Puddledock Cottage looked innocent, tiled roof melting into the woodland landscape and the garden where wild flowers had reached a compromise with the gardener's hand. Nature was tamed here, but for good or evil? It must be a fine point. As I opened the gate I could see foxgloves; the poison its leaves contain is used in countless medicines for good, but in overdose is highly toxic.

There was a similar balance between Nan the peacemaker and Nan the man who years ago murdered his wife. How much demand did he still have for his ointments and pills, I wondered. Did the village still make its way to him for potions as they had done to his mother? Some would perhaps, I thought, but most would not. His skills were of another age and the knowledge he had inherited would die out.

The more I looked at Puddledock Cottage, the less I could see Nan being willing to leave it. I'd looked up his trial with some difficulty, as Nantucket turned out to be his middle name and John his first forename. From the report it seemed a familiar scenario of his having discovered that his wife had a lover, but murder is murder. Nevertheless, that of Hugh Compton could have been committed in the passion of the moment when Nan had learned that he was going to be turned out of his cottage. That would fit with the hoax murder in the barn, if Nan had discovered where Hugh was hiding and had only just learned of his plans for Puddledock Cottage. Relief followed when I realized it was hardly likely that Nan could have killed Hugh at the chalet and then conveyed him to the pond right near his home. Why would he?

Then an unwelcome thought came to me and would not be dislodged. Hugh did not remain marooned in his chalet for all that time. He would have emerged at safe periods for exercise on the Compton estate, as he had done on the Friday night when he returned to the manor for a discussion. Perhaps he had done so overnight on Saturday or early on the Sunday morning, when no one would be around – except possibly Nan, who lived on the estate and might have run into him by design or chance.

I wrestled with this, but the possibility would not remove itself from my mind. It was no use. I had to square up to knocking on that door.

Before I could do so, however, it was wrenched open from within and I automatically sprang backwards to a shouted series of unrepeatable oaths. The feminine voice's only faintly recognizable message was: 'Lemmego!'

A pair of whirling, kicking boots (female) came out almost horizontally on the end of leather-clad legs followed by a body and familiar face squashed in and peering out from a mass of leather jacket and scarf.

'*Pen?*' I asked incredulously.

A second later, I realized that Nan was behind this ignominious exit and was suspending her flying figure solely by his grasp on the back of the ancient bomber jacket she favours.

I stood aside while he released his hold and the boots scrabbled for the security of the brick path. I then had to wait while she went through her entire repertoire of oaths and threats, while Nan stood there unmoved and in silence. When he had had enough, he went back inside and shut the door on us both.

'Good morning, Pen,' I said politely.

A snarl. 'Do you know what that – said to me?'

'I can guess. Many of your victims would feel the same way.'

'He's a – criminal. I'll have him for assault.'

'From what I could see he wasn't touching *you*, only your jacket.'

'Yeah, and that's another thing. Ruined it he has. Heard it rip. He did it, Jack. He did for that Compton guy. What say we go for it?' she asked eagerly.

'I'd rather be sure he's guilty first.'

'I'll make sure he is,' she assured me.

'Pen!' I warned her.

She had the grace to look discomfited. 'OK. But if he did do it, he's mine, Jack.'

'What did you say to upset him?'

She shrugged. 'Only asked him if he'd knocked off anyone else between his wife and Hugh Compton.'

I gazed at her in incredulity. 'Did you expect his full cooperation, Pen?'

'Yeah. Often works,' she told me seriously. 'Go in with guns blazing and you hit something somewhere. Go careful with him, Jack. He's a strange one.'

'As the pot said of the kettle.'

She grinned. 'I mean it, Jack. You mark Auntie Pen's words. There's a witches' brew boiling up nicely in Plumshaw. It's not over yet.'

'Old or new Plumshaw?'

No reply. I watched as she marched off to retrieve her ancient motorbike hidden in the bushes, a ploy she sometimes uses when on her special missions.

Time for my own special mission. The door was shut, but Nan opened it readily enough when I knocked. 'I thought you'd be coming sometime,' he remarked as I followed him into the cottage. 'I reckon you've been everywhere else.'

He didn't grin exactly, but at least I wasn't walking into enemy territory without a white flag, although he must have realized that I knew Pen.

'Want a coffee?' he asked.

I tried not to think of the foxgloves. 'Please,' I said. 'White, no sugar. Your own coffee beans from the garden?' I joked.

'No,' he replied matter-of-factly. 'I use ready-ground or instant. Best tell me what you've heard,' he continued without a pause. 'That's what brought you, I reckon.'

I'd never met anyone quite so upfront with his cards on the table. 'There's a lot of talk flying round this village about everyone, not just you, Nan.'

'That's what's best. Let it all go round and round, and then it never touches the middle, eh? The middle's what you want.' A pause. 'Like them globe artichokes. You peel off all the leaves, get a little bit of flesh on them here and there, but chuck most of them away. Then you get to the heart.'

'The problem with this case,' I said, impressed, 'is that I don't know where the heart is.'

He chuckled. 'You'll get there, see if you don't. And when you do, you'll know it. For instance, you working for the police, you know about my record like that woman did. Is that the heart of it? Not for me, it isn't.'

'Unlikely,' I said reasonably truthfully. 'It was a long time ago.'

'A long time ago's what we're all made of. Up here.' He tapped his head.

How to counter that? 'You've built on that experience, haven't you?'

'Jane, my wife, was a lovely woman, a good one, and I killed her. Didn't mean to, but it happened, like things do. I had a tough time in prison, Mr Colby. Very tough and I deserved it. But I had time to think about things. I came out looking tough, but inside I'd turned round. My dad didn't believe it, but Mum, she saw I'd turned and she taught me all she knew.'

I wasn't sure I could believe this. Not that I thought he was lying, but I was forced to consider that life had treated him gently in the last fifteen years and circumstances had not required violence from him. Until, perhaps, now.

I had to find out. 'When Hugh Compton told you he wanted you to leave this cottage, weren't you faced with the same unexpected and frightening situation?'

The gentle face changed, just for a moment. I could almost see the battle going on within him, as he chose whether to punch the living daylights out of me or answer the question.

'Yes,' he said.

Nothing else. I might ruin everything if I said the wrong thing, changing Nan the peacemaker into someone quite different. Don't speak, I told myself. Say nothing.

The battle of silence is a hard one, but I won it, and he spoke first.

'You want to know whether it was me killed Mr Compton?'

'Yes.'

'I killed once, never again. Where would killing him get me? They wouldn't let me keep the cottage then, would they?' Another long pause. 'To my way of thinking, Mr Hugh can't have been killed in the barn. Was he killed near the pond?'

'We don't yet know where. Stories, as you say, go round and round. When did he tell you about the cottage?'

'The day he disappeared, Mr Colby. That would be the Wednesday afternoon.'

Did I believe Nan? With someone like him it was hard not to. On the other hand, I was aware that he knew that. I drank my coffee, which was amazingly good, in silence, and waited for him to make the running again. It was the only way I was going to get anywhere.

There was a long pause but, eventually, as I had hoped, he began to communicate again. 'This cottage is my life, Mr Colby. Home is everybody's life. I could pack up Mum's jars, equipment and everything else and find room for them in that place Mr Hugh wanted me to go to. Maybe the family will still pack me off there. It would be the end of me. I don't know when exactly, because I'd look the same but I wouldn't *be* the same. So eventually the *me* would just die.'

I didn't comment and sure enough he continued. 'I could even take the animals' cages but I can't take the garden where Mum used to sit, or the place where I feed the rabbits. And what would the foxes do? Being near the woods, see, they feel safe here, but I wouldn't be very popular with old Farmer Wild if I started looking after wounded foxes over there. Or birds. They're fond of a bit of cereal like old Wild grows. Then there's my dispensary. Not many folks from the village come. They're too posh today with their antibiotics. Fighting nature they are. They work all right, but they pay for it in other ways. So I heals the animals instead and the birds, who haven't got no National Health Service. Can't take all that with me, can I? Besides, this is *my* home. Have you got a home, Mr Colby?'

'Yes, a farmhouse where my parents used to live. It's called Frogs Hill.'

'I like frogs and toads. Toads are good at hanging on to homes. They stay where they want to. Wouldn't want to leave yours, would you?'

'No.' The pain of that idea tugged at me unexpectedly. I'd spent many years travelling round in the oil trade and it had only been when my father's health began to give way that I came back to

Frogs Hill. Now it was my home. Leave it? Never. It would mean abandoning the Pits for a start, not to mention the Glory Boot. Harry Prince, the local garage magnate, had had his eye on buying the place from me for many a long year, waiting for the day I couldn't pay the mortgage. So far I've scraped through. It's tight though, and he knows it.

Nan was watching me with amusement. 'See? Some places you can't just up sticks and go.'

'Perhaps Bronte won't want this cottage, now that she's split up with young Jamie.'

I said it to comfort him but I wasn't at all sure I was right.

I told myself a hundred times that this was going to be about Giovanni, not about his son, Louise and me. I had seldom felt so nervous in my life. I'd faced tough situations in the oil business with equanimity. I'd faced one or two murderers and a lot of thugs everywhere from Finland to Folkestone. Therefore, I reasoned, one single Italian, however delicate the situation, should present no difficulty. We would talk things over like reasonable human beings and all would be well.

So why was my stomach churning like a misfiring engine? It was Thursday morning. A working day. A *normal* day. So why was I pacing up and down in front of the Pits as though a heart operation were going on inside? It was the equivalent in fact, as Len and Zoe were tuning a Jaguar in distress.

Why my unusual panic? Answer: *Ricardo* was dropping by for coffee.

I had with difficulty dissuaded Louise and Maria from attending this notable event. Both of them, it seemed, were anxious to protect Ricardo. Neither of them appeared to think I too might need protection. I comforted myself that that must say something about Ricardo. He must be pretty feeble all round, whereas I wasn't – not outside anyway. I'm over six foot and present a strong facade to the world, no matter the quivers inside me. I could cope – or so I bravely tried to convince myself.

And then I heard a car approaching. The latest Volvo? No. Through the gates very slowly, very carefully came a magnificent yellow 1970s Triumph Stag. Out of it stepped very slowly, very gingerly, a tall, good-looking, slim Italian in his early to mid thirties who whipped off his sunglasses to size me up. He then advanced with great confidence – which did little for mine.

'Signor Colby?'

I swallowed. I could see I wouldn't be fighting on equal terms with him, which in the circumstances wasn't fair. I was the one under attack. 'Signor Donati?'

'Ricardo, please.'

'Jack.'

We shook hands and mentally retired to our corners. 'So you found us then?' I said heartily, unable to think of anything more intelligent to say.

'It was difficult,' he agreed.

Silence. 'Come in and we'll have coffee,' I said more heartily still.

'*Grazie.*'

I supposed it must be tough for him walking into a house where he knew the love of his life was now living with this bolshie stranger, but I was more concerned with how *I* felt and what his plans might be for himself and Louise. I took him into the living room which was less personal than our comfortable farmhouse kitchen.

'Louise . . .' I began, thinking I'd set his mind at rest with the assurance that she was not here at the moment, but his face darkened as he interrupted me.

'Business, Jack. Only business.'

I'd made a false move. To hell with that, I told myself. I had a fifty per cent stake in this conversation.

'Do you live permanently in England?' I asked, wondering if this could be classified as business though it was of pressing interest to me.

'No, but I come here often. I have a flat in Blackheath.'

This wasn't good news.

My small talk now exhausted, I went into the kitchen to busy myself with fussing over the coffee, wondering where to go from here. I need not have worried. Ricardo took over, marching after me and watching every move I made. Perhaps he thought I was doctoring the coffee.

'I saw my father in prison yesterday,' he told me. 'He says you are helping to solve this terrible crime and get him released.'

'I hope to do so. I don't believe he is guilty.' That at least – I hoped – was still true.

'Of course he is not. But can you prove that?'

He was so composed that it threw me off my stride. 'Not yet.'

He hitched his beautifully creased trousers most elegantly (bet he used to make Louise iron them) as he took a seat at the kitchen table, so that I was forced to put the coffee tray there and not in the more neutral living room. 'Tell me everything,' he commanded.

I couldn't do that, especially where the fake murder plot was concerned. 'Only what I can,' I told him firmly. 'I work for the police, so I can't discuss the case against your father.'

He banged his cup on the table. 'Then I am wasting my time.' He stood up, the image of the affronted Latin.

We weren't exactly bonding, yet for Giovanni's sake we had to, so I made an effort. 'We're both finding this meeting hard, Ricardo, but we have to put your father's welfare first. It's his life at stake.' Cack-handed of me, to say the least.

He looked horrified and no wonder. 'His life? You still hang people here?'

'No, but a long-term prison sentence would kill your father just as effectively.' I couldn't see Giovanni's ebullient nature lasting long in the prison system whether he served the sentence here or in Italy. 'You're close to your father?'

'Who would not be?' Ricardo relaxed. 'He is my father so I love him. He is an extraordinary man so I admire him. He did not kill this Englishman and so I know I must try to help you. But it is hard.'

'It's hard for me too,' I pointed out.

'Why is that? You have Louise.' There was genuine anguish in his voice.

I went softly. 'No one *has* Louise. She comes and goes as she chooses.'

'From me she goes,' he said sadly.

'She went from me too, but she has come back. For how long I don't know.'

For a moment our eyes bonded, then he turned away impatiently. 'I do not understand that woman. I love her still.'

'I'm sorry. Perhaps she will go from me too.'

'I hope so.'

'Kind of you,' I retorted.

He laughed. I laughed. *We* laughed. And all was OK – temporarily.

'So now we talk only of my father. What do you wish to know?'

'I need to be sure about *why* Giovanni wrote to ask the Comptons if he could paint the car. Whether it was for just that reason or whether he had more in mind.'

He frowned. 'I do not know. Truly, Jack. He told me he had been asked to do so. I will try to find this out, when I see him.'

'Thanks.' Did I want to be grateful to this man? 'You knew he was eager to paint it?'

'Of course. He has told you now, I think, that the car used to belong to our family – the Santoro family on my grandmother's side. My great-grandfather loved it very much.'

'And when Giulio died during the Second World War, his wife would have inherited the car?'

'In those days the word inherit meant little. It was in their possession, but it was taken from them by the Fascists in the spring of 1945 after they had killed Giulio.'

'It was they who killed him? Not the Germans?'

'At that time and indeed until the referendum in 1946 the Fascists remained very powerful in north Italy, and very ruthless. After the armistice and the fall of Mussolini the Germans had moved into the north of the country, rescued Mussolini and the Italian Fascists held power there, and not the new Badoglio government as in the south. The Fascist Militia were worse than the Germans in their determination to root out all opposition, especially from the republicans amongst the Partisans. All those who were not Fascist but of mixed beliefs – they all fight for Italy. At first they fought in small groups mounting sabotage raids wherever they could to tie up the German war machine. Giulio had his own *banda* in the mountains near Parma and stayed there throughout two winters, very cold ones. Many, many of the Partisans died. While behind the German lines, they faced torture, starvation and betrayal to the Fascists and the Germans while the Allies worked their way up through Italy.'

'Did Giulio Santoro ever meet Peter Compton there?' Peter's own account had been in very general terms – perhaps too general, it now struck me.

'That I do not know. I only know about Giulio and his *banda*. The Partisans were supplied at first only by a *staffeta* – they were messengers, often girls, who would bring food and information to them in the mountains. But during the snows, this was not always possible, and it was a dangerous time, as the Germans and *Fascisti* had ski battalions to hunt them down. In the summer of 1944 the British brought in their Special Operations Executive to organize resistance in northern Italy, and it was then more effective for the British supplied the Partisan groups through parachute drops. Giulio's *banda* fell at the boundary of the British Mission Toffee area, between the two roads from the port of La Spezia, one to Parma and the other to Reggio Emilia. The *banda* was near the Parma road and mounted raids on it and also on the railway line where it enters and leaves a long tunnel under the Apennine mountains. On one raid the *Fascisti* came and Giulio was fortunate to get back safely to their mountain retreat. Not long afterwards in the spring he was betrayed, tortured and shot.'

'Betrayed to the Fascists or the Germans?'

'The *Fascisti*. Giulio was a brave man. So his car is very important to the family.'

'Peter Compton says he bought it in 1946.'

'That is right. But we know this too: when Partisans were killed by the *Fascisti*, they killed the families too. In our case, our family was lucky. The *Fascisti* took only the car, and when the end of the war came in May 1945 the car could not be traced. Later the family was told it was given to or bought by an Englishman. As politics began to change, Giulio's widow, my great-grandmother, asked for it back, but even the republican victory in the referendum did not help, because things do not change so quickly, and in any case the British were demanding Mr Compton's release. The *Fascisti* still had some power in north Italy and so the car went with him.'

'So the police could say your father's motive for killing Hugh Compton was to claim the car back, and that he was killed, perhaps accidentally, when they quarrelled on the issue.'

'My father is not so stupid,' Ricardo retorted angrily. 'How could we *prove* it was not a legal sale by 1946? Some things are not possible. A stolen work of art, perhaps, but this is a car.'

'A valuable one, however.'

Ricardo said stiffly, 'My father say that if he paints it, it becomes his in his head and that is enough.'

'Then why,' I countered, 'did he not tell us of his relationship to the original owner? Why pretend even to me that it was just the car that inspired him?'

'It is family business,' Ricardo said flatly.

'*What?*' This was beginning to sound a familiar theme.

'Family business,' he repeated. 'It is the Italian way. It is not good to discuss such matters outside the family. Already I have told you too much.'

'Even when a murder charge hangs over Giovanni?'

'*Especially* with a murder charge hanging over him. My father knows he is innocent. He knows that all he wished to do was paint the car. The Comptons cannot prove otherwise because there is no "otherwise" that can be proved.'

Oh great! 'And how,' I asked wearily, 'therefore, did this friend Umberto Monti at La Casa know about the car? He isn't family.'

'Umberto? But he is family.' Ricardo seemed amused.

I took a deep breath at this revelation. 'Would you mind telling me how he fits in as both friend and family and why Giovanni didn't reveal this either to me or the police?'

'Of course.' Ricardo's turn for the deep breath. 'Because the car and Umberto's connection with it are family business and must remain within the family. It is a question of honour.'

I thought of Pen's casual reference to the Mafia brotherhood, presumably picked up from Stephanie, but it wasn't a line I was going to press with Ricardo *or* with Louise. 'And who exactly is Umberto?'

'He is Lucia's son.'

'And Lucia is?' I asked patiently.

'The daughter of Giulio's sister, also named Lucia.'

'Thank you.' I meant it ironically, but he took it seriously.

'You are welcome, Jack. You might also wish to know that Giulio's sister married Enrico di Secchio, his co-driver.'

Game, set and match to Ricardo.

I was speechless and Ricardo followed up this triumph with: 'I would like to see this famous car. My father tells me I should. How can I do that?'

Was there no end to his nerve? I pulled myself together.

'I'll speak to the owner. But not yet, Ricardo. We have to save your father first. The Compton family is still convinced that he killed Hugh.'

'When you have proved the truth of this case, then I will come.'

'The Comptons will think that you have come to claim the car.'

'Perhaps I only claim Louise. You like that, eh?'

He might appear to be joking, I thought, but I couldn't take that chance and so I replied stiffly, 'Perhaps Louise should make her own decision.'

'Then we must fight,' Ricardo said placidly. 'We have a race, yes?'

Were we in Disneyland? Was this for real? 'I can't see that influencing Louise.'

'No, but it satisfies us perhaps.'

TWELVE

This tangled web was far more complex than would allow coincidence to play a part. The paths of Peter Compton and Giulio Santoro could well have crossed over the Alfa Romeo in Italy during the war and Peter now possessed Giulio's Alfa Romeo without the element of chance. I could understand the passion for the car that had gripped both men. Its sleek lines, even in its unrestored form, shouted style and history at anyone who looked at it and to car buffs it shouted ten times more loudly.

There was certainly something strange about this situation. For a start, Peter Compton did not cherish the Alfa Romeo as a classic car without parallel. He had not restored it or kept it in running order. Had he been so different as a younger man that he had set his heart on owning this car, then lost interest in it and left it to rot? No, one didn't forget beauties like this Alfa Romeo, any more than one would forget having met Marilyn Monroe or Helen of Troy.

Perhaps Peter had been a Grand Prix enthusiast rather than being addicted to Alfa Romeos for their own sake? No, that didn't work either. It was unlikely he had even seen the Alfa Romeo until after the war. Even if Giulio Santoro and he were on speaking terms and could have managed to reach the local villages once in a while, they would have more important matters on their mind than racing cars. Peter said he had bought the car through Sofia, so probably she had been the driving force behind his buying it. No, that seemed unlikely. Peter didn't come over as the kind of person to be 'driven' over such a purchase.

If Ricardo's tale was correct, I needed to dovetail Peter's side of the story with it. I had to tread carefully though. I could hardly justify more questioning on the Alfa Romeo when it was only my own curiosity sending me down that route. I had no proof at all that the Alfa was at the heart of this murder case and I might be in danger of taking the wrong fork because of its temptation.

Still, I cheered myself, at a church fête anything goes, and today,

Saturday, was the day the vicar had told me that Plumshaw was celebrating summer with its annual beanfeast including its gathering of classic cars. Both halves of the village would be present, which in itself should make it interesting. I decided to give my Lagonda a day out and asked Louise if she'd like to come if she wasn't working. I was highly gratified when she agreed.

She must have caught my look of amazement. 'My youth,' she informed me with dignity, 'was not misspent. At our village fête I was permitted to help run the coconut shy.'

'A great honour,' I congratulated her gravely.

'And,' she continued, clattering plates into the dishwasher, 'I also used to cut a dash at maypole dancing.'

Village fêtes come in many forms, some determined to cling to well-established traditions, others striking out for a more modern approach with bouncy castles and burgers, some turning it into a sports event and some mixing every ingredient they can think of. Plumshaw, hardly surprisingly, as it was on Compton land, veered to the traditional, but it looked fun nonetheless. The classic car section was one of the few concessions to modern improvements to the traditional fête attractions. The fête was being held in a field in front of the church, with an adjacent field for general car parking and for the classic car gathering. I drove my Lagonda into the field with style, where it received many admiring glances – or perhaps they were for Louise who was looking stunning in a picture hat and short flowing blue dress. I duly parked with the other participants, which ranged from a shabby Morris Minor to a smart Aston Martin.

A marquee had been erected for traditional tea and coffee refreshments although a hamburger stall outside it provided a rival attraction, and a roped-off area in the middle of the field provided space for – yes – maypole dancing, a dog show, an egg and spoon race and a tug of war. Not all at the same time, fortunately.

The fête was in full flow by the time we arrived and we duly enjoyed a hamburger for lunch. Only one person seemed to recognize Louise but, with true British reserve, the gentleman averted his eyes. Privacy was to be respected, which suits Louise who struggles to keep her working life apart from her private concerns. True, the picture hat didn't help much in this respect.

The crowd reflected all sides of the fashion scene, from pretty summer frocks and a striped blazer or two down to jeans and tank tops. I could see mostly families here with young children or toddlers which are always fun to watch. There were a few faces I recognized, but none of them had so far featured in the Compton versus Makepeace battle; this scene was a world away from murder.

As we began our tour of the stalls, I laughed on spotting one in particular.

'What's so amusing?' Louise asked.

'There's a coconut shy. But you've been sacked. Nan's in charge of it.' I could see him picking up the balls and taking money from customers.

'That doesn't stop me having a go.' She proceeded to drag me over there right away.

Nan nodded to me. 'Do this every year,' he told me with pride. The Nan of the Pen episode might never have existed.

'For the church?' I hadn't put him down as a churchgoer.

'Regular there,' he told us. 'Caretaker and in the choir.'

I blinked. 'Any jobs you don't do, Nan?'

'I'm not vicar yet.' He spoke so seriously that I was thrown for a moment. Then a big grin crossed his face. 'Want a go, miss?' he asked Louise, interpreting her wistful face correctly.

'Yes, please.' Louise then proceeded to miss every coconut she aimed at. Nan still gave her one, though, which she clasped lovingly for the next half an hour until I removed it and took it back to the car.

I lingered there in admiration of a post-war Riley tourer and while I was doing so I was greeted cheerfully by Stephanie, today clad in the *grande dame* mode in a navy blue silk dress. 'You're a glutton for punishment where Plumshaw's concerned,' she joked. At least, I took it as a merry jest.

'Pure pleasure,' I quipped. 'Can't keep away from the place.'

'We've noticed that. Still delving for pots of gold at the end of the rainbow?'

'That's a detective's life. Digging for golden secrets.'

She batted this one away with ease. 'The Compton family has plenty of secrets if you go back in time. There was an eighteenth-century Compton who ran off with one of Bonnie Prince Charlie's mistresses. And another who dabbled in the dew with the village maidens wearing a smock and skirt.'

'Did your mother have such a colourful family as Peter's?'

She couldn't bat this one away as easily but she tried. 'She was Italian, which is always colourful, not that I recall much of it. I was only four when she died. My father never talks about her,' she added, almost as a challenge.

Paul then arrived, having parked his 1949 drophead Bentley coupé, which I eyed enviously. Its owner, however, was less charmed to meet me than Stephanie. 'What are you doing here?'

'My Lagonda likes an outing now and then, and Plumshaw is always so welcoming. And of course the Land Rover affair is far from complete.'

He didn't like that. 'Nonsense. We've got it back.'

'We have to find out who took it.'

'I have my own ideas on that.'

'Care to share them with the police?'

'No.'

That ended that typical conversation with Paul. Brandon had already told me that, as was to be expected, plenty of Hugh's DNA had been found in the Land Rover, and so had that of the rest of the family. Giovanni's had not. That too was hardly surprising, as he had been in police custody when it was stolen.

I made my way back to the heart of the fête, where I found Louise deep in discussion with someone who turned out to be the primary school teacher in charge of the maypole dancing. I heard the magic words: 'We have the original maypole the school used in the 1920s. Nan restored it for us.'

Of course he did. Nan was the hub around which the life of the village spun. Nan sat in the midst of their interlocking loves and hates. Nan settled disputes. Nan cured their physical and emotional ills. Nan was everywhere including – it occurred to me – in the choir, which meant that if there were a Sunday morning or evening service he would have been away from the cottage while Hugh Compton's body was being disposed of nearby. A fact that of course would be generally known in the village.

I thought Louise might be asking if she could join the children in the maypole dance, but despite the eager look on her face, she must have decided not to push it. I was rather sorry, but on the other hand it was good to wander round the fête with her – especially when she attracted Hazel Compton's attention in the first-aid tent where she was on standby.

'Had an accident, Jack?' Hazel asked acidly, her eyes swivelling to Louise as I introduced them.

'I'm in perfect health, thank you,' I assured her. 'I was hoping Peter might be around.'

'He is not.'

'I'd like another chat with him.'

'I doubt if he would like to chat to you, however.'

I wasn't top of the popularity polls with the Comptons, it seemed. Just as Hazel was about to build on the introduction to Louise, Bronte came into the tent, nodded to us, and announced to her grandmother: 'I'm going home. I've had enough.'

For that, read 'I've just seen Jamie Makepeace', I thought. I had glimpsed him wandering around like a loose cannon. I meanly abandoned Louise to Hazel and hurried to catch up with Bronte.

'Hi,' she said without enthusiasm.

'I wanted a word with your grandfather. I hope he's not ill?'

'He didn't feel up to coming here. Can't blame him. I know how he feels.'

'Life is tough for you all at present.'

'Very.' She grimaced. 'I made the grand gesture. I broke it off with Jamie to stick with the family, only for them to tell me about that stupid joke they played on that poor painter. How could they?'

'Your father must have consented.'

'Under pressure from his mother,' she snarled. 'I'm sure of that. Dear Grannie Hazel is a tyrant. They didn't tell me that my father was alive and well, even though he came back one night. They just left me to worry myself sick because I'd upset them by planning to marry Jamie. And look what happens. Dad really gets murdered!' She burst into tears as we reached the manor gates and I hugged her closely for a while, hoping Jamie wasn't around to object.

He was. He came charging across the road towards us, shouting, 'What do you think you're doing?'

I let go of Bronte and faced him. 'Looking after her – which you're not.'

'I'll – well look after you then!'

'*Jamie!*' Bronte turned into a furious Boadicea, and he instantly stopped his headlong charge towards me. I let them stare at each other for a moment charged with emotion. Would they fly out at each other or fall into each other's arms? Just at the moment I didn't much care. I'd had enough.

'Where can I find Peter?' I demanded.

'Try the barn.' Bronte didn't take her eyes off Jamie.

I walked off, down the drive, straight to the barn, where I found him sitting in a picnic chair by the Alfa Romeo, a Zimmer frame at his side. I knew he had seen me enter, but he didn't take his eyes off the car even as I reached him.

'It's a great sight,' I said.

He sighed. 'It is.'

'Will you sell it now?'

'No. After my death, they can do what they like with it, but until then it stays here.'

'You seemed willing to let Giovanni paint it, if only as a means to an end.'

'And because I knew his real motive. I suffered because of that man's family. If he was intending to make me suffer this time through litigation over its ownership I wanted him to know what it felt like.'

'I've known Giovanni for many years, Mr Compton. Painting means everything to him, not possession.'

The Pickwickian side of Peter vanished. 'You are too trusting, Jack. Life has taught me not to trust.'

'Your army life or post-war?'

He turned to look at me for the first time. 'My army days.'

'You told me you served in Italy. Did you meet Giulio Santoro then?'

'I did.'

'You were friends?'

'That wasn't a word that applied. We were comrades, we were fighting for the same cause – no, let me correct that. We worked to the same end, to rid Italy of the Germans, but not for the same reasons. The Italians wanted their country back, we were fighting to save ours.'

'Were you fighting closely with Giulio?'

'I was. Giulio and his Partisan *banda* were poorly equipped and poorly organized, until Florence was freed in 1944 and SOE took over organized resistance. Up till then the Partisans could bark but they had no teeth. They had fought bravely and recklessly and undoubtedly we could not have done without them, but once supplies could be dropped in by parachute, operations against the Germans could be effectively organized over the entire area.'

'I thought you were in the SAS, not SOE.'

'You want the full story?' Peter seemed to have come to life, to have come to a decision. 'Here it goes then. All special forces united under SOE in that final effort to push the German lines back. My SAS squadron landed at Bari in the south of Italy and some of us were parachuted behind the German lines into the mountains. Giulio's *banda* was well-placed for attacking the railway line to Parma, a distance of about seventy to eighty miles. Any dislocation to German troop movements or supplies was valuable, big or small, to hinder the German ability to fight our advancing troops and as a morale booster to the oppressed civilians. They'd gone through a terrible time, and that lasted until the end of the war and after.

'I joined Giulio's *banda* in late December 1944,' he continued, 'and was in command. Giulio naturally resented my arrival, but the *banda* needed our communication set-up plus our supplies if they were to achieve anything. I did my best to work with Giulio, but it was difficult.'

'He wouldn't work with you?'

'He did, up to a point. There was only a certain amount we could do before the heavy snows hit us, but we planned an attack on the railway at Fornovo di Taro near the point where the track to Parma from La Spezia emerges from the tunnel through the Apennines. We had already tackled one further down the line at Pontrémoli where the tunnel begins. We were ambushed there, but we fought it out, and managed to escape. We thought Giulio had been captured, but he joined us an hour or so later back at our refuge. That was basically a cave, although a wooden structure had been erected in front and around it and then camouflaged with scrub. It was on the second raid that we did lose Giulio. He was taken by the Fascists and shot, probably tortured. Most were.'

I shivered at the matter-of-fact tone in which Peter recounted his experiences, probably because he had lived with them so long in his mind. 'Did you leave Italy then or stay on?'

'I was in the army, and after the war returned to England. I had met Sofia in Italy however, so as soon as I could I returned there; that would be early in 1946. She had already told me that she'd heard this car was for sale. She arranged the sale and it became mine.'

His eyes remained fixed on it. 'I didn't expect to be locked up in jail for it, but that's what happened. I had assumed Giulio's family had wanted to dispose of it after his death. I had no means of knowing that it had been taken from the family by the Fascist Militia when he was killed and that I was effectively buying it from one of their number. Nor did Sofia. They wanted cash for it – everyone did at that time. Italian politics and the whole country were in chaos and in June 1946 came the referendum on whether the monarchy should be retained or whether there should be a republic and who should rule that. The republicans won. I was already in jail by this time, but after the referendum the British stepped in and I was freed. I had been there four or five months because the family claimed the car was wrongly seized by the Fascists and I refused to return it. There had been no court case for me to state my viewpoint and that was the issue that the British took up to get my freedom. They just let me go *and* the car.'

This more or less dovetailed with Ricardo's account but sounded more of a recital than a vivid memory of the past and so, to my frustration, I couldn't see where to push the story forward. 'You've kept the car in memory of those days?'

'Perhaps.'

'Was Sofia a Partisan herself?'

'The Mesola family supported the Partisans and suffered greatly during the war from starvation and deprivation, but the farms of Kent are not like those of the Apennine mountains. Sofia chose to return to Italy, as I believe I told you. She died two years later.'

'Of an illness?'

I don't know what made me ask that, but in any case he did not reply.

He looked tired. I blamed myself and began to creep away.

'By the way,' he called after me. 'I'm still not selling the Hop and Harry. I've told Andrew, I've told the Makepeaces and I've told the police. And what's more,' he added, 'neither will I sell this car.'

I continued on my way, and he didn't even notice me leave this time. He was still staring at the Alfa Romeo.

By the time I reached the road again and was about to cross over to rejoin the fête, it was alarmingly clear that something was wrong in the village. A police car raced through, followed by an ambulance. I could see George Makepeace standing at the entrance to the car park field so I crossed the road to talk to him. Even by the time I reached him, however, I could almost see news spreading round the fête – people were stopping, gathering in groups, some hurrying past us towards new Plumshaw.

'What's up?' I asked him, aware that he was looking very shaken.

'The Hop and Harry,' he growled.

'Again? Another fire?'

'Not this time. Andrew Lee.'

'He's hurt?' What more could go wrong for this family?

'Dead. And not natural neither. Strangled.'

THIRTEEN

S trangled? Andrew? I couldn't get my head round this. George must have got it wrong, a misheard word, blown up into a certainty. Andrew and his wife had left the Hop and Harry over a week ago and their possessions – such as had escaped the blaze – were now safely elsewhere. It would be a giant step to believe that someone was killing off the Comptons and their supporters one by one, and even if by some ill fortune Andrew was indeed dead, murder seemed way off the mark. Rumours spread quickly and notoriously change with each of the relay players, and that was surely the case here.

Nevertheless, I still found myself striding along the road to what used to be the pub, half preoccupied with that and half still battling with what I had learned from Peter Compton. I tried to put that aside. I had to deal with the present situation first. The nearer I drew to the ruins of the pub the more obvious it became that there was indeed another major incident. Police cars and vans stood outside and a cordon was already in place. If I still had any doubt that George had been mistaken, it vanished when I saw Brandon. The name of Plumshaw must be a magnet for him at present.

I could see no faces that I recognized in the crowd of onlookers and, thankfully, no sign of Lucy. No press either, although they would not be long in coming. I could see Brandon beckoning to me, and he joined me at the cordon entrance. He seemed to take my presence for granted, which I supposed was flattering in a way.

'Join the party,' he grunted to me. 'I take it you've heard? Andrew Lee. Manual strangulation. Guesstimate between eleven and two today.'

So he was killed either during the preparations for the fête or shortly after it had opened, which was an unpleasant thought in itself, with the fête in full flow such a short distance away. I steeled myself to get kitted out in a scene suit and joined Brandon in what had once been the main bar of the Hop and Harry. Now it was empty of bottles and glasses, but the smell of this desolate place was still so strong that it made me retch. It was more than the smell of fire, it seemed to have the smell of death itself about it. Brandon seemed to share my distaste judging by his bleak expression. Ten days earlier, this bar had been full of life. Not now. Brandon led the way through to the snug, the small bar at the rear of the building on the left as one faced it. On the right were the kitchens, giving on to the restaurant that semi-circled the far end of the main bar.

It was only then that I realized Andrew's body had not yet been moved. The forensic team was still at work, although Brandon had told me that the pathologist had come and gone. And then I saw him. Andrew was lying sprawled on his back, although that would not necessarily have been the position he was found in. The ghastly signs of strangulation were all too evident. The tongue, the lips, the froth, the clenched hands.

'Is his wife on the way here?' I asked. Lucy was in for a terrible ordeal.

'Against our advice, yes. She's coming from her mother's place in Ashford.'

My heart went out to her, but I forced myself to be professional. 'Was he attacked from behind?'

'Most likely.'

'Any witnesses?'

'George Makepeace, the chap who found him.'

'George was up by the fête car park when I saw him. What was he doing here?' No wonder George had looked shaken; he couldn't wait to get away from the Hop and Harry.

'Walking his dog, he said. Took a short cut across the car park, peered in through the pub window for no apparent reason and saw what lay here. That was an hour and a half ago, but we told him he could leave and give a formal statement later.'

George's story sounded limp, I thought, but it could be true.

'We interviewed him over the Compton murder,' Brandon continued. 'Connected to this one, do you think? This pub belongs to the Comptons.'

My mind was racing like a Bugatti. My first pit stop was still George Makepeace. I thought I knew what his part in the Compton case was, but I'd tackle him later. Second pit stop: the police case against Giovanni hadn't excluded other possibilities on motivation – and that might include Andrew's involvement.

'If they weren't connected,' I said, 'then this attack could theoretically be by a casual looter, but it's a strange time to choose to break in. And even the most desperate squatter wouldn't have chosen this place.'

'Which brings us back to the Makepeaces, either George or that grandson of his, Jamie. Both determined to get the Hop and Harry out of the way for this development plan of theirs. Jamie attacked him, George found the body. Neat?' Brandon didn't sound convinced though.

'Not that neat. If this was all part of the Makepeace-Compton feud then burning the pub down alone would do the job without adding murder to the charge sheet.'

'Except that the fire wasn't enough,' Brandon pointed out. 'Peter Compton still won't sell.'

I tried to plough doggedly on. 'I don't see that killing the manager-cum-chef would achieve anything. He was never going to be a three-star Michelin chef.' It seemed tough to say this, with Andrew lying there, but it was a relevant point. Nevertheless, I came to a halt. My stomach was churning with the effort of debate in these terrible circumstances, and I was relieved when Brandon began to move away.

'It could affect the decision over rebuilding,' Brandon commented.

I didn't reply. Both of us knew that would surely be too much of a risk for too little gain. The method of murder moreover suggested a struggle in the heat of the moment.

'What about a personally motivated attack?' Brandon continued back in the bar.

'Possible, but again the timing would be a coincidence. There's another way it could be connected to the Comptons, though,' I added. 'Andrew and Lucy were the only people apart from the Comptons themselves who officially knew where Hugh Compton was hiding out in the chalet. What's more, if it is connected, then Giovanni is the one person who could not have killed Andrew.'

Brandon looked at me almost compassionately. 'I see your point, Jack. I always have. But we still have to hold him. This crazy fake murder has thrown a new light on it, and when that's disclosed to the defence the lions are going to be roaring. Even though we're grilling the Comptons on that score – *and* still considering charges

– there's no denying that Donati was free at the time Compton was murdered for real.'

Back to square one. 'But there's no evidence.'

'There's one very powerful motive,' Brandon pointed out. 'And no alibi. He might not have killed him in the barn, but he could have taken advantage of the situation later.'

'But Giovanni does have an alibi,' I pressed on. I'd kept Brandon up to date every step of the way. 'He was with his son.'

'Who feels as strongly about family matters as his father.' He caught my change of expression. 'It's go-slow time, Jack. Giovanni Donati is not out of the woods yet.'

The sooner I was out of this building the better, I thought, as Brandon seemed to have finished with me. It was macabre here, the burnt ruins, white-clad figures moving around like ghosts, and the general feeling of oppression. Signing the exit log set me free into the everyday world again. The crowds were fewer now, but they definitely included journalists, so I searched the parked cars. Right on cue, I spotted an ancient Vauxhall. Pen was here somewhere and at any moment she could pounce on me. Before she did so, I needed to sort out something with George, whom I could see walking back towards the Hop and Harry. I rushed to cut him off before he vanished into Pen's all-encompassing professional embrace.

First come, first served. And I was first.

'You didn't tell me you'd discovered Andrew's body, George. Must have been very tough for you.' Out of the corner of my eye I saw Pen retreating, but her body language didn't bode well for me.

'I can think of better claims to fame,' he retorted grimly. He seemed genuinely upset. 'Find a body and elect myself chief suspect for murder. Apparently first I killed Hugh Compton and then came back for poor old Andrew. I'm a property dealer and farmer, haven't got time to murder half the village. Nor to burn this place down. Nor carry out any other crimes round this place.'

'Not true,' I said.

'What the blazes do you mean by that?'

'A certain Land Rover comes to mind.'

His cheeks bulged in fury. 'What's that supposed to mean?'

'Hugh Compton's vehicle stolen from outside the manor and returned to it. Unharmed,' I added, placatingly.

'Nothing to do with me.'

'Care to have a DNA test?'

He weighed up the situation carefully before replying. 'Even if I did – joyride, that's all it was.'

I sighed. 'Let's try it this way. I suggest you took it to make a point while Hugh Compton was first missing. After his body was found, it seemed out of order, so you returned it.'

'No harm done,' he grunted.

'What *was* the point?'

'Mind your own bloody business.'

'It *is* a bloody business,' I said. 'Murder. What interests me is that Hugh was generally presumed dead after the blood was found in the barn and in Giovanni Donati's car. You clearly didn't believe he was – as your finer feelings didn't come into it when you pinched the Land Rover. How come you knew he wasn't dead?'

At that delicate point Brandon's sergeant called George in for a 'chat'. He shot me a triumphant look and marched away. I'd gone a long way with an educated guess, but now I'd been stopped in my tracks. Surprisingly, he too stopped. He turned round and shot out at me like a true Parthian: 'What's Compton's death done for us, eh? Nothing. He didn't own the joint. The old man does. I wanted to put paid to his driving the Land Rover around, lording it over us peasants for a while. Thought he'd think twice before he started that up again. And what's happened? Now it's back and he didn't waste a minute. He's off again.'

I watched him go into the incident van. What he'd said had some truth in it, but how far had his dislike of Peter Compton's feudal ways driven him? And furthermore, he could have been under the impression that Hugh owned the estate. He could also have thought that Jamie and Bronte would marry and that Peter Compton would agree to sell if Hugh was out of the way. Neither had proved true, but George could not have known that.

More urgent problems pulled me out of the maze in my head. A police car drew up, a woman PC alighted but before she could help her passenger out, Lucy had leapt out of the far side of the car – where I could see Pen bearing down on her, having been forced to give up on George. I've seldom moved faster. Once again I just made it in time to block Pen's headlong dash. I seized Lucy's arm and rushed her over towards Brandon. Before I could get her there though, she tore herself away and pushed straight through the cordon entrance and towards the pub.

Brandon is used to such situations, and urged her back to one of the vans to talk to her, but having been turned away from the door, Lucy chose the lesser of two evils. Me. She clutched at me in desperation.

'I want to know what happened,' she cried. 'No one will tell me. Only that Andrew is dead. I need to see him, however awful it is. I really do. Just to be sure it's him. There could have been some mistake.'

What to say? The man in me wanted to hold her close, soothe her and take her back to her mother, but I was supposed to be working with the police. The man won, although I led her to one of the vans, with the PC on one side, and Brandon following. Once at the van, though, she shot a second scared look at me and refused to let go. Reluctantly, Brandon let us stay where we were.

'I told him, Jack,' she blurted out. 'I told him Mr Compton's a good landlord. We'll never get another chance like this and he had to go and muck it all up. Just because of the Makepeaces. It's their fault.'

I sensed Brandon breathing down my neck. 'For the fire?' I asked.

'Who else would have done it?' she moaned. 'We quarrelled about it but he said we'd be all right. Now look what's happened.'

I was instantly alert and I itched to push her on this, but held back. The PC didn't though.

'Don't worry about it now,' she said soothingly. Brandon must be as torn as I was over this intervention. Just how hand in glove had Andrew been with the Makepeaces?

Lucy turned to the PC. 'I loved this old pub. Now Andrew's dead, suppose he burnt the pub down and grabbed the takings first? What shall I do now?'

'Rest, Lucy, rest,' I said, though part of me still wanted to push further. Was she right about Andrew or was Makepeace involved? But Lucy was beginning to collapse and needed a medic's help. The PC glanced at Brandon, who nodded, then she hurried away to organize this.

Lucy couldn't be stopped though. 'He told the Makepeaces about it.'

'About the pub?' I asked as gently as I could, every second expecting Brandon to shoot me. He didn't, but Pen too was hovering.

Lucy looked at me with dull eyes. 'Everything.'

Brandon indicated it was time for me to leave. He would send her home with the PC, after the medics had seen her. Lucy began to sob in earnest then. 'Home?' she said heart-rendingly. 'What home do I have?'

Time to find George again, now free from his 'chat' with the sergeant, and with Pen busily chatting up Martin, who didn't seem to be responding as heartily as she might have wished. George did his best to avoid me, but I wasn't having that. I needed answers.

'What's the reply to my question, George?'

'What question?'

'Why didn't you have moral objections to pinching the car when Hugh was presumed dead, but only after the body had been found?'

'What's the difference?'

'A big one. You knew that Hugh Compton wasn't dead during those first few days. You knew that he was in one of the chalets because Andrew had told you.'

He eyed me carefully. 'So what?'

'When did he tell you? Did you and Andrew come to some agreement over the Hop and Harry?'

'Business matter, that is.'

'The business is murder, George. So it's me or the police right now.'

He looked at me and surrendered. 'Met Andrew Lee often, had you?'

'Once or twice.'

'He had ambitions. He wasn't going to get nowhere in the Hop and Harry. I didn't want the Hop and Harry there at all. Suited us both. So what I said to him was that if it so happened the Hop and Harry went west, then he need not worry about a job. There's a high quality restaurant going to open up in the new development, and he'd be running it. He saw it as his great opportunity – and it was, because Compton was never going to put money into this old heap.'

'And it just so happened that the old heap did burn down. Your work?'

He looked straight at me. 'You think I done that? Set fire to the place and then murdered Andrew Lee? What good would that have done? Look elsewhere, Mr Policeman. Andrew had a loose tongue. I wouldn't have got nowhere by torching this place. And Compton's not selling anyway, so I've been told.'

There was something in what George said, but he could not have reckoned with the fact that at his age Peter was still in full control despite Hugh's death. Nor with the fact that Bronte was not going to inherit. And if he didn't burn the pub down, it would be back to Andrew, with Lucy's worst fears realized. I watched George walk away. He was only just out of sight when Pen materialized out of nowhere like the wicked witch on her broomstick in *The Wizard of Oz.*

'I thought we were mates!' she yelled. Her eyes were blazing, every inch of her body aquiver with righteous indignation.

'We are, Pen,' I said soothingly. 'Subject to the usual embargo on police work.'

'You caught me on that one,' she snarled. 'Lucy Lee your police work, is she? You nark.'

'I'll make it up to you.'

'Sure. Give me some real hard stuff on that Nan, then. I'm out to get him. And who's that fellow you were talking to?'

'Leader of the development movement,' I said promptly, knowing my Pen well.

'Yawn, yawn,' she commented right on cue. 'Unless,' she added hopefully, 'he murdered Andrew Lee? Any chance?'

'You could work on it.'

'Found the body, didn't he? Drained most of that out of him already.'

'Congratulations, Miss Vampire.'

'There's more, isn't there? Cough up, Jack.'

She was sniffing hard; it wouldn't be long before the story of the fake murder was spreading round the village. I'd have to warn Brandon. No doubt he would be working on Lucy's implication that Andrew was more closely involved in the burning down of the pub, but add George Makepeace's information – or misinformation – into the mix and I needed to move quickly.

I was in no shape to enjoy the rest of the village fête and even less when I remembered I had completely forgotten Louise. It seemed to me I'd been at the Hop and Harry for hours, but to my amazement only an hour and a half had passed. Nevertheless, I could see many of the classic cars had already left, as well as the visitors' cars, and I walked over to them to see if Louise was sitting in the Lagonda. She wasn't, but at least the Lagonda was still there. So was the Bentley and Paul was sitting in it, probably waiting for his wife.

'I envy you this,' I told him.

'My pride and joy,' he replied, which somewhat endeared me to him. No one who owns a car like that can be all bad. Nor, it occurred to me, as dull as Paul had struck me hitherto.

'Have you been at the Hop and Harry?' he asked me. 'I heard what had happened. A bad show. Strangled, is that right?'

'You heard rightly.'

'That poor girl. Plumshaw has done badly by her.'

I took the opportunity 'She'll be in a bad way now. No home, no job. Could your father-in-law help?'

He nodded right away. 'I'll see to it. I'll have a word with Hazel.'

I must have looked surprised. 'Not Peter?'

'Ultimately, but always politic to go through Hazel. Especially as Plumshaw is a family trust. Hugh ran the farm, estate, pub, woods and so on, but the final ownership lies with Peter. He's just appointed Hazel in Hugh's place.'

'Not Bronte now she's broken off with Jamie Makepeace?'

'She inherits the whole caboodle after both Peter and Hazel's deaths. She has the right to live in the manor if she wishes though and she inherits Puddledock Cottage after Peter's death with the right to live in it if she so chooses. Unless of course she marries a Makepeace. Different arrangements then.'

'Yourselves?' It seemed steep to exclude Stephanie.

'Don't worry on our account,' he said drily. 'We do come into it. We'll be running the estate for Hazel. You seem very interested in us, Jack. Anything else I can tell you?' He spoke with deep irony but I promptly took him up on the offer.

'Thank you. Yes, there is. I'm obviously interested in the Alfa Romeo's story since it affects Giovanni so greatly. Peter told me that it was your wife's mother, Sofia, who arranged the car's sale from the Fascists who were holding it, although she came from a Partisan family.'

He was looking at me warily. 'I believe that is so, but at that time such things weren't easy to pigeonhole.'

'And yet your wife referred to Giovanni as a Mafioso. Was that merely a term of abuse or did she mean it literally?' This must be where Pen had picked up her 'man of honour' reference, which meant Stephanie had endured interview by Pen too.

He stiffened. 'Perhaps. There was no love lost between the Santoro and Mesola families. The Mesolas referred to the Santoros as the Brotherhood. It's possible they had Sicilian connections or that the Mafia was already beginning to spread its influence into the north of Italy. But to me the implication seems clear enough.'

It didn't to me. I still wasn't convinced.

'Incidentally, you will undoubtedly be interested to know,' he continued, 'that the trust specifically excludes the sale of the Hop and Harry land for Peter's lifetime and fifty years thereafter. A poisoned chalice, don't you think?'

Including for Nan, I realized. With Puddledock Cottage in effect gifted to Bronte, he would have nothing to gain from Hugh's death. But did he know that?

FOURTEEN

'We should talk,' Louise said at last, obviously worried at my continued lack of communication once we reached Frogs Hill. I'd driven back from the Plumshaw fête almost in silence, poleaxed both by the horrific events of the day and by the twists and turns that were unexpectedly emerging in this case. Case? Could I even define what case this was? Was it Giovanni's? Was it Hugh Compton's? Or was it Plumshaw's itself: its manor, its old style, its new style and every damned thing about it?

After my dismay at realizing that while at the Hop and Harry I had completely forgotten the fête, the manor and even Louise, I had compounded this by stopping to talk to Paul. When I returned to the fête itself, it had seemed at first glance still to be in full swing, which nearly finished me with its stark contrast to the horrific scene so relatively close by. In fact it wasn't. It had thinned out considerably and those remaining were obviously discussing the news. I found Louise helping to clear up in the refreshment marquee.

I had explained my absence and she had sympathized. 'After all,' she said, 'I can get immersed in a role as much offstage as onstage, and that's only a make-believe world, whereas yours is real.'

'The dark side of Plumshaw erupting,' I'd agreed.

'That poor woman. How will she cope with his death on top of what's happened to the pub?'

Thunderstorms follow stifling heat, I thought, as now back at Frogs Hill I carried drinks into the garden. Old Plumshaw assumed its sunshine and fêtes would go on for ever, but it had to face the fact that some change at least was inevitable. If only it wasn't. If, if, if . . . If only Giovanni could be back, laughing, quaffing his glass of wine and wielding his paintbrush amid his adoring fans and family. With all his irritating faults, how much I longed for that. If only . . . but first I had to do my best to solve two murders.

'How much longer can they go on holding him after all the new evidence?' Louise asked at last, when I mentioned his name.

'None of that absolutely rules him out,' I told her despondently. 'In theory he could have carried out the murder with Ricardo or with Ricardo providing an alibi.'

'Without that fake murder scam he wouldn't need one, as there's no other evidence, except that he set up the appointment with the Comptons in the first place.'

'Agreed. It would be tricky to prove that the idea had been deliberately planted by them at La Casa.' Trust Louise to put her finger on the salient point. That's what makes her a fine actor. She looks at a part, a speech or even a line, decides its heart and its mood in relation to the character and then pitches her performance accordingly. 'And,' I continued gloomily, 'it's a powerful motive too. The more I look at those of other possible suspects, the more they vanish like the Cheshire Cat's grin. The Compton trust, which Bronte would surely have known about, knocks most of them out anyway, whether Comptons or Makepeaces.'

'The Makepeaces might not have known about that, and if they heard about Hugh's hideaway from Andrew they could have taken advantage of that.'

'Nan would be in the same position with Puddledock Cottage, which Hugh was intending to hand over to Bronte. At least Paul and Stephanie knew for sure they would not inherit quickly, if at all.'

'Wrong,' she came back at me. 'If Hugh died, they might have *thought* they would because the trust would be rejigged, and Bronte then seemed out of the picture. Hazel on the other hand—'

'Is in her seventies,' I retorted, weary of this merry-go-round. 'She's hardly likely to butcher her own son.'

Louise pressed on. 'You know what Sherlock said about the improbable.'

'Only if the impossible is eliminated,' I shot back. 'But we haven't done that.'

'Peter Compton,' she said promptly. 'You can eliminate him, at least physically.'

'I agree. And sorry, Louise, I'm going to eliminate Hazel too.'

'Which brings you back to Giovanni. He's not impossible.'

Stop right there, I wanted to say, but I had to deal with it. 'But *very* improbable.'

'I'm glad of that,' she said awkwardly. 'You know that he and

I don't get on, Jack. It goes right back. Ricardo seemed in his shadow and because he thought that himself it annoyed me. He had no confidence in himself and Giovanni would never see that. Ricardo's gifts lie in management, but as they weren't in art Giovanni never encouraged him. Art is all to him and he tried so hard to turn Ricardo into an artist, that Ricardo felt he was a failure. He's good but not in Giovanni's class. Parents can be devils when they are so arrogantly convinced their children's lives can be laid out on the same track as their own and don't even dream that they might be wrong. Once upon a time that was understandable, because that was economically the only path open, but now? No way.'

I was on soggy ground here. I didn't want to sink, but I forced myself on. 'When you were with Ricardo did he talk much about his family?'

'Very little, because he was also caught up in this family forever concept. Family first, family forever and repel all invaders. I had no wedding ring and so I was excluded. Worse, in his view, I didn't want one. Not that it bothered me. Ricardo and I were happy – until we weren't.'

Not exactly what I had wanted to hear, but I struggled on.

'Did Ricardo say anything about the Santoro family having connections with the Mafia before or after the war?'

That really did it. Louise was furious. 'You're way off beam, Jack. Out of order.'

'You're sure? There was a mention of it by one of the Comptons.'

'Then the mention was wrong. I'm as sure as I can be. The idea's ridiculous. Ricardo is straight, and if Giovanni wasn't I would have picked that up in my two years living with Ricardo.'

She really knew how to hurt. I put my defences up. 'You didn't know about the imprisonment of Peter Compton, so you might have let this go by too. For instance, could Giovanni's father have had any connection with the Brotherhood?'

The stony face changed to cool triumph. 'As Giovanni's father was in the Italian navy, it's hardly likely, is it?'

'No.' I had to go on, even if I wasn't sure where I was going. 'Did Ricardo talk about Italy during the war, even if not about family matters?'

'Not much,' she snapped. 'Somewhat before our time.'

'I know Giulio's sister married his co-driver Enrico di Secchio, so perhaps there were brothers too.'

'Maybe,' Louise retorted. 'But not in the Brotherhood.'

She meant it as another put-down, but it occurred to me that this might have been how the possible misconception about the Mafia might have begun. Stephanie was only a child when her mother died but she must have kept in touch with the family thereafter. It could be something she had picked up rightly or wrongly from them. Perhaps it was a complete red herring, though. I couldn't see how this factor might have affected Hugh Compton's death.

I realized I was getting to the desperate stage of needing to find something, *anything*, to cling to that might shed a new light on the case. Another tricky situation. One last go: 'Did either Maria or Ricardo ever mention the Alfa Romeo before Giovanni heard about it from his cousin?'

'Not that I remember, but of course I might have let that go by me too. Time for supper?'

It was and we called an armistice. Louise made an early departure for work the next morning, Sunday or not, but to my relief I found a *billet doux* left on the kitchen table. I hadn't ruined our relationship for ever, for which I was profoundly grateful.

There were two big kisses scrawled on it – and a few scribbled words. These read: 'Did either of them mention Floria?'

Who on earth was Floria? I had a vague memory of Maria mentioning a Floria, then amending it to Lucia. Or had that been a quick recovery from a slip? By 'them' I presumed Louise meant Giovanni and either Maria or Peter Compton. It didn't matter too much, which was fortunate as she was on set and that meant no phone calls, no mobiles and no texts. The princess was up in her ivory tower until this evening. There was no instant way to contact Giovanni; Maria was out when I rang La Casa and Ricardo was on voicemail.

The word 'communications' conveys a mistaken image. One assumes they are always helpful and available, but as with other areas in life it takes two to make them work, one to initiate and one to receive. And today, I was doing all the initiating without any cooperation from the other side. Brandon wasn't answering, his Sunday team couldn't help, and Dave wasn't around. Unfortunately for Zoe, she was. There was a late 1920s Model A Ford roadster from which she would not be parted, even on a Sunday. Either that, or she had had a row with her boyfriend, Rob. I saw her arrive, gave her ten minutes and then strolled over to the Pits to greet her, trying to look nonchalant. Zoe glanced up and her body language suggested no help was required. Finally she grew restless as I didn't budge, continuing to watch her every move, and threw three words at me: 'Talk away, Jack.'

As she had picked up the right signals, I did. I went as far as I could, given that this was confidential work for the police – although it was true that no mention of payment had yet been made by Brandon, save for the Land Rover case. I ended my diatribe, which concentrated on the Alfa Romeo story and finished with the Brotherhood via a side track to Andrew Lee's death and his probable involvement in the arson attack on the pub, with a plaintive, 'Where do I go from here?'

Zoe actually stopped work and considered the matter. 'Harry Prince.'

'*What?*' As I mentioned earlier, Harry Prince is Frogs Hill's bête noire. A local garage magnate, he longs to buy us out lock, stock and barrel, meaning the farmhouse, the Pits and of course the Glory Boot, and is eagerly awaiting the day that I throw in my hand through lack of money. So far I have eluded this by the skin of my teeth, but I never congratulate myself that he is no longer a threat. Thus the idea of going to sup with this devil without a very long spoon was unappealing. 'What about him?' I asked cautiously.

'If there's a big development in Plumshaw afoot he of all people will know something about it. He'll be looking for his angle or be busily pulling strings behind the scenes. Bet you he knows all about the Comptons and Makepeaces and the man at the pub who was murdered, *and* he might have heard gossip about the Alfa Romeo.'

'Why should he help me with inside information?' A reasonable question given the delicate relationship between us.

'For your bright eyes, Jack. Besides, his wife likes you.'

I like Jackie as well, although that's all there is to it. Harry knows that, so there's no unease between us on that score. Only over Frogs Hill.

It could do no harm, I reasoned, so I parked in Pluckley and walked over to Harry's home at Charden along a bridle path. It would be good for my soul, I thought. The countryside tends to put

life in perspective and this particular track took me past the barn
that had once contained my Lagonda, the subject of the first of my
cases and the one that had brought me face to face with DCI Brandon
for the first time.

The walk did succeed in calming me down, even if it did not
produce any miracle cures for my problems. This countryside might
endure for ever, unless the concrete jungle spread its tentacles as
far as this. Long after the woes of Plumshaw were solved, if not
forgotten, it would remain, just as once it nurtured Neanderthal
ancestors.

At last the huge iron gates of Château Prince faced me, as I
pressed the keypad entrance. His Majesty came out to greet me in
all his rather endearing pomposity. Harry is not a tall or a slim man,
so this can be an impressive sight.

'Good to see you, Jack.'

'And you, Harry.'

These courteous fibs over, he took me round to the conservatory
at the rear of the house where Jackie greeted me benignly and we
caught up to date over a tray of coffee and biscuits. Catching up is
usually an interesting process, as Harry deals with modern cars as
well as dabbling in classics and he can impart – if he so chooses –
many sidelights on the criminal car underworld. In return – subject
to obvious restrictions – I can fill him in on the other side of the coin.

'Heard you're involved with that Alfa Romeo,' he eventually said.
'That Plumshaw business is looking weird.'

'As usual, you heard correctly, Harry.'

'Another death, I gather. Linked to this development they're
planning.'

'Quite possibly.' This was both true and a tactical move since
Harry doesn't like being mixed up with trouble – even if it's on his
own pitch and even if he initiated it. 'Did you know Andrew Lee,
the man who was murdered yesterday?'

'I did, as a matter of fact.' Harry was finding his coffee spoon
extremely interesting judging by the way he was fiddling with it.
'Running the Hop and Harry pub, wasn't he? He used to joke about
it. Weird chap. Said I was a dead ringer for Henry the Eighth.'

Then he realized he had revealed too much. 'Not that I knew
him well. Andrew, I mean, not Henry the Eighth.' It wasn't like
Harry to lose his grip, and Jackie was giggling.

'Of course not,' I said politely, though I could see Andrew's point. 'What's your interest in the Plumshaw development?'

'Always interested in progress,' he told me heartily, back on safe ground. 'No doubt it will go through. Compton will sell up the land.'

'I wouldn't be too sure of that.'

He tapped the side of his nose. 'I would. We'll find a way somehow whether he wants to sell or not. There'll be shops, garages, restaurants, a cinema maybe, and industry. Jobs, Jack, jobs. I've heard about chaps who'll make his life hell if he doesn't sell. Wouldn't like that to happen to the old man.'

Nor would I and I wondered who would be paying these 'chaps'. Unless it was just bluster on Harry's part. It's never safe to assume that with him, however. I had noted the use of 'we'. So had Jackie, who winked at me.

'Another restaurant? Another garage? Martin Fisher won't like that.'

'Progress, Jack. That's what I told Andrew.'

I could have pointed out that Andrew had possibly died as a result, but this would not have been a good tactical move. All the same, these 'chaps' Harry knew might have been behind Andrew's death.

'Who do these chaps belong to?' I asked casually.

He shrugged. 'For hire, Jack.'

'By anyone in Plumshaw?'

'Now how would I know that?'

So the answer was yes. 'Andrew was caught out of his depth,' I said.

'But I don't believe that's the case, Jack.' Harry nodded sagely. 'Word gets around, you know. Bad do about that fire,' he added.

'If it's not "these chaps", any idea who did it? What's the gossip?'

At that he looked shy. 'Not my place to speculate, Jack. You know me.'

I did. Whether he knew or not, he was bowing out of the situation – which meant his hands were clean, or shortly would be. Harry then decided he had another appointment and left me with Jackie, although he kindly commented as he left, 'You know, Jack, progress is like charity. It begins at home. See what I mean?'

I thought I did and I didn't like it. He was confirming my reluctant conclusion that it was Andrew himself who had burned the pub down. It was true that although his wife had been present, their young son had conveniently been away and Andrew had discovered the fire himself. Moreover its seat had been at the other end of the building from where they slept.

All circumstantial evidence of course, but if I believed what George Makepeace had told me about his job offer to Andrew, I had a nasty feeling Harry could be right. And yet it didn't entirely satisfy me. After all, George Makepeace wasn't the only person who might see the benefit of removing the Hop and Harry from the battleground of the access road to the new development. All sorts of people and businesses might have wanted to spur the discussion onwards.

I walked back along the bridle path, conscious that, despite a pleasant chat with Jackie, my visit to Harry had opened up yet another problem rather than providing a stepping stone to the truth. Not unusual where Harry is concerned, and I supposed I should be grateful for the nudge about Andrew's involvement. I cheered myself with the thought that this line would be for the police to follow up, especially as the insurance company would be down on them like a ton of bricks if they didn't do so. And they too would be investigating other interested parties.

And then there was the matter of Floria. When Louise arrived home, I tackled her immediately – or as immediately as was possible given that we had a lot of loving reconciliation first.

'Now,' I said, 'tell me about Floria. Who is this gorgeous-sounding woman? Tell me all.'

'I don't know.'

'What do you mean you don't know?' I yelped at this let-down.

'I really don't. I just remembered overhearing Giovanni mention that name to Maria. He shut up like a clam when I came in. Not family,' she added, somewhat wryly I thought.

'Laugh, darling, laugh,' I advised. 'Did you get any idea of when this lady was around?'

'No – yes, I had the impression it went way back.'

There's nothing like a Monday morning for gloom. On this one, I had a late start, since I had to run an urgent errand for Len, picking up a battery. Louise had left early as usual, so I couldn't badger her any more about Floria or anything else. Not that I thought she was hiding anything, but the mind can often produce nuggets one by one if it so chooses.

When I returned and checked my phone, it seemed everyone wanted to speak to me at once. Dave Jennings had rung. Martin Fisher wanted to speak to me urgently. The Comptons had put in their claim and so had Bronte and Stephanie. I'd even had a call from George Makepeace.

My adrenalin shot up to maximum. Something significant must have happened. I rang Dave Jennings first, as he might provide the easiest path to finding out what it was.

'Heard the news?' he asked me, unhelpfully.

'No. I've been out for a while.'

'Get back in. Brandon's arrested someone for the Plumshaw murder. Jamie Makepeace.'

'*Which* murder?' I was racing this information through my mind in top gear.

'Andrew Lee's.'

'*And* Hugh Compton's?'

'Not that I've heard.'

My mind stopped at a pit for quick refuelling. This didn't mean that Jamie was in the clear over Hugh Compton, I reasoned, only that Brandon didn't have enough on him to go for it. That implied he had plenty over Andrew's murder. I couldn't see it, however. Not Jamie. No – rethink that, I thought. I *could* see it if Jamie had flown into one of his hot-headed rages, but that could not apply to two murders. I could see why he might also have had a go at Hugh, if he believed that Hugh was behind Bronte being cut off without a penny if she married him, or if they had had a row resulting in Hugh withdrawing the offer of Puddledock Cottage. Why kill Andrew though? Because he had evidence that Jamie had killed Hugh? It fitted, but it didn't convince me.

I dutifully returned the rest of the calls, but they all had the same information they thought I should know. Bronte was the worst to handle. She was in tears and insisted I prove Jamie innocent. He was, she told me over and over again.

Stephanie had her own angle. 'Hugh seems to have been forgotten in this concentration on Andrew's murder. Find out what's happening, Jack,' she demanded.

'I'll do my best.' What else could I say?

'Do so. He's a loose cannon that boy and Bronte's well out of that mess. Hugh was having second thoughts about letting her have Puddledock Cottage. When my father dies she will have it anyway, and Hugh thought she should wait because that awful man Nan was making such a nuisance of himself. Jamie and Bronte were set on having it though, so don't let the police overlook that for a motive.'

I had my chance because, instead of answering my call, Brandon came to see me in the afternoon. He didn't choose the Pits this time. 'I've forgotten what gardens are like,' he remarked, looking round mine appreciatively.

'Is your wife the gardener in your home?' I asked.

'Elaine has to be. Gardeners need to be on a regular beat like Uniform. No use dashing out for ten minutes at a time.'

This was unusually personal for Brandon and I murmured something about Louise adding her loving touches to my basic efforts.

'You're a lucky man, Jack. Go gently,' he added, to my astonishment. Advice too! We were indeed breaking new ground. 'You told me she knows Giovanni Donati,' he added.

'Yes. Any change there?'

'That's what I came to tell you. It's going through the channels now. It's odds on he'll be released, charges dropped. For your ears only,' he emphasized.

Good news at last. 'Does that mean Jamie will be in the clear?'

'Not yet. We need DNA. The rest of the evidence is iffy. He's no alibi yet – says he was at the fête but we can't pin down any witnesses to exact times.'

'I saw him myself, must have been about three-thirty. But that doesn't rule him out from your point of view.'

'No. First he denied being at the pub at all. Someone saw him there around two o'clock and then he admitted he went there to collect some stuff for Andrew, couldn't find him and left. When we challenged that, he finally confessed he saw Andrew, realized he was dead and took fright.'

'That would tie in with his being het up, to say the least, when I saw him. What about the Compton case? Any link there?'

'We're working on it. Can't tie Jamie Makepeace into the arson case either, although I'm pretty sure whoever torched the place killed Lee as well. I don't see George Makepeace in that light.'

'Nor do I. Then who?' I had a feeling that the answer was staring me in the face, but I couldn't put a name to it.

'Nothing yet. We've got till tomorrow evening unless we ask for an extension on Jamie Makepeace.'

'And Giovanni? Any idea when?'

'Sorry, Jack. Don't get the champagne out yet, but have it ready.'

We did get it out in fact. When I had brought Louise up to date after she reached home, she decided we needed to cheer ourselves up with a bottle of Prosecco.

'I've been thinking about this Floria,' she began, somewhat tentatively. 'How would you feel if we invited Ricardo over here and asked him about her? We could ask Maria too,' she added hastily, perhaps seeing warning signals in my expression. 'Ricardo could pick her up. You could ask them anything you want then.'

Dumbfounded, I wrestled with myself. Did I want to see Ricardo and Maria here with Louise, which would make me an outsider? Then I remembered Brandon's advice: go gently.

'Why not?' I forced myself to reply. I couldn't tell any of them the news about Giovanni, so if he was released there would have to be another celebration. As for this one, I would at least be playing on home ground. I told her the news about Jamie though, emphasizing he'd been arrested for Andrew Lee's murder, not Compton's.

The gathering was arranged for Saturday lunchtime. It wasn't going to be an easy one, but I had to realize it wouldn't be easy for Ricardo either. He must have dressed with great care to look so splendidly casual, I thought as they arrived. His designer shirt and chinos, together with Maria looking her best petite self in black, sent out a signal that they intended to be on the winning side in Louise's eyes, which meant I had to be on the lookout for point scoring.

In unspoken agreement, he and I did the macho thing: we shared the barbecuing, wielding our tongs like true knights of old, stabbing away with great pleasure at the innocent victims before us. Louise made the salads and dessert and Maria sat there glowing with joy at seeing Ricardo and Louise together. Clearly she thought I would be history if her darling Ricardo wanted Louise to return to him.

All seemed to be going well, however. No one asked when Giovanni would be released, to my relief, and at last, when Maria was fully replete with desserts, I was able to ask the big question: 'Who was Floria, Maria? You mentioned her to me once.'

In a trice Maria presented her obstinate face. 'I did not. I do not know.'

'Ricardo?' Louise asked firmly.

He was standing with a piece of toasted cheese at the end of a barbecue fork which he waved like a samurai sword. 'It is not important, Louise.' He was pointedly ignoring me, but clearly ill at ease.

'It is family,' Maria roared.

My call. 'Giovanni is in prison. Unless you tell me *everything* you know, whether it is about the Comptons or your own family, he will remain there and it will be your fault.'

Tough but true. I thought at first I would get the barbecue fork stuck in me, but an encouraging smile from Louise to her former paramour worked. Maria picked up on that and surrendered, albeit not happily. 'Enrico know her,' she said, glaring at me.

'The ancestor of the owner of La Casa?' This cousin was omnipresent.

'*Si.*'

'Who was Floria?' I demanded, hopeful that I might slowly be getting somewhere.

'Enrico died five years ago. I know nothing.'

I slumped in despair and Louise, bless her, took over. 'Please tell him, Maria. You might be the means of saving Giovanni.' She too was ignored.

Then Ricardo decided to score a point. 'Tell him, Mama.'

Even then she wouldn't budge. 'I do not talk about Giovanni's lady friends.'

Louise had another go. 'Floria could not have been one of Giovanni's lady friends. If Enrico knew of her she was much more probably Giulio Santoro's lady friend.'

'Family matter,' Maria snapped again. 'Giulio married man.'

Ricardo then stepped up for his big moment of glory. He squatted down at her side, cream chinos dangerously near somewhat muddy lawn. 'Papa is in prison, Mama. If this Floria would help, you must speak.'

'She will not help.'

Ricardo's even bigger moment. He stood up on his manly feet, looking the picture of the heroic warrior and annoyingly free of mud. 'Then I will go to ask Papa.'

'He not know either.'

Time for me to rise to my own manly feet. I'd had enough. '*Tell me*, Maria, or I stop helping Giovanni. They will charge him with murder and he will be away from you for months, years.'

She was almost swayed, but I wasn't going to get my moment of glory. 'What shall I do, Ricardo *mio*?' she pleaded, clasping his hands.

'Tell him, Mama.'

Mother and son gazed at each other in torment. Mother gave in and Ricardo got the glory. That's life. Worth it, I suppose. 'Floria,' she told us, 'was Giulio's girlfriend.'

'Not his sister as you said when you first mentioned her?'

I received a withering glance. 'No. His girlfriend in the war.'

Promising, I thought. 'Could she have had anything to do with the Alfa Romeo story?'

She shrugged. 'I do not know.'

Unless she had, I couldn't see what relevance she would have. Floria might be a massive red herring and I had put myself through this agony for nothing.

And then Ricardo swept back on to the battleground, obviously determined to win more laurels. 'Enrico would have known more about her.'

'Pity he died five years ago,' I snarled.

Maria was beginning to look bored. 'I ask Umberto,' she snapped.

'Why would he know?' It seemed highly unlikely that he would know details of the love life of his grandfather's brother-in-law.

'Enrico lived with Umberto. Very close.'

FIFTEEN

L a Casa. Everything seemed to be pointing to La Casa. Did the Comptons know about Umberto Monti's family connection with the Santoros? I began to wonder. They certainly knew there was a connection of some sort. Did Peter know about Floria?

From great reluctance, Maria was now determined that I should meet Umberto at the very first opportunity. Having dissuaded her from setting off to La Casa right that very minute, we agreed to ask Umberto when it would best suit him for me to arrive. Tuesday was his choice. Ricardo would be unable to come with us – what a shame! – as Umberto had chosen a weekday afternoon during that precious interval between the last of the lunchers' departure and the preparations for evening dinners commencing. Ricardo had smugly kissed Louise's hand on leaving on the Saturday, devotion pouring out of his eyes. Louise picked up on my reaction and had giggled.

'Old times, Jack,' she said, after he and Maria had roared off in the Stag down Frogs Hill Lane. 'They don't go away, they just get superseded by better ones.'

This cheered me up greatly and it was with a light heart that I set off to La Casa on Tuesday. The sun was shining, it was June, and although Louise could not come with me, I would be seeing her that evening. I could almost convince myself this was a day off and nothing to do with the Plumshaw case. I've often found, however, that days off pay off. Unexpected gems of inspiration and informa- tion seize the opportunity to emerge without competition from everyday preoccupations. Given that the paths of the Comptons and the Santoros had crossed in Italy, and its present generations had clashed over the Alfa Romeo, I might even find that proverbial crock of gold.

Even if it only turned out to be a good pasta.

'Bravo, Jack. You are here!' Maria was all smiles for me today and proudly presented me to Umberto. He was roughly the same age as Giovanni, but shorter, stouter and, it became clear, jollier, whether by nature or profession.

'I ask Umberto about Floria,' Maria told me, even as I was ushered to a table with a feast of tea and delicious cake on it. 'He knows nothing.'

Well, that was a great welcome. 'Thanks a bunch,' I said wryly. At least I'd get a slice of that cake.

'Do not worry, Jack.' Umberto clapped me heartily on the back. 'Maria jokes. I know some but my grandfather knows much more.'

I was relieved, but plunged back into confusion. 'Enrico di Secchio is still alive?'

'No, but he leave behind many interesting tales. Photos, letters. He lived here with Mamma for two years before he died and often he talk of his great friend, Giulio. The friend of his youth. We all have friends of our youth, yes?'

I agreed, though I could think of one or two I was glad to have left behind.

'And it is good,' Umberto continued, 'that Maria is married to Giulio's grandson. She is a good cook, yes?'

'She is.' No argument about that. Giovanni travelled a great deal but was never so happy eating away from home as he was at Maria's table.

'I tell you what I know about Floria,' Umberto continued. 'I am surprised when Maria tell me you want to know about her, because it is long ago and how can that be why Giovanni is in prison?'

'I don't know that it is the reason. But there are undoubtedly missing ingredients in the story behind this case so it is useful to check the original recipe.'

Umberto chuckled. 'You are right, Jack. So I tell you because this is for Giovanni.'

Maria's eyes promptly filled with tears, and Umberto hastened to console her with a large slice of cake before beginning his story. I received one too. 'My grandfather Enrico,' he began, 'is a son of the Conte di Secchio. The family supports the monarchy, which in 1938 meant supporting Mussolini. Very wealthy family then. Enrico buy the car for Giulio and they are great friends. They both serve in the army during the war, and then after the armistice there is a new government under the king and Badoglio. But only in the south has it any power because in the north the Germans come and the new government is not strong enough to oppose the Fascists who have power again. Giulio became a Partisan in the mountains, but

Enrico stay in Parma where he must pretend to work for the Fascists, although he really works for the Partisans. As did Floria. She was a messenger taking provisions and other supplies to the Partisans in the mountains. She was more than a messenger though; she stayed with the *banda* and helped them fight when she could. She was brave, she was funny, she was gentle, she was beautiful. That's what my grandfather said. Giulio fell in love with her. This was not good because he had a wife and a child at home, but it happens.'

Maria snorted her disapproval and I squeezed her hand.

'Giulio went to the mountains in the autumn of 1943. His *banda* mounted several good attacks, but did not achieve very much because of lack of armaments. Then in the spring of 1945 the British come, and arms too. The operations are getting bigger for there is more at stake. They needed to attack the Germans from behind their lines, so there would be fewer Germans to fight the Allied armies as they came up from the south of the country.

'Floria was caught by the Fascists as she brought supplies up the mountain to the arranged rendezvous. She was tortured and shot, but gave no information away. Only a week or two later, Giulio himself was caught on a raid with his men. He too was tortured and shot.'

He paused, so I quickly put my burning question to him. 'Peter Compton, the father of the dead man and owner of Giulio's Alfa Romeo, was in the group at that time. Did you know that?'

'I did. But patience, if you please, Jack. In the time between Floria's capture and Giulio's, Giulio made his way down to the village to find Enrico and ask what had happened to Floria. Enrico told him she had been betrayed, but he did not know by whom. Giulio told him that he was sure of the truth, and he wrote it down for Enrico. I have all papers, Jack. I have photographs. You can see them all. But here is what Giulio himself wrote. Here is the story of Floria.'

He went up to his living quarters and brought down a notebook browning with age but still readable. 'In English I will tell you what it says,' Umberto told us. 'Giulio writes that Floria had been betrayed by one of his own band, who had only recently joined them. He must have regretted it, Giulio writes, but he too loved her and was jealous of Giulio. It had been Giulio he intended to betray that evening, but Floria arrived early and it was she who was captured, not Giulio.

They had arranged to meet at a shack on the mountainside, but Floria came early and was captured instead.'

'Who was his betrayer?' I knew the answer of course.

'The English officer, Peter Compton.'

I spent several hours with the papers he had laid out for me in his living room. Maria chatted to Umberto's wife while I was oblivious to anything but what was in front of me. Letters, diaries, and photographs, much of the hoard irrelevant. Letters between members of the di Secchio family, letters to the Santoro family. I couldn't take it all in. But I did read enough to learn what happened to the Alfa Romeo. Enrico heard it had been taken from the family and found out after the war who had bought it. That was how Peter had been clapped in prison to await a hearing. After the referendum that turned Italy into a republic however, Enrico was not in such a powerful position; the British managed to get Peter released, as he himself had told me.

What moved me more were the photographs. There were some of the 1938 Mille Miglia that collectors would give their all for. There was a photo of a young Enrico and Giulio in the Italian army at their barracks. One crumpled photo of Giulio's *banda* after the war was won, and one – through serendipity – marked 'Floria' on its reverse. She was dark-haired, smiling slightly at the taker of the photograph – perhaps Giulio? It was a face with strength as well as beauty and I could well understand that both Peter and Giulio were in love with her.

Where to go from here, I wondered as I drove home. Either the Plumshaw case had no relevance to this story and the answer was to be found in the village politics, or the answer might well lie in the story of Floria. Could I really believe that Peter was so jealous of Giulio and Floria that he betrayed them both and then returned after the war to buy his car as the final vengeance? A vengeance that he was still pursuing all these years later? And yet Enrico's story and what I had read in Giulio's own words rang true. Peter Compton had not mentioned Floria at all.

By the Wednesday morning I was ready to face Plumshaw again. I had things in perspective now. With Jamie released, tension must have relaxed on Andrew Lee's murder, though goodness knows what agony Lucy must be going through. On the Compton front, I was primed for battle. Nan should be my first target as he sat between the two villages.

There was no sign of him at Puddledock Cottage although his car was there. No answer to my knock, nor was he in the rear garden. He couldn't be far away, however, so I made my way to the church where, if I was lucky, this might be one of his caretaking days. I found him carefully sweeping the path from the lychgate to the porch and he broke off readily enough.

'I heard Jamie Makepeace has been released. Good news for the village,' I began.

Nan considered this. 'Not for whoever killed Andrew,' he pointed out. I'd forgotten Nan tended to take things literally.

'Any news on your cottage?' I asked.

'Why would there be? I'm staying there. That's what I told the Comptons. They said they'd think it over, but there's nothing to think about. I told them to take that special tea of Mum's. It'll buck them up a bit.'

I laughed, though Nan looked surprised at that. 'Still see your job as peacemaker in the village?' I asked.

'Sometimes you can't have peace till you've sorted out the war.'

'The current war has run into a brick wall surely, with the burning down of the pub and Andrew's murder. There are even rumours that Andrew burnt it down himself.'

'I heard them.' He picked up his broom again.

'Do you believe them?'

'Not my business, but George wouldn't have done it. He plays hard but he plays fair. Jamie too.'

I couldn't tell him about the most pressing problems in my mind – the car, the Comptons and Giulio Santoro – but I could express one in general terms. 'What do you do, Nan, when you have a problem that is tricky either way and you don't know whether there's right or a wrong, but a lot hangs on it?'

'I listen,' he answered me predictably.

'To both sides separately?'

'Yes. Then let them talk it through together.'

'And if they won't?'

'I wait.'

'And if still nothing happens?'

'Something always happens.'

Was that going to be true in the Compton versus Santoro story? Not so far. Nor was it as regards the village. Jamie had been released without charge. No one else had been arrested for arson or for Andrew's murder, and the nameless face still refused to identify itself. Was something going to happen, as Nan said, or should I make it happen? I'd go with the latter. If Nan's back seat plan worked, so be it, but I couldn't afford to take that chance. Besides, in my deck of cards I might be holding an ace with Floria and it was time to play it.

I left my car in the church car park and strode along the manor drive. I tried my best to feel like a Time Lord coming to settle the disputes of nations, but if I succeeded there was no one around to be daunted by my approach. A cat looked up and continued to wash its paws, uninterested in my arrival, but that was all. I noticed that cars were parked outside the manor so someone must be at home.

No one answered the doorbell for some time, and the cat had a 'told you so' look on its face. Just as I was turning away, however, Hazel opened the door.

'I'd like a word with Peter if he's around.' Not a very Time Lord type of opening for hostilities, but even a Time Lord would be thrown off course by the look on Hazel's face.

'What about?' The sharp eyes and her small tense figure were fully alert although I judged she wasn't hostile, only in gatekeeper mode.

'Floria.'

She frowned. 'Floria who?'

'Peter will know.' I played my ace, with mental fingers crossed that I was on the right track.

I thought I'd blown my chances, but, perhaps curious herself, she returned to me in a surprisingly short time. 'Come in,' she ordered, and led me to the same room as on my previous visit. This time, however, it seemed Peter and I were to be alone, to my surprise and relief.

'Call me if you need me,' she told her husband, banging the door behind her to make a point.

Peter Compton didn't look delighted to see me. The Pickwickian benign expression vanished right from the word go. 'Sit down.' He waved a hand to the armchair opposite him, studied me for a while and then barked: 'Who told you about Floria? That painter?'

'No.'

No comfort to him, it seemed. 'Who then?'

'The descendant of Giulio's co-driver and brother-in-law, Enrico di Secchio.'

'You've been busy,' he remarked. It didn't sound like a compliment. 'Tell me exactly what you've heard. Forget how old I am. I'm not going to keel over so you needn't pull any punches. I've plenty of punch left in me.'

I took him at his word, and related as neutrally as I could the story that Umberto had related, ending with: 'He told me that the person who betrayed both Floria and Giulio was you. I also saw a document, apparently written by Giulio himself, which confirmed it.'

I don't know what reaction I expected, but it wasn't this. He didn't move an inch. He didn't seem outraged or even surprised.

'Now allow me to tell you what really happened,' he said. 'I have the advantage of having been present. Enrico was not; he only heard Giulio's false claim. It is quite obviously false. What possible reason could I have had for betraying Floria? I was deeply in love with her. If the accusation is that I had planned for Giulio to be arrested that day and by chance it was Floria who suffered, I can only say that that too is ridiculous. Would I have risked that, knowing that Floria was on her way to the rendezvous? If Giulio had been arrested thanks to me the enemy would have known someone else would be arriving and they would wait.'

A good point, I thought, as he paused, although that didn't mean it was true.

'No, Jack,' he continued, 'the person who betrayed Floria was Giulio himself, to save his own skin. I told you about the operation at Pontrémoli after which Giulio returned later than the rest of us. I thought this was strange at the time. He was either trapped by the Fascist militia or more likely had told his friend Enrico who worked with them about Floria. He was not a clever man. He bargained Floria's safety for his own. Floria and the Mesola family from which she came—'

'Floria was a Mesola?' I interrupted. 'She was Sofia's sister?' Why had this been kept from me? By accident or by design?

Peter was unfazed. 'She was,' he continued steadily. 'The Mesolas were thorns in the flesh of the militia and the key to the whole

Partisan resistance movement in the area. By catching Floria, they would have not only her family in their power but a lead on all the other Partisan sympathizers in the civilian population. Giulio arranged to set a trap for her; she was caught and shot. Two weeks later Giulio met the same fate – of course he did. He had played into their hands and it was only by luck that Floria's family and the rest of us survived. We instantly moved refuge.'

This surely had to be wrong. 'Why would Giulio betray her?' I asked. 'He loved her.'

'Through arrogance and hatred of me. He was convinced he was vital to the *banda* and had been resentful of me from the start. When Floria turned to me rather than him, it was the last straw. I was parachuted in to lead his men, which was hard for him as he had been with them for well over a year by the time I joined them. It was hard for me too, even though I was the officer in charge and he was dependent on me for communications to Mission Toffee about supply drops of food and armaments. I knew I wanted to marry Floria after the war, despite the short time I had known her, and had told her so. Giulio, with his Italian pride, could not take rejection. When Enrico's Fascist friends talked to him, he was all too quick to take revenge on me.'

'Did he admit that to you?'

'He refused to speak of Floria during those two weeks before he himself was captured. He was impossible to work with. He became a risk for us. Too much of a risk, Jack.'

'*Too* much?'

'He was a danger to us all, with his hatred of me. The *banda* could not afford to lose me. It was five men's lives against one.'

'Are you telling me . . .?' I had a terrible feeling I could see where this was leading.

'Yes, Jack. On our next operation Giulio led us from the front on my orders. I knew there was a risk that the operation had been picked up by the enemy. I sent him in first. A good method of ensuring one's personal enemy's fate, if I remember the biblical story of David and Bathsheba correctly. I betrayed Giulio.'

SIXTEEN

I have never fancied myself as Solomon but here I had to make a judgement on two different stories that converged at some points and were directly opposed at others. Both dated back roughly seventy years. Both were stories of love, betrayal and death and still as chilling today as they had been at the time. I tried to imagine myself in the same position, with Ricardo, myself and Louise as the absent Floria. I couldn't do so, perhaps because the background of the Second World War was impossible to recreate for a non-soldier seventy years later. Europe at war had dominated centuries for our ancestors, but now was hard to envisage. Perhaps our great-grandfathers, grandfathers and fathers had felt the same way in 1914 and 1939.

The two stories I had been told could not both be true. There was no avenue for compromise here, and yet I had to go forward. How to find the right path? Did I side with Santoro or the Comptons or should I try to rise above both of them? I told myself that what mattered was not what had taken place in the Apennines all those years ago, but what had happened *now*. The story of Floria certainly lay behind the fake murder plot but how could it have led to the deaths of Hugh and Andrew?

The Compton case too had its forks, especially since Andrew's death. Were the Comptons responsible for Hugh's murder *and* Andrew's, whether linked or not to the Second World War story, or had the village feud been behind both of them? Forks in the road don't always have an escape route via a link lane if you make a mistake. Sometimes they wind round and round and round taking you further and further from the true path. It seemed to me I was doing exactly that on both forks of the Plumshaw case – unless of course I spotted that link.

A night's sleep found me no further forward, until Brandon drove sedately through the Frogs Hill gates, with his sergeant, a nice-looking girl called Judy. Could Brandon be galloping to the rescue with some helpful hint? Apparently the boot was on the other foot, because he immediately wanted to know what I had to tell *him* about my Compton visit. He must have had wind of it, because I hadn't yet called in to put him in the picture. I took them both into the garden, brought some coffee – which won me a beam of thanks from Judy – and began.

'Run through that again,' was Brandon's immediate comment when I came to a halt on what I thought was a pretty good summary of what I'd learned from both sides. Judy, at least, had an admiring look on her face, which is always encouraging.

The second run through achieved little more with Brandon, though it's always hard to tell with him. 'Ancient history,' he commented. 'Can it really have anything to do with this case?'

I was tempted to say that he had obviously thought so when he ascribed it as a motive for Giovanni. I restrained myself. What I said was: 'It explains the reason for the Comptons' fake murder plan.'

'Still old hat for the real one,' he said. I wish I could add 'dismissively' after that, but it wouldn't be true. He was being completely objective, and as I thought the same as he did I could hardly disagree.

Even so, I did mutter under my breath: 'Old hats wear well.'

He heard me. 'They wear out too.'

Judy giggled, but a stony face from the boss quelled her into silence and note-taking.

I made amends by sharing my fork analysis with them. 'There could well be a linking road,' I concluded.

'It's taking its time. Like the forensic results.' Brandon stared at my favourite rose tree (Louise had planted it when I first met her). 'Two murders in one village for two reasons is overdoing coincidence.'

'Plumshaw *isn't* one village,' I pointed out. 'The concerns of new Plumshaw aren't always that of old Plumshaw.'

Brandon remained unconvinced. 'A united motive does away with coincidence. Those Makepeaces had reason to do away with both of them. So did Nantucket Brown. All of them saw their futures being threatened. I'd have said that Andrew Lee was our man until proved wrong. That brings me right back to Brown.'

I couldn't fault his reason. Nan stood to lose his cottage, which was his reason for being. And yet you can fit a Ford engine in a

Porsche and it would still look right from the outside – but it doesn't make it a Porsche. Nan sat in the middle of the two cases, like that ill-fitting engine. Strong hands like his must have put that engine into this case.

I won't say the answer came to me in a blinding flash. I was still crawling along that left fork to new Plumshaw, and trying in vain to find a turning back to the right fork. I couldn't find it. I was left with one fork only and that did not please me one little bit. Now the signpost pointed right, and someone stood right in the middle of the road. Someone I had overlooked. I'd overlooked him because – oh hell, for the worst of reasons. I *liked* Martin Fisher.

I felt a traitor. Martin, I admitted as I sat in the police car with Brandon and Judy driving to Plumshaw on Friday, had motive, means and opportunity. That didn't mean he was guilty, but Brandon had got straight on to his case, and had already interviewed George and Jamie Makepeace again. This morning I had the call I dreaded. Half of me wanted to dash straight into the Pits and hide. The other half knew I had to accept his suggestion that I accompanied them to Plumshaw.

His motive? Try as I could I could not avoid it. Martin's garage was independent, and not doing well. The new housing development could bring nothing but good for him. But a huge new industrial estate into the bargain would surely mean that Martin's local garage would soon have competition in a major new chain garage opening up? Would he like it any more than Andrew? Andrew had been promised a lucrative future in the form of running the new restaurant, so Martin could equally well have had a bribe in the form of cash or even a new garage. But killing a Compton for it? He must have been torn. The Comptons were customers of his and he had been hankering after restoring the Alfa Romeo.

'Sorry, Jack.' Brandon looked over at me as his driver turned the car into the Plumshaw Road. Behind us came another police car with Judy and uniformed PCs. I was also aware that behind that was a familiar Vauxhall. Pen was on the story, but she wasn't going to get this one. 'He was a friend, wasn't he?' Brandon continued.

'Yes.' How was I going to break this news to Len and Zoe?

Martin made it easy for us, once we drew up at the garage. He took one look at the police car, saw me getting out, saw the back-up car arrive, and looked undecided whether to run or stay. To do him justice he stayed. 'Come in,' he said courteously to Brandon and myself, ushering us into the cramped garage office. Judy followed us in. Pen didn't make it in time. The doors were closed on her. At least I had had no accusations of Judas from Martin, for which I was grateful,

'A few questions—' Brandon began.

'I'd no choice,' Martin interrupted. 'He was blackmailing me, taking me for all I'd got, which is precious little. One house mortgaged up to crisis point, one business rapidly failing, one marriage already failed. Not much of a life history, is it?'

Brandon looked startled. 'Hugh Compton blackmailed you?'

Martin did an about turn. 'Good grief, no. Andrew Lee.'

'He was blackmailing you over Compton's death?' Brandon asked sharply.

Martin looked really worried for the first time. 'No. *Nothing* to do with Compton's death. He knew I'd burnt the Hop and Harry down.'

'Steady,' Brandon warned him. 'You're admitting arson?'

'Might as well. It was the only way – or so I thought – to get Compton to sell the land. I even failed at that. He still doesn't want to sell. You have to admire the old man,' he added bitterly. 'But then blasted Andrew started on me.'

'Hang on,' I managed to say, not to Brandon's pleasure since I'd been told to keep my mouth shut. 'Why did you want the Comptons to sell up? Your garage would do well with the new development.'

'No way. I've only got a lease on the land. It's up next year and George says he won't renew. Wants to knock it down for the access route with the Comptons playing up over the Hop and Harry. But he would get me the first offer of the new garage in the development – if it went ahead.'

As I'd thought. Martin stood no chance now and I was right, because Brandon stopped him at this point to caution him. 'You may want your solicitor present before you say more.'

'No I don't,' Martin retorted. 'I just want to get it over. I knew Andrew was doing a final sort out at the Hop and Harry so I went over to give him the payment he was demanding. He'd boasted about having proof that it was me fired the place. When I handed over the money that I'd only just managed to scrape together he said he was putting the price up next time. I tried to appeal to him as one future beneficiary of the development to another, but he just sneered at me, taunted me for being a loser and doubled the price. I just snapped. Left him where he was and got out quickly.'

'You've left some of the story out, Mr Fisher,' Brandon said, as Martin seemed to have finished. 'Andrew Lee was blackmailing you over the fire perhaps, but also over Hugh Compton's death, wasn't he? Had he seen you loading the body into your van?'

'No. *No*. I wouldn't kill him, not Hugh,' Martin said vehemently.

'You said you'd burnt down the pub, because it stood in the way of the new development. So did Hugh Compton.'

'That's different. I couldn't stab anyone, but I've always had strong hands. You know that, Jack.'

I did and shivered. I had seen those hands pulling apart the rear axle of a tractor.

Martin turned to me as we left the office, a look of desperation in his eyes. 'That Alfa Romeo, Jack. That's why I'd never have killed Hugh Compton. You can understand that. I misled you. He *had* offered me the chance of restoring it if he could get his father to agree. I wanted to do it, but I reckoned that Frogs Hill would be better. I knew I wasn't good enough for that car. The story of my life. Make sure you restore it, Jack. Do it for me.'

The Alfa Romeo. It all came back to that, although its mystery still eluded me. Despite Martin's denials, Brandon remained convinced that he had the link between the two murders. The problem was that though he had found forensic evidence to link Martin with the death of Andrew Lee he could find none to link him to Hugh Compton's murder.

'I'll find it,' he told me matter-of-factly. 'And thanks for your help. Put in a bill.'

I was being paid off but to me the job was only half done – not that I had a problem with being paid anything at all. I had thought I was doing it for free. But I did have a problem with the 'get lost' factor. Hunting for Hugh Compton's murderer had led only to the arrest of a friend on another charge.

Days passed slowly. Len and Zoe had been as struck dumb as I was at Martin's arrest and the news that he had now been charged. All three of us have a simple faith that no one who loves classic cars can be that bad at heart. I managed to persuade them that Martin wasn't that bad at heart, only deeply distressed, but they didn't buy it. I didn't myself either.

I continued to feel despondent about it, especially because I knew what they did not: that Brandon was hunting down every stick and stone in Plumshaw to prove Martin was guilty of Hugh Compton's murder too.

And then, on Wednesday, five days after Martin's arrest, Giovanni blew into town.

Up the lane came the unmistakable sound of the Ferrari Daytona; it was driven by its lawful owner, both now free of police custody. As it came through the gates, Giovanni looked strained but very happy as he shouted out to us: 'Hey, everyone. I free again!'

It was a brave attempt and I rushed for the champagne. Even Len had a sip or two, regardless of any effects this might have on the final stages of the Lanchester's restoration. I'd known Giovanni's release was imminent but didn't know when, so this was a welcome surprise.

'Where's Maria?' I suddenly thought to ask. 'At La Casa?'

'In Plumshaw,' he told us blithely.

I goggled at him. 'What's she doing there?' I had a vision of her on a one-woman hunt for the murderer I was still convinced existed there.

'We stay at the hotel.' He looked very pleased with himself. 'I come here to invite you all to a party.'

'You did say Plumshaw?' I asked faintly. 'The Larches Hotel, I presume?'

'*Si.*'

'But a party, Giovanni? With all that's happened? Is that wise?' Giovanni now knew all about the reason for his release and about the fake murder plot. At first, so Brandon had told me, he had treated it as a big joke himself. Then he had realized what the joke had meant for him and cried. Then he had said briskly, 'So now I am free. That is good. Thank you.'

It wasn't like Giovanni to harbour grudges, but to throw his new-found freedom in the Comptons' faces looked perilously close to that.

'You come, Jack. I owe you my freedom. You bring Louise, you bring everyone, all these nice people.' He waved his arms at Len and Zoe.

'When is it?' I asked.

'On Saturday.'

'Evening?'

'No, no. All day. We start when we get up, we finish when we go to bed. Very late.'

I had to say it. 'But, Giovanni, have you given any thought to the Comptons?'

'Yes,' he answered me. 'I invite them all. I tell the police I do not wish to bring charges or for them to do so. I wish to show that I forgive Mr Peter Compton and his family.'

I believed him. The trouble was, would the Comptons? Would they see any reason to forgive *him* yet, while Hugh's murder was still unsolved? However sure Brandon was that Martin had committed both murders, I was equally convinced he hadn't. I had known Martin a long time and lying wasn't one of his fortes. He was the sort of person who would tell a customer exactly whether there was any hope for his car before setting to work on it and refuse to touch it if it was hopeless. Nor did he baulk at telling someone they'd bought a pup instead of a bargain.

I had another worry too. It bothered me that no one had even glimpsed Hugh Compton while he was living in that chalet. It was a busy car park and he could have left the chalet during Saturday night as well as the night before and walked along that footpath to the manor. Brandon had no line yet on where he had actually been killed. There were no traces of blood in the chalet and he had not been killed by the pond. The chances of his being already dead when he left the chalet were therefore very small and it was much more likely that the poor man walked to his doom in the woods, although so far no trace had been found there. However he would have been walking across Compton fields and according to the Ordnance Survey map there was no public footpath there. That didn't rule out his being attacked by someone from the village, but it made it far less likely. His route could have taken him round the back of the manor past Plumshaw Cottage and across the woods to the pond – or Puddledock Cottage.

This added up to the probability that he was killed either by

someone who was very familiar with the Comptons, such as Nan
or Jamie, or by one of the Comptons themselves.

And Giovanni was going to invite them all to a party to forgive
them for the 'joke' they played on him.

I'd passed by The Larches Hotel many times without giving it much
thought. Now I examined it in a new light as Louise and I arrived
for Giovanni's party, opting for a twelve o'clock arrival. The hotel
blended rather well with old Plumshaw, I thought, with its red brick
facade, gables and well-proportioned windows. It wasn't too osten-
tatious and, apart from those Huggy and Puggy monstrosities in
the children's play area, it clashed with neither old nor new
Plumshaw. It was essentially a bed and breakfast establishment and
I doubted whether it was doing particularly well. Nevertheless,
since his release Giovanni had not only contrived to have them
serve three meals a day to himself, Maria and Ricardo – for yes,
we were to be blessed with his presence of course – but had
informed the hotel that Umberto would be arriving to provide a
banquet for all his many guests all day long.

The married couple who owned it had apparently surrendered
like lambs. Fortunately The Larches possessed a large conservatory
at its rear as well as a breakfast room and a visitors' lounge. It also
had a very nice garden, an oasis in the wilderness that would doubtless arrive beyond its red brick walls if the development plan went
through.

I had mentioned my misgivings over this party to Brandon but
he didn't pick up on it. The attitude seemed to be that if there was
a murderer around, I could cope with it. 'Give the station a call if
you need back-up,' was his parting offer.

At first all seemed well. The buffet lunch was superb, the Comptons
had turned out in force and it seemed that their object too was peace.
A guarded one, but nevertheless peace. Did that mean that they too
had decided to overlook the fact that no one had yet been charged
for Hugh's murder? It appeared so, for on the other hand none of
Giovanni's clan mentioned the fact that he had been falsely accused
in a fake murder plot. There was no sign of Peter Compton himself
here, and I wondered whether that was significant.

'Unfinished business, would you say?' Louise whispered to me,
eyeing the panna cottas with great interest.

'If you want one have it now,' I advised her. 'There could be storm clouds ahead.' I had just spotted what she had not. Jamie Makepeace was joining the party, not it seemed to attack Bronte, but to support a triumphant George Makepeace.

The buzz of conversation stopped. George brought an old-fashioned megaphone with him and was preparing to use it.

'Listen to that,' he boomed. 'Now what you got to say?'

Almost simultaneously the racket began. Over the top of the far garden wall I could see what the noise had made all too clear. A JCB was at work. What on earth was it demolishing? I wondered. This didn't bode well, with George preening himself.

'It's the start,' he continued. 'I'm knocking down that old scrap-yard of mine, ready for the houses.'

The stunned silence seemed to displease him.

'Needn't worry, folks. It's all right and legal. You're going to get a hundred and fifty houses there, with or without the Hop and Harry land. Planning application will be approved. Oppose it all you like, but it will go through.'

Hazel found her voice first. 'You've no access road.'

'Don't you worry your pretty little head about that, Mrs Compton. We've got that sorted,' he roared back. 'No thanks to you though. I've bought up Martin Fisher's lease, so we'll have that. Didn't he tell you?'

He looked round with a pleased smile. 'Just the beginning, folks.'

Money has no conscience, many friends, and all too few enemies, I thought, watching the Comptons' reactions. Bronte simply marched up to George, ignoring Jamie, and grabbed the megaphone.

'My grandfather,' she shouted over the din, 'wants us all to go to the barn to look at the Alfa Romeo. Let's go *now.*'

Giovanni didn't look too happy about this, but I grabbed the opportunity. It wasn't making much of a statement to walk out on George, but it was worth it. We made a solid phalanx of old Plumshavians, formed of the Italian brigade and assorted friends. Jamie did his best to tag along with Bronte but she firmly removed his hand from her arm. I couldn't even guess at what would await us once we reached the barn, but it couldn't be worse than this. I walked with Louise and fumed when Ricardo chose to walk on her other side. I felt her pinch my arm reassuringly and I cheered up.

The barn symbolized this whole case, and perhaps Peter was

aware of it. He was patiently sitting outside the barn as we arrived. Mr Pickwick, to my relief, had returned. He stood up to greet Giovanni very courteously. 'Signor Donati, welcome back.'

'*Grazie.*' Giovanni was cautious and no wonder.

'I hope, Signor Donati, that you will still wish to paint the Alfa Romeo.'

Was this another fake plot, I wondered. What on earth could be behind it? Was it a straight offer? Maria looked ready to explode. Ricardo looked out of his depth and the rest of the Comptons flabbergasted.

Giovanni was in no doubt however. 'No. *Grazie.*'

'Is that because you no longer own it?' Peter looked tired and genuinely sad at this outcome to what – unbelievably in the circumstances – seemed to have been some kind of offer of amends.

Whether it was or not, Giovanni for once seemed wrong-footed. 'I never wished to own it. I do not wish to own it now; I only wished to paint it.'

'Then why not do so?' Peter asked.

Giovanni spread his hands in a gesture of despair. 'Because this is now dark for me. Not light, as once it was. It brought death.'

'It's a car, Giovanni,' Louise said gently.

'Cars are feelings, cars are emotions, otherwise why do I paint them?' Giovanni replied vehemently. 'And this one is surrounded by hate. There has been enough.'

Peter sighed. 'Let us look at it together, Signor Donati, and see if you feel differently.'

Giovanni was clearly unwilling, but to my relief I could see Maria urging him inside. I followed the group into the barn and watched Peter and Giovanni as they stood side by side by the Alfa Romeo.

It was still in the same place, but it looked completely different. It was clean for a start, its black paint glowing for the first time in all those years, its chrome radiator grille gleaming with pride. It seemed to be saying: *I'm ready. I am here.* I heard Giovanni gasp. Even Ricardo looked impressed.

They were all silent until at last Peter spoke.

'We must talk of Floria,' Peter said at last. 'It's time, Signor Donati. Your grandfather betrayed her to the Fascists, but—'

'No,' Giovanni said flatly but without rancour. 'You betrayed her. That is what Giulio believed, what Enrico confirmed. You could not

bear to see her with Giulio. Perhaps you thought you were betraying
Giulio, not Floria, but the result is the same. They were both lost.'
Peter must have been prepared for this. 'That is not the case,
Signor. I loved Floria, and could never have risked betraying her.
Giulio did that, and that is the reason that two weeks later, having
heard about Floria and knowing the truth, I put your grandfather in
a position of danger on our raid, knowing he would most certainly
be captured by the Fascists.'

Giovanni went very white. 'You admit that? Because you did not
succeed the first time you do it that way?'

'Enough,' Hazel said angrily. 'This will lead nowhere. It is seventy
years ago. No one can know the truth now.'

I did not believe that. There was an answer somewhere, even
though I believed both these stories.

Which meant what? Either there had been no betrayal and these
were misconceptions, or a third party had been involved. Enrico?
Surely not, but if it wasn't him then . . . Slowly I began to realize
who that third party must have been. I must have exclaimed out
loud, because the attention of the group was suddenly on me.

'The truth *will* be known,' I said firmly in answer to Hazel. 'It
can't lie buried for ever. Barriers have to be knocked down, just
like that JCB is doing. The rubble has to be cleared, and there it
lies. The solid unadorned ground.'

Hazel looked at me, with a face full of fear. She too had realized.
'Not Hugh too?' she asked me almost pleadingly.

'It's the only explanation. The true explanation.' Did the truth
connect with Hugh's murder, or was it a story that had died long
ago? But Giovanni's family had not forgotten, and nor had Peter's.
Such stories do not die.

No more was said. I had time to reflect as Louise and I returned
with Giovanni and his family to The Larches. I thought the Comptons
would not come with us, but they did, including Peter. They drove
ahead of us in the Land Rover, perhaps to annoy George Makepeace
even more. Louise looked at me anxiously as we walked along, but
I could not even begin to tell her where I was on this case. I wasn't
even sure myself, but I remembered that there hadn't been much
blood found on Hugh's clothes. I'd assumed that was because of
his immersion in the water, but I might have been wrong. I remembered that he had seemed to have dressed in a hurry – in the clothes

he had been wearing when he was in the barn with Giovanni. I put this information together with all I had learned since.

By the time we arrived at the hotel, the noise from the JCB had stopped and in order to ring Brandon I stayed on my own outside the hotel, walking up the drive through Martin's garage premises to the development area. And a sad sight that was. The JCB had been demolishing an old farm building, the rubble from which now lay in heaps by the rear wall of the hotel garden. Even Huggy and Puggy in the play area had their backs to this desecration. I stood there for some time looking at it. I wondered whether this would be the fate of old Plumshaw itself sooner or later and if I could possibly be right over what fate Hugh Compton had met. It seemed unbelievable now, and yet Brandon went instantly into action, Saturday or not.

I stood there too long.

The roar of the digger started up and the whack on my back from the bucket sent me sprawling on to the piles of rubble. As I struggled to regain my feet, I saw that huge bucket rearing up to fall down on me. I saw the driver intent on positioning it for its deadly task but I couldn't get a foothold in time. No escape to the left, nor to the right, nor ahead. My legs didn't seem to belong to me. Terror, pure terror took hold of me. I could see nothing else but that bucket above me. I was unaware of anything else but that bucket.

Then my legs were seized, sending me sprawling again. This time I found myself being dragged and bumped over the brick and plaster rubble. I was miraculously hauled, painfully but safely, to one side as the bucket crashed down inches from where I lay, courtesy of Paul Ranger in the JCB.

I opened my eyes to find I was lying in a heap across my saviour, smothering him. I tried to roll off, bit by bit – and the world had indeed gone crazy. It wasn't a man beneath me. It was a woman. Pen was letting off a string of oaths. I tried feeble thanks as we looked up to see the bucket swivelling dangerously above us. I flung myself, pain and all, to one side pulling Pen with me, so that once again we fell together on the debris as the bucket descended inches away from us.

When I managed to look up after that it was to see not Paul Ranger, but Jamie Makepeace, in the cab and the engine running down. Despite cuts and bruises, we were safe. Paul Ranger was lying prone on the ground.

I had another go at feeble thanks to Pen for saving my life. She ignored them.

As she staggered to her feet, she gripped me by my jacket, eyes ablaze and hissed, 'What's the story, Jack?'

Giovanni and Maria stayed on with Umberto for some weeks. I heard little from Brandon, whose plain-clothes man on the job had quickly materialized to help Jamie restrain Paul Ranger, once he had recovered from Jamie's knockout blow. All I knew was that Paul had been charged with Hugh's murder and the attempted murder of one Jack Colby (plus that of 'courageous *Kentish Graphic* journalist Penelope Roxton'). Paul had admitted all charges.

I had tried to tell Brandon I still wasn't happy as I thought there was a missing link. Brandon had told me he *was* happy, but if I could find this link then he'd be just as happy to consider it.

I set out to find it. What I considered first was whether I should drag Giovanni into this. I decided not to do so, because this was between me and the Comptons. If I could sort this out, it might even be possible to see the Alfa Romeo in a different light, and persuade Giovanni that the light had returned and he could now paint it.

I arranged a meeting with Peter and this time I welcomed Hazel's presence, as it might be some comfort to him. He began to apologize to me for his family's actions but I stopped him.

'We need to get to the truth, Peter,' I said gently.

He looked at Hazel, who nodded, so I took my courage in both hands and began:

'It all stems back to the Mesola family, doesn't it, Peter? Your first wife, Sofia, and her sister Floria.'

He flinched, but answered me. 'Yes.'

'Sofia was in love with you during the time you were fighting with the Partisans, not just after the war?'

'In love with the idea of a British officer who might marry her and get her to England afterwards,' Hazel snorted.

Peter didn't comment on that, but simply replied, 'I believe she was.'

'Could it be that it was she who betrayed Floria, not Giulio? That it was she who changed the time of the meeting so that Floria would be captured and informed on her to the Fascists?'

I held my breath. This had to be the answer, but every finger I had was crossed. I thought Peter would not reply, but eventually to my relief he did. 'It is possible. During the past weeks I have come to see that. Whether it is true or not, though, there is no getting away from the fact that I betrayed Giulio, believing him to be guilty. If I was wrong, I should find that hard to live with.'

'Tell him, Peter,' Hazel urged him, when he stopped.

Peter looked at her, seemingly past the ability to argue. 'As you know, my first marriage was not happy. Stephanie adored her mother, however. Although she was so young when she died, she grew up to hate the Santoros, believing that her Aunt Floria had died through Giulio Santoro's treachery.'

I could see now what might have happened. 'She continued to see the Mesola family after her mother's death, so it might have been from them rather than her mother that she had inherited this hatred of the Santoros.'

'That is possible. They were honourable people. Stephanie does however have a memory of her mother talking of the Santoros with hatred. After her mother died, she remembers asking her grandparents who the Santoros were. All she can recall is that she was told that Giulio's brothers had come to the house not long before her mother died, and coupled with that memory of Sofia's hatred of the family, Stephanie became convinced that they were also responsible not only for Floria's death but for her mother's. Sofia had taken an overdose of sleeping pills, and Stephanie had the impression from the way the family talked that it was not by accident.'

Giulio's brothers. It was all beginning to come together now, as I'd suspected. 'Could that be why your daughter believes that Giovanni's family belonged to the Mafia?' I asked. 'A confusion between the Santoro brothers and the Brotherhood?'

Even if that childish mistake had turned the brothers into villains, however, it surely could have nothing to do with Hugh's death. True, it had affected the fake murder plot, with Stephanie, like Peter, intent on getting vengeance on the Santoro family, but murder was a far different matter.

'It's possible,' Peter granted. 'But there is something else you should know, Jack. The Alfa Romeo. When I first met Sofia she knew that I was working with Giulio. He talked about the car with great passion during the long nights in the mountains. It helped us

all, something not to do with the war. I knew all about the 1938
Mille Miglia and the Alfa Romeo, because I was in my late teens
then and followed every step of the thrilling 1930s racing scene.
Sofia knew how much I admired the car despite my feelings for its
owner, and so I now suspect she could have asked the Fascist militia
for the car in payment for her betrayal of Floria. She knew I wanted
to marry her sister. At the war's end, marrying Sofia was the price
I paid for the car. I was fond of her, of course, but I did not love
her and she knew that. The car won me over. Only later I wondered
how she came to get it, but we are often fearful when the truth is
too terrible to contemplate, and I shied away from it. It lay between
us though. Poor Stephanie. All that, and now having to cope with
the fact that her husband killed her half-brother.'

How could I say to him after this that I did not think Paul had
acted alone? That he was probably not the instigator of Hugh's
murder and had only acted to safeguard his wife. Stephanie, for
whatever reason, had herself killed her half-brother.

I was present when Brandon interviewed Stephanie under caution
at Charing HQ. She didn't seem to care that I was present too. I
think she was anxious to talk in order that we should sympathize
with her point of view.

'I am Italian,' she told us proudly. 'My mother told me I should
be proud of my family. But it was her parents who told me when
I had grown up what my mother had done. So then I did not even
have a mother and it was the Santoro brotherhood who killed her.
I did not have a father. He cared only for Hugh. Everything was
Hugh. He was the heir, he was the one who carried on the Compton
name. I never told my father he was wrong about Giulio betraying
Floria. Why should I? He betrayed me, he did not care for me, only
for Hugh. And we are so poor too. Paul does not earn enough, and
my father would not sell the only thing that was worth money in
this place – that car. He told me it had memories for him. But I
had memories too.'

Her cry of distress was chilling. 'So I told my father,' she ranted
on, 'how he could get his revenge for Floria's betrayal by Giulio,
and we set up this plan. Hugh went to La Casa, where we knew
Enrico had lived and that his descendants still ran it, and we told
the owner about having seen the Alfa Romeo in a friend's barn. He

wasn't to know it came from us and we knew the story would reach
that terrible Santoro man, Giovanni Donati.'

'But you had your own plan: to kill Hugh for real, and let Giovanni
take the blame?' Brandon asked.

'Why not?' She seemed genuinely surprised at our looks of horror.
'The Santoro brothers killed my mother. I know that. It was quite
easy to kill Hugh and he deserved it. I went to the chalet on Saturday
evening, invited him to come during the night and stay at Manor
Cottage for lunch and the next two days until his planned return. I
killed him there. Paul helped me get the blood cleaned up and the
clothes changed to those he wore in the barn that night, and we
moved the body. It was quite straightforward.'

I had one more visit to Peter Compton at his request. I had wondered
how much more emotional battering this frail old man could take,
but the subject today was, he assured me, all pleasure.

'I'll survive long enough for this,' he told me.

It *was* all pleasure. I was far from being the only guest in the
barn. Giovanni was there, as were Maria, Umberto, Bronte, Hazel,
Peter, Len and Zoe – and Jamie Makepeace. Even more pleasant,
Louise was there, but not Ricardo. This could have something to
do with the fact that we had arranged it for a weekday, which he
could never have managed. My idea? Of course not.

As we stood admiringly around the Alfa Romeo, Peter said, 'I
have come to a decision about its future. I want you to have it,
Giovanni. I owe it to you.'

Giovanni's face lit up. 'No, I do not wish to own it, thank you,
but I have another plan which will make it light again after its
darkness. First I will paint it as I remember it first, unrestored, and
then I will paint it restored.'

Peter looked pleased. 'That is good. What then?'

'I ask Umberto whether he would want it, and he say no too if
you ask him. You sell it and half the money you keep for this farm
and the other half you give to a prison charity. We both suffer, Mr
Compton. We both know what it is like to lose liberty.'

It was quickly agreed. I had remained silent, not knowing whether
I had any stake in this or not. Apparently I did. Peter turned to me.
'As for you, Jack. I want Frogs Hill to do the restoration.'

*   *   *

That evening Giovanni, Umberto and I went for a celebratory drink in the Half Moon pub in Piper's Green, while Louise, Maria and Umberto's wife looked after the restaurant. We drank quite a lot, and it was agreed that we would get a taxi back to La Casa, where we would drink another bottle and then sleep it off.

'And now,' Umberto told us after finishing it, 'there is something that you do not know, Jack. Nor you, Giovanni. But I know, because I kept back one letter from the Mesola family. Too sad. But Giovanni must know. Sofia Mesola did not die by accident, nor by suicide, nor by the hand of Giulio Santoro's brothers. They went to see the Mesola family to tell them the truth about Floria, that her own sister had betrayed her because Peter Compton wanted to marry Floria, but Sofia wanted Peter Compton for herself. Learning the truth, her parents killed her, gently, peacefully, for the honour of the Mesola family. Today this could never happen, but in those days when war was still so near to them, when the Partisans and civilians had suffered so much, it could.'

I was silent and it was Giovanni who spoke in the end.

'It was many years ago,' he said. 'We keep this to ourselves, eh? It is the champagne perhaps that talks.'

Which left me just one matter outstanding from the Plumshaw case: Nan.

I went to visit him at Puddledock Cottage one last time. 'You can stay on here?'

He smiled. 'Yes. Miss Bronte say I can. She and Jamie are to be married. Good, yes? But they will live in the village or Manor Cottage. Not here. Good news.'

'It is. I'm told the trust has been rewritten yet again. With Hazel as trustee in charge?'

'No.' He looked at me shyly. 'I am the trustee. And it is completely rewritten. I can do with all the land what I think best.'

So there it was at last. A possible reconciliation for old and new Plumshaw. Just one thing though: 'Does that mean you will have the last say in whether the Hop and Harry land is sold or whether it's rebuilt?'

He smiled. 'Yes.'

'And how will you do that?'

'I will listen, and then I will choose.'

*   *   *

I was waiting at the track for my rival, and like a warrior knight of old my charger was at my side on the starting line. I was about to fight for my lady's hand. (In theory anyway.) My lady Louise had in fact retired into the café at Old Herne's Club in disgust at being dragged into such a juvenile battle between Ricardo and myself.

Len and Zoe were here with me to cheer me on. Or rather cheer our Black Beauty on. We had spent the last three months restoring the Alfa Romeo, from grappling with the seized engine and struggling to get the drivetrain out to giving its glowing black paint and gleaming chrome radiator grille and hubcaps their final polish.

Unlike the thousand miles of the Mille Miglia race, Old Herne's track consisted of two former airfield runways linked together in a curve at both ends. Hardly a gruelling task to do four laps round it – especially as Ricardo's yellow Triumph Stag was roughly an equal match in speed for the 1930s Alfa Romeo.

'There he is,' grunted Len. I saw Zoe's eyes widen and thought it was because she could see, as I did, Louise sauntering out from the café. It wasn't. Certainly it was Ricardo now saluting Louise with one graceful hand, but it wasn't the Stag.

Ricardo had cheated. He was driving Giovanni's red Daytona Ferrari. That red monster would be round Old Herne's in half the time it took the Alfa, forty years its junior.

He drew up on the starting line with splendid aplomb and laughed as he saw my face.

'All's fair in love and war, Jack!'

Should I complain? Accept the challenge? I took one look at Louise's amused face and chose the latter.

'Tortoise and the hare, Ricardo!' I yelled back at him. This morning I had patted the tortoise emblem on my Gordon-Keeble's bonnet for luck, so now I was calling on it even harder. It was the Red Devil against the Black Beauty and if I were thrashed at least I'd go down fighting.

Louise refused point blank to start the race, but Len nobly stepped in and dropped the flag. We were off – Ricardo much more speedily than me. Half of me minded very much, the other half didn't. To feel this Alfa Romeo in my hands on a real track was an experience I will never forget. I remembered an old cliché about the Alfa Romeo. You don't steer her. You just keep your hands on the wheel and wish her round bends. And here I was wishing like crazy.

Even if Ricardo did lap me as I was midway through Lap Three. The tortoise did its best but it wasn't going to catch the hare up before the end of the race after the fourth lap.

Fortune favours the brave, it's said, and though I was feeling far from being a brave warrior by how, fortune dropped in with a vengeance. The dulcet voice of Louise, beloved by fans all over the world and especially by me, intervened. 'Bravo, Ricardo!' her mellow tones shouted as he passed her shortly before the last bend. I could see him turn, see him go too fast into the bend – and spin off into the undergrowth.

The tortoise drove sedately past him and crossed the finishing line triumphant.

To do him justice, Ricardo drove back on to the track, completed the lap, climbed out, shook my hand and kissed Louise's hand with perfect poise.

'Next time,' he said, 'I win.'

I had to ask Louise when we were alone: 'Did you shout out on purpose?'

'As if,' she retorted, and took my hand.

The Car's the Star
James Myers

The Starring Cars

1937 Alfa Romeo 8C 2900B

The 1930s was a triumphal time for Alfa, racking up eight Mille Miglia and four Le Mans victories as well as an outright win at the 1935 German Grand Prix by Nuvolari. The 8C 2900 was designed in the mid-30s for racing. It used a 2.9 litre uprated version of the inline eight-cylinder engine featuring dual camshafts, dual magnetos and dry sump oiling. It sported two Roots type superchargers fed by two Weber carburettors. In its competition form, the engine produced 180+ horse-power. The chassis featured fully independent suspension.

Just over thirty 2900Bs were built in 1937 and 1938 (plus one more from spare parts in 1941). The bodies were made by Carrozzeria Touring and Pininfarina.

1972 Ferrari Daytona Spyder

The Ferrari 365 GTB/4, generally known as the 'Daytona', was a grand tourer made from 1968 to 1973. It replaced the 275 GTB/4 and in its turn was replaced by the mid-engined 365 GT4 Berlinetta Boxer in 1973.

The 'Daytona' name no doubt came from Ferrari's 1-2-3 victory in the 1967 '24 Hours of Daytona'. The Daytona was a traditional front-engined, rear-drive car with a 4.4 litre V12 engine producing around 360 horsepower. It was styled by Pininfarina and is still one of the fastest road cars ever with a top speed of 175 mph.

Jack Colby's own classic cars

Jack's 1965 Gordon-Keeble

One hundred of these fabulous supercars were built between 1963 and '66 with over ninety units surviving around the globe, mostly in the UK. Designed by John Gordon and Jim Keeble using current racing car principles with the bodyshell designed by twenty-one-year-old Giorgetto Giugiaro at Bertone, the cars were an instant success but the company was ruined by supply-side industrial action with ultimately only ninety-nine units completed even after the company was relaunched in May 1965, as Keeble Cars Ltd. Final closure came in February 1966 when the factory at Sholing closed and Jim Keeble moved to Keewest Developments, the firm Keeble then formed with Geoffrey West. The hundredth car was completed in 1971 with leftover components. The Gordon-Keeble's emblem is a yellow and green tortoise.

Jack's 1938 Lagonda V-12 Drophead

The Lagonda company won its attractive name from a creek near the home of the American-born founder Wilbur Gunn in Springfield, Ohio. The name given to it by the American Indians was Ough Ohonda. The V-12 Drophead was a car to compete with the very best in the world, with a sporting twelve-cylinder engine which would power the two 1939 Le Mans cars. Its designer was the famous W.O. Bentley. Sadly, many fine pre-war saloons have been converted to Le Mans replicas. The V-12 cars are very similar externally to the earlier six-cylinder versions; both types were available with open or closed bodywork in a number of different styles. The V-12 Drophead also featured in Jack's earlier case, *Classic in the Barn*.